# NOW
# I SEE YOU

# NOW
# I SEE YOU

## Priscilla Holmes

modjaji books

Published in 2014 by Modjaji Books

PO Box 385, Athlone, 7760, Cape Town, South Africa

www.modjajibooks.co.za

© Priscilla Holmes

Priscilla Holmes has asserted her right to be identified
as the author of this work.

Edited by Máire Fisher

Cover artwork by Carla Kreuser

Book layout by Andy Thesen

Printed and bound by Megadigital, Cape Town

ISBN 978-1-920590-75-8

Ebook ISBN 978-1-920590-86-4

In memory of my mother, Gertrude Amy Kench
and to Jack with all my love

# 1

Julia stared into the bronze mirror at the entrance to Mama Ruby's, at the reflection of someone she barely recognised: herself. Despite what had happened earlier, despite her battered body and despair, she looked so normal. She should look like a ragged refugee from a broken country, hiding in a dark railway station, waiting to escape, waiting to be free of oppression, of violence. Every time Magnus planted her at one of these dinners, charity soirées, or cocktail parties, she asked herself why she kept coming.

Or did she just enjoy facing public humiliation?

Tonight, as usual, she looked elegant, poised, calm. Her long red hair swinging to her shoulders, her face pale, but immaculately made-up. She was actually smiling at Ivan Ivanski, just as if nothing had happened. As if her body wasn't aching and bruised. Nothing ever showed. Magnus hurt her only in hidden places. He stood behind her, solicitously helping her with her coat, pulling out her chair. She stared at him in the mirror. He smiled back, his eyes cold. She hated him.

They sat at the best table in the restaurant. The wishy-washy lady, with cast-down eyes, offered Julia a welcoming bowl of rosewater to rinse her hands. A large chandelier showered golden light on the crowd; candles blossomed in enormous iron holders imported from Zanzibar; waiters whirled past dressed in bright robes and turbans. People came from all over the world to eat here. The square outside the restaurant bloomed with fairy lights strung around the tall plants. Diners sat beside flaming torches, drinking from enormous goblets as the evening swirled around them.

Julia sat next to Ivanski, opposite two executives and their wives from a major mining group. Magnus had positioned himself beside Ollis Sando, the powerful lawyer, rumoured to be in line for the presidency in the upcoming elections. Sitina Sando, a tall beauty from Ethiopia, sat next to her husband, constantly touching his arm and smiling up at him. They were a couple in the golden lap of the world. Since their recent marriage they had been on the covers of all the glossy magazines and newspapers in South Africa. Julia couldn't stop a sharp twist of envy as she watched the tender way Sando looked at his wife, the way he touched her face and smiled at her.

Magnus was talking to Sando in his usual bombastic yet obsequious way, pushing up his chin, gesticulating.

'What about a trip to our game lodge next month? We've got a place at Madikwe, you know, right on the Botswana border, awesome game viewing. Do you enjoy the bush?'

Julia watched him through narrowed eyes, feeling the back of the chair pressing into her bruises. Sando answered quietly, not meeting Magnus's patronising stare.

'Sounds good, Magnus, we'll think about it,' he murmured, his eyes wandering the room.

Magnus turned his heavy gaze on Sitina. 'Do you like the bush, Sitina?'

She smiled tightly. 'I do, actually, we're regulars. Luckily we have our own private lodge near Kruger.'

Magnus sat back, deflated.

Julia smiled to herself at the put-down.

She thought Sando attractive in an unfinished Michelangelo-sculpture kind of way. His strong nose, full lips and large well-moulded hands seemed expertly formed, but the rest of him, heavy shoulders, torso and legs had not been liberated from the original slabs of black marble. He was all raw power.

Ivanski leaned towards Julia. 'You are looking very beautiful tonight,' he said. 'I believe red-haired women are –'

Whatever the Russian believed about redheads, Julia never discovered. Cutting across the chatter and laughter of the restaurant came a violent crash and a volley of gunfire. The ceiling exploded, great shards of glass tumbling down onto the traumatised diners. Shrill screams erupted, people leapt up, tables overturned, plates and glasses shattered. A thin man dressed in a black tracksuit was standing on one of the tables dominating the room. He wore a black mask tight over his head, with tiny slits for his eyes, nostrils and mouth. His movements were jerky; he held a semi-automatic weapon in one hand. He shouted in a high, tinny voice, demanding that people empty their pockets, and throw their bags, cell phones, wallets, jewellery, and put them on to the table.

He fired again, just missing a man attempting to get to the door. People shrank back whimpering. Julia watched women crying as they tried to take off necklaces with shaking hands. One woman sobbed as she struggled to ease her emeralds and diamonds over swollen fingers. A man yanked shimmering South Sea pearls from his wife's neck. His wife turned away from him in disgust. Another man fumbled a heavy gold watch off his wrist. Probably a Rolex, Julia thought. This was a well-heeled crowd. The man jumped down from the table, shocked diners shrank back. Waving his gun he ran from table to table, sweeping the jewels and watches into a black refuse bag.

'*Nyet*! Stop this!' Ivanski was on his feet, shouting.

The gunman strode to their table; hit Ivanski in the face with the butt of the gun. Blood spurted over white linen and crystal. The Russian fell back and hit his head. He slumped and twisted on the floor. Julia heard him moaning.

The gunman raised his weapon and sprayed more bullets across the room, shattering the mirrors, creating maximum noise and panic. Terrified diners dived for cover. Men yelling, women screaming. It was chaos.

Security alarms blasted the air so loudly that Julia's ears hurt. The man hesitated and then darted forward, dropping the bulky black bag. He stood right in front of her. She could almost see his mind clicking and shifting. Before he even moved, she knew. He was coming for her. The world shifted on its axis.

He grabbed Julia around the neck, pulled her off the chair and pushed the gun under her chin. He was immensely strong, his arms like iron bands as he pushed Julia's head back at a painful angle. 'Don't struggle, bitch,' he said, 'you're coming with me.' He sounded like Bugs Bunny, or Donald Duck. A friendly character from Julia's childhood.

He turned to the cowering diners: 'Try anything and I'll blow her brains out.' He took the gun from under her chin and released another round into the ceiling. The noise was shattering.

He grabbed Julia's hair, pulling her so close that she could feel his hot breath on the back of her neck, smell the sharp scent of his excitement.

Nobody moved.

He thrust the refuse bag into Julia's shaking hands 'Hold this,' he squeaked. She clutched the heavy bag like a life line.

The man jammed the gun into her throat and dragged her back across the entrance and out into the square. Shocked bystanders fell back to let them pass.

He frog-marched Julia, using her as a human shield. As he dragged her across the tiles of the square, security guards raced towards them, their breath steaming in the cold night air.

'Get back! Any closer and I'll kill her,' the cartoon voice squealed.

At first the guards fell back, uncertain. Then they edged forward, step by step, matching their quarry's pace. Julia blocked their line of fire and they could do nothing but watch, helpless, as the man retreated across the square, pulling his hostage with him.

'Don't shoot!' Julia cried to the guards.

People stood frozen, watching, their faces blank with shock.

The man thrust her towards a shabby white van parked on the edge of the square. He opened the back, forced her in and jumped in after her. She fell heavily on the floor. It smelt of old vegetables. The van sped around the corner with shrieking tyres. Julia bounced around in the back, hitting her head, twisting her wrist as she tried to steady herself. Suddenly the van screeched to a stop. The man pushed the door open, prodded the gun into her kidneys, thrusting her out of the van. She fell heavily, toppling towards a dark ramp, the man right behind her.

'Go, go, go!' he shouted. The van revved. Julia caught a glimpse of another masked man in the driver's seat, before the van drove off, tyres shrieking.

The man crouched low and ran hard, dragging Julia behind him. She slipped and smashed her ankle against something steely. Pain shot up her leg. Now she was dragged, half hobbling, while her abductor shrieked in his Bugs Bunny voice, over and over again, 'Hurry, hurry up, bitch.' It was a cartoon nightmare.

At the bottom of the ramp was a gated parking basement. Her abductor clicked on a button on the wall. The gate opened. He dragged her inside. It was dark, but he seemed to know where he was. With the gun pressed into her back, Julia stumbled between rows of cars, until they reached a doorway. The man pressed a switch. Doors opened. Julia lurched forward into yawning darkness.

They were in a lift. It smelt of food. The doors clanged shut and they dropped at least four floors. Would she still be alive when the doors opened again? The man pressed a button. The lift jerked to a halt, and hung shaking in mid-air. They were suspended in darkness.

For a while the figure next to her did nothing. Julia stood very still. The only sound, her panting breath. The man was blacker than night. Then he moved his hands all over Julia's face, his gloved hands rough on her chin and neck. Her heart banged at her ribs like a trapped animal. She closed her eyes and kept very still. He ran his hands over her head. 'If you want to keep this pretty face, just do exactly what I say,' the man squeaked.

She shuddered at his touch. She flattened herself against the wall of the lift. She could hear him breathing near to her. Too near ... She opened her eyes and tried to focus, looking and listening with all her senses.

After a few minutes the dark figure pulled off his ski mask. Julia saw the gleam of skin, bright narrow eyes. Her attacker spoke in a perfectly normal voice. Bugs Bunny was gone.

# 2

Three months later

15 June 2006

The snow softened the harsh concrete skyline, decorating the buildings opposite my office with birthday cake icing.

Snow in Johannesburg. It didn't happen often, even at the high altitude. Big thick flakes. Like the snow in the valley. Only when it snowed there, round huts turned into iced cupcakes; kids threw snowballs and slid down mountain paths on tin trays.

I shook my head. Jozi was my home now. The land of mountains and isolation was far behind me. And that's where it could stay.

Zak Khumalo walked in, blowing away all thoughts of the lonely valley of my childhood. A big personality, some of the girls in the unit said. An overinflated ego was more like it. As always he walked past me, managing to touch my shoulder without dropping anything out of a bulging folder tucked under one arm. As always he was brimming with the awareness of his own charm. 'Morning, Detective Inspector Tswane,' he said. 'How're you doing?'

'It's snowing,' I said quietly. 'Do you remember the last time? When we were called to the Inanda Club to investigate the assassination? All that blood, it looked so red on the snow.'

'I remember,' Zak said, his face sober. 'He was a real loss. Our next president – if he'd lived. But hey,' he smiled at me, 'did you see the headlines in *The Star*? "Snow turns city of gold into city of ice" – focus on that image, DI Tswane, forget the blood. You'll feel better, trust me.'

Take it from me, the last thing I would ever do was trust Zak Khumalo. Most of the female officers thought he was so hot. They were all jealous that I was working so closely with him. I looked up at him and he smiled, that quick flash of white that had all the girls swooning. He smoothed his hands over his shaved head.

Something you need to know about me, I don't give compliments easily. Zak Khumalo was strikingly handsome; there was no getting away from it. His body wasn't too bad either ... and he didn't hide it, flat muscled chest under a thin black T-shirt, tight trousers moulding long, well-defined legs. Yes, Zak Khumalo was attractive alright, if you like the brash arrogant type. Not that there was any point in looking at any man in the Eagles – the Serious and Violent Crime Unit, to give it its official title. When you were on Divisional Commissioner Matatu's team, you didn't form close relationships with your colleagues. Not if you had any sense.

'The boss wants to see you in his office, immediately,' Zak said.

'Thanks for *telling* me immediately,' I said, pushing past him. 'I could have done without the weather forecast, trust me.'

Khumalo laughed and shook his head as I left the room.

***

I stared at the boss in disbelief.

'I can't go there,' I blurted. 'Couldn't somebody else take this case, sir? I can't.'

'You can't *go* there? You can't do it? What does that mean?' Matatu's eyebrows rose. He was a huge man with a great slab of a face and enormous hands. He rocked back in his chair and looked at me with annoyance. 'You are assigned this case, DI Tswane. It's not a choice.'

Matatu wasn't about to listen to arguments. He had changed in the last year, become harder, less quick to smile. He'd been suspended, under suspicion in a recent investigation. Whispers of corruption had circulated, rumours were rife. I had never doubted his innocence. In the murky world of police corruption, Matatu was an honourable man. But he had come under heavy fire as the sins of his bosses were investigated. Much as some people wanted to pin the blame on him, he had emerged unscathed to head up a new unit of the Serious and Violent Crimes section of the South African Police Services.

It was good to have him back at his desk, but the experience had taken something from him. He'd become a tough taskmaster, unwilling to accept any dereliction of duty. There would be no whisper of fraudulence in his crack unit. Discipline had never been tighter. And I was feeling just how tight it was.

'Detective Inspectors don't have choices. They obey orders. Do you understand?' Matatu asked.

'Yes, sir.'

Matatu stared at me, as if he was trying to look through me and beyond the walls of his small shabby office. I kept my eyes fixed on his silver pen as it fluttered through his fingers like a magician's wand. 'You know the area, you speak the language. You are a senior officer in this unit. You're going. Tell me, where is your home exactly?'

If I had been a valley girl I would have said 'North-west of the Great Fish River' and Matatu would have known what I meant. But then again, if I'd been a valley girl I would never be having this conversation, let alone looking my boss in the eye. It wasn't respectful for a village woman to look into a man's face.

'Nguni Intile – an ancient valley, to the west of Umtata. Very rural,' I said. 'I haven't been back for a long time.'

I closed my eyes for a moment and there it was – as clear as the day I left. The remote valley where the top activity for women was walking up from the river with a twenty-litre bucket of water on your head.

Matatu searched my face. He didn't have to say anything. I knew what he was thinking. Most people who came from places like the valley returned to their homes whenever they could. They might have to spend days on overcrowded buses, walk miles through the bush, climb mountain peaks and ford dangerous rivers, but they went back. So what the hell was wrong with me?

But the boss didn't comment. Just shook his head. 'I'm briefing you now; you'll be chief investigator, so listen carefully.'

As Matatu turned to the map of the Eastern Cape pinned to the wall opposite his desk, I glanced around. The room was a smokescreen for what lay behind the simple office. The special unit's headquarters didn't look like a sophisticated power centre. That was the whole point. It was what the boss wanted visitors to think. The Eagles Unit was designed so you saw nothing but hallways and doors, unless you walked through one of them. Matatu's inner office opened into a beehive of activity. Behind him doors of plate glass and steel stretched out, the central sections frosted so it was difficult to see any detail of what was going on behind them. I could just make out men and women, some in uniform, hurrying through the workspaces.

'The case is centred in your home area,' Matatu indicated on the map. 'You'll be interviewing people you might know. The local police have requested our help.'

'What's happened?' I asked.

'Serious robberies. Two men working the whole area. It's been going on for two months now. Armed hold-ups, bank heists, millions of rands stolen from different locations right across the Eastern Cape, mostly in small towns. Yesterday it went seriously wrong; they killed a man in a small seaside town, Kenton-on-Sea. That's why we're involved.'

'Only two of them?'

'So it seems. But they're clever. Not the usual hit-and-run-like-hell tactics. These guys are smart. They've got a different plan for every heist. Then they just vanish into thin air, or so the locals tell us.'

'Any CCTV footage?'

'Plenty. Camera footage shows they're heavily armed – Uzis, Smith & Wessons or Glocks. They're always masked. Alien masks pulled tightly over their heads. And – this is strange – they always talk in the same high voices, like cartoon characters, in Disney films.'

'Like Donald Duck? You inhale helium to do that. Your voice goes squeaky and high for a short time.'

'How many people know a thing like that?'

'Anyone who's ever blown up balloons, just one of those things you pick up.'

Matatu rubbed his temples with his fingers before he spoke. 'DI Tswane, there's one more thing. There was a witness to this murder. The only person to come forward who has actually seen the perpetrators.'

'Who?'

'Your grandfather, Chief Solenkosi Tswane. He refuses to cooperate with the police. He won't talk to anyone but you.'

Life's like a chessboard. Just when you think you have a game plan, one piece moves and everything changes. My palms prickled. It was always like this. The valley had left thorns in my hands.

'Keep me informed,' Matatu said. 'I want to know what's going on. If you need more people or resources, talk to me. I want regular progress reports, whenever you can establish contact.'

'Yes, sir.'

I closed the door quietly behind me. No point in exposing myself further to the boss's scrutiny. He'd given me my orders and I'd follow them, even if going back there, leaving Jozi, was the hardest thing I'd been asked to do in a long time. I stood there for a few minutes trying to come to terms with what was going to happen next.

If there was one thing I knew all about, it was leaving. Usually when someone left the valley their leaving was accompanied by cries of grief. Clothing was torn, heads shaved. But not for me. After the ritual punishment ordered by my grandfather, I had left forever.

I fled alone and in the dark. And I swore never to return.

Now the outcast had to go back. The valley people usually displayed their hands to the sky in happiness when a loved one returned. This would not happen for me. There would be no stamping feet, no killing of an ox. As the chief's granddaughter I had been a sort of princess in the valley, a loved one. But now it would be different. News of my arrival would be announced in the valley. But who would care?

After my briefing with Commissioner Matatu, I needed to clear my thoughts. I walked outside for a moment. It would soon be dark. Johannesburg nights came quickly. I heard the last birdsong of the day and watched long, mauve shadows creeping across the walls of the building. The snow was melting, leaving soggy patches on the road. The winter sun slipped below the rim of the world, leaving the sky blood red and ominous.

I walked back to my building and took the lift to the underground shooting range: a bright well-lit place with sand walls surrounding six individual practice stands.

I selected a .38 Special, narrowed my eyes behind the safety goggles, and shot ten rounds into the heart of a life-size target hanging on a wire ten metres away.

As I stood back, judging my aim, Zak Khumalo appeared in the next stand.

'Glad you're on our side, Thabisa; you're almost as good as me.'

I ignored him. Zak Khumalo might secrete some hypnotic scent that drove women crazy, but I simply found him irritating.

'Yes, and to think my grandfather wanted me to stay home and do beadwork,' I said as I turned to leave.

He laughed softly. 'That's a great idea. Beautiful black women with grey eyes should stay put. Trust me; you'd be safer at home.'

'Unless I had you to protect me, I suppose?' I said sarcastically.

'I'll always protect you, DI Tswane, you know that.'

'Oh ja? Like you did last week with Botha?'

'Listen Thabisa, if you'd entered the building with me like you were supposed to –'

I looked at him in outrage. We'd been on a job together the week before, chasing Mike Botha, a suspected murderer and known drug dealer, who had jumped bail. It had meant storming his girlfriend's apartment in Hillbrow.

The lobby of the building was small, full of rubbish. It stank. You could reach up and grab a handful of grease from the air. An old washing machine, a filthy armchair, black bin bags containing God knows what. The door looked as if it had been kicked in a few times and I'd sighed when I looked at it. I had spent quite a few years knocking on doors like this.

I'd been about to follow Zak inside the building when a figure lurched out of the shadows, smashing into me from the side. We both crashed to the ground. The impact knocked me breathless; my weapon skidded off into the dark, beyond my grasp. Then Botha's hands had curled round my throat, squeezing.

'Don't move, bitch,' he hissed.

I smelt him coming before he touched me; his breath sour, his body odour like ripe cheese. That's one of the things that gets to me about my job, the baddies often smell really bad. I wanted to vomit, but his hands constricted my throat and I couldn't breathe, let alone throw up. I lay still for a moment. Then with all my strength I brought my knee up hard into his soft gut. He gasped, relaxed his grip for a moment. I turned, grabbed the pepper spray from the back of my belt, and shot into his face. Howling, he reeled into the street, hands tearing at his eyes. His howling turned into choking and gasping, and he fell on all fours. As he crumpled forward, Zak appeared from the building. In a few seconds Botha was handcuffed and shoved into the car.

Before he dragged Botha away, Zak had glanced at me.

'You okay?' he asked. 'You should have gone in with me, you know that.'

I'd almost smiled. Under all the swagger and macho exterior, perhaps Zak was a grown-up professional after all.

'I'm fine,' I said. 'I didn't need your help. It was under control.'

He looked at me with a small half-smile.

'You having fun?' he asked.

'Oh, ja. A real blast.'

Now, a week later, I could see his eyes gleaming in the darkening light. Everything about him – T-shirt, bulletproof vest, shaved head and the 9mm Glock – was black as night. He blended into the dark like a shadow. Invisible. But I could feel his eyes on me.

I stuck my .38 into my webbed hip holster. My cuffs and spray were stuck into the back of the belt. I was in full uniform, but I knew Zak saw straight to the black lacy underwear I was wearing underneath.

'Zak,' I said, 'enough, okay? Stop looking at me like that. I could use a bit of real encouragement. About police matters, that is.'

He stepped forward, stood close, put his finger under my chin and locked eyes with me.

'Anything you like, Thabisa,' he said, moving his finger down my neck.

'Cut it out, or I'll report you for sexual harassment.'

He stepped back, dropped his hand.

'I understand, Thabisa, you just can't trust yourself around me.' His laugh was soft and low in his throat as he walked away. 'Still got your bank-teller boyfriend?'

'He's a trader, not a bank-teller.'

'Same shit.'

Adrenaline tripped into my bloodstream and I had to breathe slowly. I didn't want to risk grabbing my gun and shooting him by mistake.

In the cloakroom, I washed my hands quickly, not wanting to look in the mirror. I knew what I'd see there. A wary young woman scared of the past. The conversation with Matatu had brought back memories of my childhood, memories of the remote valley where I had grown up. Thoughts floated to the surface of my mind and burst like bubbles.

In the Eastern Cape, beyond the Xuka River, over the Qabe Mountain pass, deep down where the river runs straight off the mountains and into the valley, is my home. Nguni Intile. Nestled in a time-worn crevice, surrounded by rugged red cliffs. If I close my eyes I can see northwards, where the great Drakensberg Mountains rise and thicken into a blue, jagged wall. This is the place where I was born. It's hard to find the way in ... but even harder to find a way out.

For as long as anyone could remember, the valley had been a remote cut-off place. Even when the trappings of civilisation trickled into neighbouring villages and the young men returned from the mines with radios and crazy city stories, the people of the valley clung to their traditions. They would have been lost without them. Or that's the way I used to see things. Back then when I thought the valley was stifling me. It felt like there was no way out. Even the landscape held me trapped. The long-promised new road from Engcobe came to a complete halt once it met the copper-coloured earth of the valley. You still had to scramble down a dangerous mountain path to get to the village.

We never saw a car in the valley. The only traffic jam was caused by cattle being taken to graze by the young boys trusted with this important task. The valley was a place where time had stood still for decades. History and time had passed it by.

Valley people cherished their isolation. Just as they tended their cattle, made their complicated bead-work, and married whom they were told. These things could be counted on. You knew the water from the mountain streams was as pure as the first snow. You knew that Chief Tswane would punish wrongdoers in the traditional way. That you rubbed your body and clothing with red clay until you glistened to show you were amaQaba, that you worshipped your ancestors, their spirits were always there in the valley. That was all you needed to know.

But I was different. My grandfather, Chief Solenkosi Tswane, had chosen me to be the one who went to school. That's when everything had changed.

Everyone thought he would choose a boy. After all, they were the ones who fought, made a noise and told the girls what to do. But I was his only descendant, everyone else was gone and blood meant everything. So he chose me.

Me, the little tomboy who climbed trees and came home wet from the river, her belly full of star apples and bush fruit. The one who played *ndize*, finding the best places to hide from the boys, finding them easily when it was her turn. I hunted scorpions, dressed the family goat in a bead headdress and rode her like a horse. I was the chosen one. The one who had to climb the mountain every day to go to the farm school. Ten kilometres there and back. In all weather, even when it snowed or when the spring rains flooded the river and I had to wade across, my school dress on my head, to keep it dry. The other kids felt sorry for me, especially the girls. It made me different. They were happy doing their beadwork and helping their mothers. But I loved to learn. To see letters forming words, numbers that always made sense when you added them up, I loved that; making sense out of patterns and squares, just as I loved to hear my teacher tell us about the world outside. For most of my childhood I believed that the world didn't go beyond the mountains that framed our village life. But once I went to school I knew there were other places out there and they were calling me. When I won the scholarship and went to live in Grahamstown, I saw that world and I liked it.

At eighteen I matriculated. And then my grandfather tried to marry me off to a neighbouring chief. I couldn't believe it. After all the education, all the dreams I had dared to dream, I was to be sold to an ancient friend of my grandfather's. A man almost three times my age. Just as my eyes were opened to the real world, I had to follow tradition and do what was expected. When all you know is nothing, all your expectations are nothing. But I had escaped the bondage of valley women, only to find it had me in its time-honoured trap.

'I have good *lobola* for you,' Chief Tswane said. 'Fifty cattle when you marry Bundo.'

'No,' I said, 'I won't marry an old man.' I shuddered to think of ancient hands roaming over my body. A toothless old man sharing my bed.

'You will marry who I say,' my grandfather insisted.

'No, I won't. I'm going to college. I'm not marrying anybody.'

Besides smelling like a goat, Bundo was almost as old as my grandfather and already had three wives. It wasn't going to happen.

But nobody ever refused my grandfather. It was unheard of in the valley.

I could understand that I was my grandfather's only hope of strengthening the family bloodline. No other members of the family remained, apart from my great-aunt, a lady in her seventies. But that didn't mean I had to kneel down and accept this fate. I just wouldn't do it.

'I will return one day and help the village, I promise,' I said. 'But for now *tat'omkhulu* – grandfather, I have to qualify and get a job. Then I can think about marrying.'

'You will marry who I say,' my grandfather repeated, louder this time.

I pressed my lips together until they hurt.

'I will not marry this man. I am leaving.'

'I command you!' Solenkosi Tswane was almost incoherent with rage, but I persisted.

'You have educated me to think for myself and now I am refusing.'

My grandfather drew himself up to his full height, pulling the red blanket around his skinny shoulders.

'How can you leave our valley?' he hissed. 'This is where our ancestors live. If you leave your village you will forget who you are.'

I stared down at the ground, saying nothing.

'Go then,' said my grandfather, turning away from me. 'You are no longer a child of the valley.'

I rose from the floor where I had been kneeling. All valley women knelt to their chief.

'There is nothing more to say. Goodbye.'

As I was leaving the homestead, Grandfather called out: 'You will be punished for this. This is our way.'

That night the village women came for me.

Women I thought friends, women who had taught me the ways of the valley, the ways of the beads, led by my grandfather's chief wife, Ngosi. They inflicted a ritual punishment I would remember all my life. I still bear the scars.

The old women came first, Ngosi, followed by Mkolo, Lulama, Odwa and Dumile, the gossipy *gogos* – the old ladies of the valley. They had taken the small blades from the Great Kraal, the blades used to inflict severe punishment. The last one to be cut was a man who had killed his neighbour. And now I was the criminal.

The younger women, my friends from childhood; Azile, Dinda, Popi and Pinda, held back, to start with. They were crying. Their mothers made the first cuts while Ngosi held me down. They were all waiting for me to scream, but I didn't cry out although I had to bite my lips until they bled. Ngosi shouted, 'This is your punishment, this is our way.' Lulama made the first cut. The women were ululating and shouting like a pack of dogs. I saw Pinda weeping, trying to run away from the hut, but her mother held her back. In the end they all cut me.

Afterwards, as I lay bleeding on the floor of the hut, Ngosi said 'I told him this schooling would bring trouble. I warned him.'

I left the valley with dozens of small bleeding wounds crisscrossing my back and grief in my heart. I left everything behind me that night; the bones of my ancestors, my childhood, all the familiar things of my life. I knew I could never be the same, that once I had left the valley I would have to become a different person. So I did.

I had not been back to the valley since.

Once I started working, I sent regular cheques to my grandfather, the way anyone who leaves always does, but they were never cashed. My throat ached with unshed tears when I thought about it. And now I had to go back and face it all over again.

I remembered the elaborate ceremonies, which involved the messy sacrifice of animals. I shuddered at the thought. I'd hated those ceremonies; I didn't like the blood and the screaming of the animal about to be slaughtered. There was a great deal of ululating, dancing and foot-stamping. This was not my thing, even when I'd been little, with my black curls jumping off my head like tightly coiled springs.

I forced my thoughts to the present day. I had to stop thinking about the past, get on with my life and do my job. I returned to my office, and settled down to read the files on the Eastern Cape criminals. I sat at my desk engrossed in them, until I checked my watch and realised how late it was.

Paul would be waiting; I'd better get home. It was his birthday and we had planned to meet friends for dinner. I snapped the files shut and left the building.

As I walked into the car park the snow started falling again. Fat snowflakes spotted the tarmac, covered my braids and landed on my lashes. It was bitterly cold. I shivered as I got to my car and saw the slush on my windscreen. I knew my heater wasn't going to cope and I would be freezing all the way home.

# 3

I drove away from the office through sheets of snow, and as I'd expected, my car heater put up a fight, but it couldn't cope. I pulled over in front of my flat and finished my make-up in the car, frowning at my reflection in the rear-view mirror. I hoped the snow wouldn't ruin it all again – a girl's whole life changes when her mascara runs.

The city roared with life: traffic, snatches of rap music, shouts, laughter, squealing tyres. I felt the rush of it. Suddenly the streetlights blinked off. As the snow kept falling, the lights in my block vanished. The whole of Randburg disappeared. Another common occurrence – a Johannesburg power outage.

There was a bad vibe coming off the city tonight, buzzing off the grey concrete and the wet tarmac. I glanced at the bruised sky. Paul would be angry that I was so late.

My throat was dry, my heart jumping anxiously. I was determined to sparkle tonight. I imagined him opening the door to greet me, seeing my glossy lips and braids caught up in a twisty ponytail. How could he resist me? I wanted him to say: 'Hi babe, you look beautiful. I know you're late, but it doesn't matter, just as long as you're home safely.'

If only he would look at me the way he used to at the beginning of our relationship. And then ... I'd look up at his slightly skew nose and full lips, and I'd kiss him, slip my hands under his shirt, feel his back, run my fingers up to his shoulder blades, then down, beneath the waistband of his trousers ... We hadn't enjoyed that sort of evening for a long time. Too long.

As I crossed the road, the snow turned to rain, fierce drops burst on my warm skin. I was soaked before I reached the stairs. The lift was out, of course. Just what I needed at the end of a shitty day. I swung open the door to the steps. Flashing my police torch, I pounded up four flights, two steps at a time. I wrenched the door open. Paul had lit all the candles; the apartment was full of weird shadows.

'I'm sorry,' I said, spraying the carpet with snow and rain drops. 'I'm sorry I'm late. There's this new case and my boss wants me to ...'

'I know, Thabisa,' he said. 'That's just it. It's always the job, never me.' He looked down and I saw the bags at his foot. All packed. Ready to go.

He turned away from me. I stepped towards him, so close I could touch him. But I didn't. I knew it was over.

'Come on, Paul,' I said quietly. 'I know it's difficult. But we can work it out. Let's go to Melrose Arch, find the others, get dinner. We can talk ...'

He stood stiff, unresponsive, not looking at me. Then he picked up his bags.

'There's really no point, Thabisa. It won't work.'

His words bobbed around the room, floating on the silence between us.

'There's someone else, isn't there.' It wasn't a question.

A man seldom leaves a woman unless there's another one waiting in the wings. I knew the answer before his eyes shifted.

'Thabisa, get a life, okay? You're a woman doing a man's job. Police work isn't for women. It makes them too tough.'

A twist of rage formed in my chest.

'You're too independent,' he continued. 'A real woman looks after her man, washes his shirts and, God forbid, even makes a meal occasionally.'

I took a deep breath.

'Get out.' I opened the door of my apartment. Paul had lived here in comfort, rent-free, for the past seven months. I held the door open, turned my face away, didn't look at him. I felt his shrug as he walked past me.

'I could have loved you,' he said.

'For a free-loading scumball you've got a hell of a cheek,' I yelled. 'And besides, how could you possibly, ever, have loved me? You're too much in love with yourself.' I kicked the door shut behind him. As it slammed, all the lights came back on again. An omen. It had to be. I just hoped it was a good one.

A police officer in the SVCU doesn't work regular hours, but my job was what I wanted, more than a love life, more than family and more than anything. When I'd met Paul Ngomo a year ago I thought it might possibly work. We met at a friend's place and got along well, to start with. Really well. We were both rural kids from the Eastern Cape, both making it in the big city – Jozi, the place to be. Paul, a banker, was smart, good-looking; he read the women's pages in *The Star* newspaper without making sarcastic comments. He frequently assured me that my career was as important as his and yet, under the modern veneer, the twenty-first-century, modern-man look, he was just another typical macho male. At first it was okay, but then he started leaving dirty dishes all over the kitchen, dropping his stuff on the floor, just leaving it there, until I got the hell in and picked it up ... What kind of idiot did that make me? He never cooked a meal, just sat there with his knife and fork in his hands, waiting for me to feed him. I suspected another woman when I saw him flipping his cell phone shut when I walked into the room, the sudden sliding away of his eyes when I looked at him. Then there were phone calls in the night, nobody there, just heavy breathing ... of the feminine sort. He had every excuse under the sun when I confronted him. Like an idiot, I believed most of it. Some woman at work was stalking him ... yeah, right! I glanced around the flat, scanning to see what he'd taken. A few DVDs were gone, some books, and most irritating of all, my favourite Miriam Makeba CD. Bastard.

What was wrong with me? Why did I pick these losers all the time? They were attracted to me like heat-seeking missiles. This had happened at least twice before. Where were all the good guys? The real men who wanted an equal relationship, who wanted to share my life instead of wanting to take it over?

I seemed to be doomed to become a sad single. Nothing seemed to go right with men. But then I thought, he's the loser here. Not me.

With Paul gone, I felt the apartment's space reasserting itself like water flowing gently over smooth pebbles.

I changed into a tracksuit, kicked off my shoes, cleared the image of Paul's angry face from my mind and sank into the squashy, cream sofa. Wriggling my toes comfortably into the cushions, I realised, with surprise, that I was actually relishing the solitude.

If I had to be totally honest, the last few months had been a strain. I'd been painting over the cracks, pretending things would improve. Now, as my anger slowly retreated, I felt a flood of relief that it was over.

I'd had enough of relationships. From now on my life was going to be a male-free zone.

# 4

## 19 June 2006

I arrived in Grahamstown at lunchtime. The streets were full of farm workers and labourers who had come into town for supplies. I glanced around. Hawkers squatted on the pavement, peddling fruit and vegetables; there was hooting and chaotic shouting at the taxi rank as taxis, cars, mini-buses, vans and motorcycles butted and pushed against one another, jostling and blaring their impatience. Smoke drifted from mobile kitchens and the enticing aromas of open-air cooking mixed with petrol fumes. I noted a darkened sports café, with a bare concrete floor and pool table, full of unemployed young men with disturbingly bloodshot eyes. They called out loudly to any young woman who passed.

There's trouble wherever you look.

I entered the Grahamstown Police Station through a barred security door. It was a grim double-storey, red-brick building, enclosed by eight-foot palisades. There were rolls of barbed wire everywhere I looked. People don't like the police – and buildings like this help to explain why.

It had been a bumpy plane journey from Johannesburg to East London and the drive from East London to Grahamstown had been the last straw. Why hadn't somebody met me? I'd travelled on the same plane as well-known politician Ollis Sando. He had been surrounded by bodyguards when they boarded, but I'd caught a glimpse of his tall, immaculately dressed body, the shaved head and wide, strongly carved lips. I recognised one of his bodyguards: Don Jacobs, a red-faced Afrikaans guy, bulging with muscles under his navy jacket. He'd worked with me back in the days at the Pretoria Police Station. He greeted me and we found ourselves sitting together at the back of the plane while Ollis Sando and his henchmen sat up front.

Don had changed for the worst since the days I knew him. He'd been a quiet, reserved sort of guy then. Now he seemed brash and arrogant. He was big, the muscles going to fat. He ordered a steady supply of red wine and I watched his eyes get more bloodshot throughout the journey. 'Off duty,' he said, when he saw my raised eyebrows as the cabin crew delivered his fourth drink. 'My detail starts tomorrow at six sharp. Plenty of time to sleep it off.'

'Why aren't you up there with the others?' I teased him.

'Not enough room. We're a small army these days,' he grinned at me. 'You look great, Thabisa. The SVCU obviously suits you. I heard through the grapevine that you're working there now. Hand-picked by Matatu.'

'Thank you, Don.' I smiled. 'Great outlet for my personality, eh? But how did you get to know that?'

He grinned. 'I still get all the *skinner*. What are you doing in the Eastern Cape?'

'I'm in Grahamstown for a couple of weeks,' I said. 'Working on a case.'

'Something to do with that missing woman, Julia McEwen?'

I turned away and stared out of the window. I was surprised by his question. He knew better than to ask me, surely? 'Why would you ask about her?'

'She's still in the news. Didn't you see the documentary on *Carte Blanche* last Sunday night? All about the little rich white lady being abducted from one of the larniest restaurants in Jo'burg.' Don moved his arm against mine and nudged me in an unpleasant, conspiratorial way.

I turned to face him again. 'I can't talk about my work – you know that – but no, for your information, it's not Julia McEwen. It's something else.'

He looked at me intently. 'Everyone in South Africa is wondering what's happened to that poor bitch. Her husband's a rich man. You'd think he'd be offering huge rewards for her return. But there's been nothing that I've heard of. Probably glad to get rid of her. Bet he's got a newer model lined up – what do you think, hey?' He nudged me again and winked. Horrible. I wanted him out of my space. Not easy on a crowded plane.

'He did offer a reward, just after it happened, but it's been three months now and still no trace of her. Nothing to do with me though.' I shifted away from him slightly. I wanted to shut him out, take some time to get my thoughts in order. 'You need to remember you're out of the force now, Don. You shouldn't be questioning a police officer.'

Don grinned. He loomed over me, twice my size, breathing his hot wine-breath against the side of my face. I shrugged further away, opened my newspaper and started to read.

He leaned closer. 'I'm not prying. Just interested. Where do you stay in Grahamstown? A bed and breakfast or what? There used to be a safe house in Hill Street, I remember from the old days.'

I sighed, folded up my newspaper and leaned back. The only way to deflect this guy was to get him talking about himself. One of the qualities Matatu appreciated about me was my ability to listen, wait patiently until the answers started coming. I never threatened or cajoled; I just waited and soon enough the information started flowing. Might as well practise my skills on this oaf, if only to stop him poking around in matters that no longer concerned him.

'Come on Don,' I said, 'let *me* question *you*. What's it like to be on the Ollis Sando protection team? Do you go everywhere with him?'

'Yes, mostly. He's a powerful guy. Nobody crosses him, but he needs protection.'

'Is he good to work for?'

Don looked away for a moment. When he glanced back there was an odd glint in his bloodshot eyes that warned me he wasn't comfortable with this conversation. I waited quietly for him to answer and soon enough he filled the silence. 'Well, "good" isn't the right word to describe Sando. He's difficult, demanding, determined, but you've got to admire the guy. Either way, this is a pretty good job. I'm well paid. It beats police work.'

'You think he'll make it as the next president?'

'Yes, or he'll die in the attempt. That's what I'm doing, making sure he lives to get what he wants.'

Don ordered another glass of red wine from the drinks trolley, leaned back and drank it one swig. Then he closed his eyes. I looked out the window as the plane flew over the Drakensberg Mountains. The valley was down there, somewhere, waiting for me. I could feel it.

Just before we began our descent, I went to wash my hands. When I got back to my seat Don was fiddling about in the overhead locker.

'Just checking my luggage,' he said. 'I'll lift yours down for you when we land.'

'I don't need you to do that,' I was annoyed. 'I'm perfectly capable of lifting my own stuff.'

'Always the gentleman, that's me,' he said, then turned away and looked out of the window.

I felt uncomfortable near him. Funny how people can change.

\*\*\*

In the police station, the Director's secretary sat behind a brown metal desk, head bent over a stack of files. 'I'm Detective Inspector Thabisa Tswane, from the Eagles – the Violent Crimes Unit. I'm here to see Director Mandile.'

'Thabisa? Thabisa, it's you! A blonde head came up. 'It's me, Bea Malan. We met at Mossel Bay when you were a cadet, remember?'

I recognised her immediately. Beatrix Jacoba Malan, known to everyone as Busy Bea. She was older than me, a little heavier in the waist than the last time we met, but still the same old Bea.

Most stations required their administrative staff to wear conservative clothes. Not Bea. She had always been outrageous, but so efficient it didn't matter. She had a Rubenesque body and her wardrobe looked three sizes too small. Today she wore a fire-engine red sweater, not a good choice for somebody who carried most of her body weight on her chest. Bea wasn't a fitness fanatic.

Some things never change, and thank God they don't.

'Bea, how amazing,' I said. 'What are you doing here?'

'Same thing as Mossel Bay. Thabisa, you've done so well. I knew you would. Congratulations.'

As Bea swivelled her chair towards the Director's half-open door, I smiled. The clinging red top was only part of it. A red mini-skirt and white, knee-high boots edged with fake fur completed the look.

'Detective Inspector Thabisa Tswane is here,' she announced loudly.

The door opened and Director Mandile appeared. A thin ferret of a man, with tight lips and narrow eyes. He didn't smile or look directly at me.

'Good day, Detective Inspector,' he said. 'We've been waiting for you. We were all too busy to come and meet you in East London. I believe you're going to help your poor rural cousins catch these two criminals? I must admit we didn't expect a woman to come and save us.'

I narrowed my eyes and did some mental deep breathing to remain impassive, refusing to rise to the bait. Before offering a handshake Mandile asked to see my identification documents, then spent an insulting length of time examining them, as though certain they were fraudulent. Only then did he grudgingly shake my hand and escort me past Bea's desk.

'This is a high-profile case,' he said. 'No doubt you'll find it good for your career.'

I had encountered a few Mandiles along the way. In a male-dominated society, it was inevitable. The only way to cope was keep calm, and just imagine stamping on his foot, or – even better – his head.

'Director Mandile, we just want to catch these guys as soon as possible,' I said. 'This assignment has been given to me because I come from the area and the chief witness is my grandfather.'

'Yes, yes, we are aware of your grandfather. We do, however, have a further witness, the security guard who was outside the bank at Kenton-on-Sea. They hit him on the head. He's in hospital here with concussion.'

'Before I see him, let's go through the information we have.' I smiled coldly and flipped open my file.

Mandile moved aside slowly, so slowly that I had to squeeze past him through the doorway. My fingers itched to push him out of the way. He was just the sort of man modern women can do without. He pointed to an uncomfortable chair and slid behind his desk, staring at me, running his beady little eyes over my face and body with a sneer.

What a little shit.

'Right, let's look at what's happened until now,' I said. 'I've been through all the documentation, but refresh my memory. I'd like to go through things a step at a time. Where did this start?'

'The hoists began in Umtata and progressed across the Eastern Cape, petrol stations, stores, a bank in Port Alfred and another here in Grahamstown. What makes the Violent Crimes team think just one woman can sort out these crimes anyway?' His eyebrows rose in his ratty little face.

Just what the world needs, one more male chauvinist policeman.

'Let's focus on the case, shall we?' I said. 'Otherwise Divisional Commissioner Matatu might have to be informed that cooperation is lacking at this station.'

He swallowed his annoyance with bad grace. 'Up to now these criminals – black males we think – have been very polite to their victims. They speak in strange, high voices and say things like "have a good day" and "sorry we have spoiled your weekend", stuff like that.'

There was a silence before I leaned forward and said, 'How can you be sure that these guys are black when they're disguised?'

'My dear DI Tswane. It's quite obvious that you are new to this area. To the demographics of the crimes here. In the last two years, of the roughly 3,000 criminals that have been arrested, 90% have been black, 10% white, Indian or coloured. Therefore, we feel quite confident in our assumption that these crimes were committed by young black males. Of course, they *could* be white males,' he smiled thinly, 'but the chances of this are slim. Very slim. It is most likely that they are, as I said, black males. We shall proceed with the investigation presuming this to be the case until we have evidence to the contrary.'

'In the Violent Crimes Unit we are told not to *assume* anything ... ever,' I said.

Mandile's narrow eyes grew narrower and he looked away, twitching with annoyance.

'How do they get away without anyone seeing them?' I asked.

'Nobody knows.'

'But how can two masked people, running away, carrying bags, not be noticed?'

'That's why you're here, isn't it?' His eyebrows rose above a fake smile. He waved his hand dismissively. 'To find these things out?'

I mentally clenched my fists and forced an answering grin. 'What happened to all this polite conversation at Kenton-on-Sea?' I asked. 'Something must have gone wrong?'

'Apparently a customer in the bank tried to apprehend them. He pulled out his firearm to defend himself and they shot him.'

'So, Director Mandile, despite the gunshot, the alarm sounding, and all the panic, they shot a man, walked out of the bank, calmly stole a car, drove away and nobody saw anything?'

'Things move slowly in the Eastern Cape. People leave their keys in their cars in these small places.'

'Wouldn't happen in Johannesburg.' I closed my file.

'Miss Malan will accompany you to the hospital to speak to the security guard. She has organised accommodation for you, just ask her for what you need. Unfortunately, I will be unable to go with you. I have several pressing matters to attend to.'

'Ja, right,' I said. I turned away, imagining Mandile's glare of deep dislike burning holes through my uniform.

Bea was at her desk, grinning, as I walked out. She was obviously the station's information wizard, with several powerful computer monitors on her side table. The neat files stacked on the top of cabinets, pens and pencils in military lines on her desk all emphasised her competence.

'So,' I asked, 'you're coming to the hospital with me, right?'

'Looks like it.'

I remembered Mossel Bay, back when black police officers were made to use separate toilets. In her role as station administrator Bea had taken no notice of these rules and regulations and made sure I used the same facilities as the others. I hadn't forgotten her kindness.

'What's with Director Mandile?'

'Bitter and twisted,' said Bea cheerfully. 'Thinks he's been passed over for promotion and hates women police officers.'

'Oh great,' I said. 'Just my luck.'

'He's incompetent as well as being embittered,' Bea said quietly. 'What a combination. It's a nightmare, but I love my job, and he's not going to get to me. Every day I look at him and think, this too shall pass. And hopefully, soon, it will. I don't trust him, Thabisa. Talking of which –' she lowered her voice and spoke even more quietly. 'Mandile has been giving information about you to somebody. That's how I knew you were arriving today.'

'Who to?

'I don't know, but he definitely gave your name as the investigating officer on this case. He closed the door of his office, but you know me, I've got ears like a hawk, I can hear through thick stone walls. He was discussing you with someone.'

'So what?' I shrugged. 'It's no secret that I'm here.'

But I tucked that piece of information into the back of my mind. I would think about it later.

***

The hospital was full of screaming children and pensioners in threadbare clothes. They hardly glanced up as we walked by, despite my police uniform and Bea's startling red outfit.

Basani Korulo, a young man in his twenties, lay propped up in bed with a large bandage around his head.

After perfunctory greetings, I spoke to him in isiXhosa. '*Ubabonile!* – Did you see them?'

'Yes, *sisi*. I have seen these people in the movies about creatures from other planets. Aliens. They had rubber masks on their heads. They were thin. The tallest one hit me on the head with a gun when I tried to stop them entering the bank.'

'Did they speak?'

'No, *sisi*, they just hit me.'

'What happened?'

'I fell down. Then later, I heard a gunshot in the bank. Then I saw them leave the bank with the black bags. Like the ones we use for rubbish.'

'And then?'

'Then they disappeared.'

'In what direction?'

'Into the air, *sisi*. They disappeared like spirits into space. The ground was shaking.'

I sighed. Basani's description reminded me vividly of the valley and all its superstitions.

'Come now, Basani, think. They couldn't just disappear. They are not spirits. Spirits don't rob banks and shoot people. Spirits don't hit you over the head with guns.'

Basani looked at me from under his bandage. '*Sisi*, they are spirits.' His voice was a stricken monotone.

'No, Basani, they are bad men. Try to remember ...'

The curtains around the bed flipped open. A tall blond man in a white coat, a stethoscope snaking around his neck, stood in front of me. He looked tired out, with dark rings under his eyes 'I'm going to have to ask you to leave,' he said in a strong Australian accent. 'This patient isn't fit to be questioned. He's concussed. You'll have to come back later, Police Constable ... you are?'

'Detective Inspector Thabisa Tswane, Violent Crimes Unit, Johannesburg, 'Doing my job,' I said, flashing my police ID. 'And you are?'

'Tom Winter, Basani's doctor,' he said. He ran kind blue eyes over me and smiled. 'You've got grey eyes,' he said. Something about his quick shy smile made me take note. It was almost as if we had already met and shared a private joke.

I was used to this reaction to my eyes. I stared back without expression.

'Please forgive me for being so familiar,' he continued, undeterred, 'but it's so unusual. And so beautiful.'

'When can I come back to question him?' I asked, trying to ignore the steady, admiring gaze of the doctor. 'He's a witness in a murder case.'

'Maybe tomorrow?' the doctor suggested. 'Please call me and I'll see if it's possible.'

I gestured to Bea and we left the ward. I felt flushed and annoyed.

'Handsome doctor – I wouldn't mind him taking my blood pressure,' Bea said.

'I didn't notice.'

'Yeah, right,' said Bea. She almost ran to keep up with me.

'Why don't people *see* things for what they are, not a load of fantasy?' I asked. 'That guard has no idea. It's all superstition and spirits, smoke and mirrors.'

'Well, the poor thing has concussion,' said Bea. 'And besides, he's not the only one. It's the same story wherever these heists have taken place. People say they just vanish into thin air. Those weird alien masks really spook them.'

'Can you buy masks like that easily around here?' I asked.

'In any toy shop,' said Bea.

As we got into the car, Bea asked, 'Do you want me to come to the valley with you tomorrow when you talk to your grandfather? We've got a four-wheel drive you could ask for.'

'Thanks Bea, that's very kind, but the four-wheel drive is only part of it. You have to hike the last six kilometres through the mountains. The final bit's almost abseiling.'

'Oh shit. No offence, but I don't think I can help you there,' said Bea. 'Listen, Thabisa, why don't you leave your bags with me for now? You can come around and have supper with me tonight and pick them up. Then I'll drive you back to your place. What about it? We can catch up.'

'Thanks, that's great,' I said. 'It's so good to see you Bea. Thanks for being supportive about your boss. I'm glad to have a good friend to back me up.'

***

When I arrived at Bea's cottage, I half-expected a colourful den filled with beads, rainbow throws and lots of cushions, but Bea restricted her outrageous tastes to her wardrobe. Like the office, the vibe in her house was clutter free and organised, with stripped pine floorboards, rugs, bookcases, a comfortable sofa and chairs.

I could smell garlic in the kitchen. Jazz played over a small sound system. Bea motioned me to the sofa and offered me a glass of Merlot. Then she curled her legs under her in a comfortable, deep armchair and beamed at me.

'I'm so glad you're here,' she said. A heavy striped cat that looked half-wild crept out from behind her chair. It gave me a suspicious glare, and then leapt onto Bea's lap. Bea stroked it between the ears. 'This is Rasputin,' she said. 'My best mate.'

'He's gorgeous,' I said. 'But what happened to your husband? Graham, wasn't it? You two seemed so good together. What went wrong?'

'He left. The usual thing – finds a younger version of me, has an affair, I find out, there's a big drama. I'm better off without him, believe me.'

Bea sliced her hands through the air for punctuation as she talked, but I could see the hurt behind the humour. 'So, you see, I had to throw him out, just like all bad rubbish, he had to go. But never mind about me, Thabisa, I really want to hear about you,' she said, sipping her wine.

'I joined the Serious Crimes Unit when I left Mossel Bay. I was picked by my boss, Commissioner Matatu, a great honour for me. I really enjoy the work. It's just the love life that isn't working properly.' I grimaced, remembering Paul.

Bea laughed. 'Whose love life can work in this sort of job?'

'I've had a couple of serious relationships, but the guy always disappoints me. You get sucked in, think this time it might just work. Get serious and then, pfff!' I flicked my fingers, 'He's gone. Talk about thin air. My boyfriends do a better vanishing job than any wannabe aliens ever could. I don't want to get involved again. It's too much of a hassle. Rather stick to work.'

'Difficult when you look like you do,' said Bea.

'Come on, Bea, I'm nothing special.'

'Your eyes are something special for a start. The rest of you is pretty good as well – you must have loads of men interested in you.'

'My eyes were a nuisance in the valley. They thought I was a witch.'

I leaned back in the chair, watching Bea stroke the purring cat. My light grey eyes were a remarkable thing in the valley. They unnerved the older villagers and reinforced the suspicion that I was destined to be a *sangoma* – a traditional healer. From an early age I learnt that I only had to turn my eyes on them, stand still and stare, to make them scatter and run.

But it hadn't worked that way the night they beat me and drove me out of the valley.

'What about the valley?' asked Bea. 'Do you go home?'

'I haven't been home for a very long time,' I said. 'My grandfather is still alive, but we have no contact.'

'But why? I thought he'd be proud of you.'

'Quite the opposite. He's disappointed in me at every level.'

'I suppose he wants you to go home and marry a local boy?'

'A boy? That would be a bonus. He's more interested in selling me off to old men who make good *lobola* offers.'

'How does it work, in the valley?' Bea asked. 'Doesn't anything ever change there? Forgive my curiosity, Thabisa, I've wanted to ask you before, but it seemed too inquisitive and you were so guarded about your background. I don't want to pry, I'm really interested.'

'I haven't been back for ages but I'm sure it's still the same – no electricity, no running water. The women still carry water up from the river on their heads. Just like it was a hundred years ago.'

'It sounds like the place that time forgot. Surely people must leave, to get married, to get work?' Bea asked.

'Yes, I guess these days most young men go off to the cities for jobs. They'll come back twice a year for a week or two to plant *mielies* in December and harvest in April. And to make babies with their wives. That's the way it is. The valley is full of children, women and old men.'

'It sounds a bit oppressive to me.' Bea took another sip of her wine.

'There are lots of places like it in South Africa. Tucked away in the hills and valleys. The young men go up to Gauteng to get work. When they come back they bring modern stuff, like portable radios and CD players. But it's all still very traditional.'

Bea leaned forward in the chair. 'I can't imagine what it must be like to be part of a place that's so cut off.'

'It's different, believe me.'

'How does your grandfather cope financially?'

'Traditional leaders get a government grant. Then there are tributes from the villagers. I send money to him monthly, but he never cashes the cheques.'

'Really? Oh my God, that means he's seriously upset with you, Thabisa.'

Bea got up and moved into the kitchen and I followed. 'Spaghetti bolognaise okay?' she asked, chopping an onion with speed and precision.

'Great. My favourite. I'll lay the table.'

We worked in companionable silence for a few minutes.

'What about the rest of your family? Do you have any contact?' Bea finally asked.

'You know both my parents are dead. My two uncles as well. My grandfather and I are the only remaining members of the family bloodline.'

'Doesn't he have other wives? Your grandfather?'

'Yes, but he's eighty-five, Bea, so it's unlikely there will be any more children. He's been a failure at procreation. He had five wives, but only three kids.' I laughed bitterly. 'So no pressure on me.'

'Well, you never know, Thabisa, he could still surprise you ... stranger things have happened!' Bea rolled her eyes. We both laughed.

'What about his siblings? Didn't he have brothers and sisters?'

'Only one, my great-aunt. Mama Elsie Tswane. She left the valley when she was very young, went to live in Jozi, but her husband died in an accident. Now she works in Port Elizabeth. She goes back to the valley regularly; heaven knows how she does it. It's quite a climb, believe me. She must be well over seventy by now.'

'How long have you been away?'

'Fourteen years,' I said quietly. I was finding the whole conversation painful. 'I've almost forgotten the valley. Jozi is my life now and I love it.'

This wasn't strictly true; the valley seemed to be with me a lot of the time. So many things reminded me.

'So when you go back, do you reckon it'll all be the same? The women doing all the work, like before?' Bea asked. She spun lettuce, emptied it into a bowl and then picked up a knife to slice tomatoes.

I laughed. 'Believe me – nothing will have changed.' I shook my head. The more I tried to stop thinking about the valley the more it was pushing in on me. 'Take my word for it, Bea, the last thing you ever want to be is a valley wife. You can forget all the luxuries you take for granted: electricity, running water, hopping into your car and going to Pick 'n Pay if you've forgotten to buy milk. The women do all the domestic chores, by hand – on foot.

'And the men?'

'The men herd cattle.'

'Is that all?' Bea looked shocked.

'Oh no, they also have very important business to attend to. After they've done with the herding, they have to go to the chief's house, drink beer and talk.'

We looked at each other for a moment. Then we exploded with laughter.

'You're kidding!' Bea said.

'No way! The valley's a man's world, Bea.'

'Thank God I've always been independent.'

'Well, we've both made our own way.'

We smiled at each other; two working women out in the world – a world of jobs and special skills, where we knew the language and knew how to play the game.

We chatted as Bea swirled pasta, tossed salad and poured more wine, all to the accompaniment of music playing on the FM radio. It was, appropriately, 'The Flight of the Bumble Bee'. Perfect music for cooking pasta in this cosy cottage kitchen.

After supper, Bea percolated coffee and we sat and chatted about the old days. The atmosphere was light and we laughed loudly together, resurrecting stories from the past.

'Do you remember that old battle-axe ... what was her name? The stores' manager. Hilda Cloete, wasn't it? Remember how she only gave out four sheets of toilet paper at a time?'

Bea stirred whipped cream into her coffee and grinned at me.

'What about those terrible stockings they made us wear at the station?' I laughed. 'Bare Beige for black women police officers, to make our legs look whiter.'

Bea shook her head. 'And we white ones wore black stockings, can you believe it? What were they thinking?'

'You can still buy Bare Beige at Woollies, if you ever want a pair,' I laughed.

'Thanks Thabisa, I'll go first thing in the morning!'

It was after eleven when Bea drove me home. 'Bye, sleep well,' she called as she dropped me off at the Hill Street safe house.

'Thanks for supper,' I called back.

The moon told its usual lies, made the ugly, flat-roofed cube of a house tolerable if not beautiful to the forgiving eye. I wondered why all police safe houses were so unattractive. This was no quaint 1820s settler cottage. The house was a one-up, one-down place, filled with heavy dark furniture and a gruesome brown and red carpet.

I opened the door, stepped inside and froze. It was only a slight noise but it didn't belong in the cottage. A prickly sensation on my neck told me I wasn't alone. As I felt for my gun, a figure stepped out of the shadows.

Black on black.

In the faint trickle of light from the street I saw he wore a ski-mask and black tracksuit. Before I had time to react he reached, grabbed my shoulder, spun me around and punched me hard in the kidneys. Paralysing pain sliced through me and I fell forward, gasping for breath. Strong hands fastened round my neck, dragging me down the narrow hallway. I fought back, wrestling, kicking and punching, but my attacker was stronger. He dragged me down and straddled my chest. I gasped for air. A voice from a child's cartoon squawked in my ear.

'I'm warning you, get off this case, Thabisa Tswane, leave Grahamstown and don't come back. Otherwise you'll die. Here's a taste of what you'll get.'

I heard the click of a lighter, and then flames danced on the back of my hand. The pain was intense. I tried to yell but it came out like a cry. I tried to pull my hand away, but the man held on.

'Do you understand what I'm saying? Do you ...?' His squeaky voice hissed in my ear.

'Who are you?' I whispered.

Silence.

Finally he stood. I felt him move past me. I grabbed at his leg, but he kicked my hand away.

'Bitch!' he shrilled.

Then he laughed. High pitched and eerie, like a horror movie.

A door slammed, footsteps sounded, a shot was fired. I heard Bea's voice shouting: 'Thabisa, Thabisa ... are you alright?'

I cradled my hand. It throbbed all the way to my elbow, and for a few moments I could do nothing but hold it against my chest and bite my lip.

Then Bea was kneeling beside me, holding me, crying: 'Oh my God, Thabisa, what happened? I was checking my messages on my cell phone outside, when this man, this burglar, shot out of your door and fired at the car. Are you okay?'

I sat up, still cradling my hand. 'It wasn't a burglar. He attacked me. He – he knew my name.'

'Oh, shit, Thabisa, we'll have to report this. I'll call the station now.' She was already on her mobile. 'He's a lousy shot, whoever he is. He could have killed me but he smashed the windscreen of the car behind me instead.'

All melted into slow motion, a police siren outside, police radios spluttering and crackling.

'Here she is.' Bea was standing in front of me, next to a tall man. I glanced up and saw it was the Australian from the hospital. His eyes lit up when he saw me and then his face darkened when he saw my blistered hand and wrist.

'Who did this to you?' he asked, his voice tight and angry.

'Line of duty,' I said. 'I'm fine.'

Looking at me, not saying a word, he cleaned the burns. Then he took off his gloves and wiped his hand across his forehead.

'You'll be all right,' he said. 'It's pretty painful, eh? Shall I give you an injection to take the edge off it?'

I bit my lip and nodded.

Afterwards, he asked again quietly: 'Who would do this to you?'

'I don't know,' I said. 'It was dark.'

He took my bandaged hand in both of his and looked straight into my eyes. 'Be careful, okay?' he said. 'Just be careful.'

Bea bustled around me, making tea. 'Come home with me tonight, I've got plenty of room,' she said.

'It's fine, I'll be okay here,' I said.

'No, Thabisa, please,' Bea insisted.

'Honestly Bea, I'd rather stay here. But thank you anyway. I really will be fine.'

Bea frowned. 'I've asked them to leave a patrol car outside for the rest of the night.'

***

I lay awake for a long time, unable to sleep. My muscles were twitchy, my mind uneasy. Why hadn't I pulled out my gun? Why had I let myself be overpowered so easily? Who knew where I was staying? Who was this person who had squawked my name, warned me off the case?

But most of all, why did he smell so strange? Something sweet and familiar, it clung to my clothes. I knew that smell, I just couldn't put a name to it.

# 5

**Three months earlier**

**11 March 2006**

'Oh my God, you're a woman!'

'Shut your mouth. When we get out of the lift, walk in front of me. I've got the gun on your back,' the woman said.

The lift descended. The doors opened into a basement car park. The woman frogmarched Julia to another lift on the far side, inserted a card and the doors hissed shut. They rose quickly until the doors opened to a dark, gloomy lobby. The woman unlocked a door, pushed Julia inside and slammed it shut. She switched on a light. They faced one another in a narrow hallway.

A tall blonde woman in her thirties stared at Julia.

'Please. Let me go,' Julia said. 'I won't tell anyone about this, I swear I won't.'

The woman didn't answer. Her face remained blank.

She gripped Julia's wrist, pulled her across the hallway into a bland, musty, room and pushed her down on a thin mattress. It covered an iron bedstead. She yanked at Julia's arms, spreading them wide. Julia felt cold steel closing round her wrists. The woman was handcuffing her to the bed.

Julia cried out as the cuffs bit into her flesh. 'Please,' she begged, kicking and pulling away. 'Please don't! No, please.'

Silence.

Then the woman stuffed a gag into Julia's mouth and taped it round her head. She choked and gagged on the rough material. It tasted like a dishcloth.

The woman didn't even glance at Julia before she walked out and slammed the door shut.

Julia was alone. Coffin darkness closed in around her. Despite the fact that she was lying down, stretched out on her back, it felt like she was falling. A dizzy plummeting, without end. An hallucination, or maybe she was falling apart from within.

She lay motionless, her wrists manacled to the sides of the bed. The night became damaged footage of an old black-and-white horror movie. It was airless, hot, and Julia was clammy with fear. She longed for a drink of water. She tried to cling to reality. She forced herself to think. Remain calm. Try to find an explanation for what had happened. Her eyes darted around the room, from wall to wall to the faint strip of light seeping in under the door. Where was she? Why had this happened to her? Could she escape? She wriggled around trying to free her hands. Every time she moved the handcuffs dug deeper into her wrists. She felt her skin split. Blood trickled onto the mattress. For what seemed like hours, she listened for any sound from the woman. She had no idea what time it was or how long she had been here. She tried not to visualise what was going to happen to her. She replayed her abduction over and over in her mind. The woman, who had seemed to be a man, had been relentless. She was strong. The way she dragged Julia from the restaurant, manhandled her into the lift and now into this room, without saying a word, was chilling.

Her isolation sharply amplified all the noises around her. Through the door she could hear surreal sounds, heightened by her imagination. A tap whimpered, pipes moaned, she even imagined she could hear pots and pans squeaking in a kitchen somewhere, but no sound of human voices. Outside, the throb of traffic and the wail of police sirens drifted up from the street below. A snatch of music floated up into the night. She was in a city teeming with people, but she was quite alone.

Her arms were stretched taut on either side of her body and her imprisoned hands prickled with pins and needles. She had to keep clenching and unclenching her fingers to increase the blood flow, but with every movement, the cuffs bit deeper. No matter how hard she tried to concentrate on something else to pass the time and distract her from her predicament, fear crept in, threatening to overwhelm her.

The best way to keep panic at bay was to think about her childhood and her parents. She hadn't thought about them in years. She remembered her young self. The indulged, only child of wealthy, older parents. Her beautiful, restless mother with her bridge parties and swirling social life. Her silent, distracted father, always deep in business transactions. She had her ponies, her dogs, her music lessons, her school and a dozen caring domestic helpers. But her parents remained distant, almost unaware of her.

She often watched, crouched at the top of the stairs, when they entertained. Men drinking, puffing smoke out of their mouths, women, like her mother, with hard, sad eyes, wearing glittery clothes and dancing, moving languidly to old-fashioned music.

'Pretty easy life you've had,' Magnus had said when they first met. 'Nothing seems to have happened to you.'

Nothing.

Her parents had tried to stop her marrying Magnus – he came from a dubious background – but she, young and naïve, thought she could handle him, change him. He wanted her money, of course, and much, much more.

Magnus. She tied to force him out her mind, but he forced his way back in. As much of a bully absent as he was present.

She shuddered. The handcuffs unearthed memories she would never be able to block. She remembered the latest discovery, just a few weeks ago, of the pornography that made it clear he was fascinated by the sadistic humiliation of women and children.

She hated the smell of him.

She hated his touch.

She hated what she had become since knowing him.

She tried to go back to her childhood again. To the lonely memories. Anything rather than think about the man who called himself her husband. Or worse, remember what had happened before they dressed for Mama Ruby's.

*** 

Chiffon, light. Floating. Running the scarf through her fingers. Winding it around her wrist. Releasing it, watching the colours light on the air. Scrunching it in her hand. Sliding into her bag.

And then ... what came after.

After the elation of the moment. After the security guard's hand grabbed her shoulder. After the store manager's insulting questions. After the phone calls, the police station, the arrest, the shame of it all. After the silent drive home, Julia had stumbled into her bathroom, opened the cupboard that contained all her treasures, and wept.

Thirteen bars of soap, an umbrella, twenty-two pairs of sunglasses, eighteen lipsticks, a dozen scarves, piles of underwear. All the things she had stolen over the past few months. Seven potato peelers too. Not that she had ever peeled a potato in her life.

It never seemed like stealing. Whatever she took wasn't enough. It couldn't fill the greedy, aching, thrilling hunger in her chest.

This time they'd called the police. Although for a moment, when the store manager's eyes roamed over her diamond-stud earrings, pin-tucked Paris shirt and crocodile-skin shoes, she had thought he might relent again. But he just gave her the sort of pitying look she associated with social workers.

'I'm sorry, Mrs McEwen,' he had said, then picked up the phone. He called Magnus.

Her husband's face had been impassive as they drove home from the police station. When they arrived home he dismissed all the staff for the day, even the four gardeners. Without a glance in her direction he went to his room and slammed the door.

Julia ran a bath. She knew what would happen next.

She glanced at herself in the mirror but the woman with the red hair and fearful eyes who stared back gave no sign of recognition.

She relived the morning's events. If only she hadn't picked up the stupid scarf without checking the coast was clear. She had been successful for too long, got complacent. It was second nature now to enter the store, flash her smile at the security guard and sales assistants, before deftly lifting something off the display and putting it into her bag.

The scarf wasn't even silk – just a cheap thing, probably made in China. It seemed so dull, so boring, to meekly queue up and pay for it, rather than seize the moment, feel alive, when most of the time she felt half dead. This was the only thing that made her feel switched on and in control. The rest of the time she felt dead inside. Why not just take the fucking thing?

But things had spiralled out of control, unleashing a cascade of horrors: arrest, shame, prosecution, Magnus's silence.

Now she could hear his footsteps on the tiled floor. She turned. He was wearing a bathrobe; his face was grim. He looked at her for a long moment. He reminded her of a bull she had seen as a child, its head lowered, pawing the ground, charging. Killing one of her father's grooms.

Magnus reached out, grabbed her wrists and pulled her towards him.

'Bitch,' he hissed into her face. 'You've humiliated me. You've made a fool of me. I own this city, and now I look like an idiot who can't control his own wife.'

He tore her shirt open. She fell back, twisting away from him. He dragged her back, ripping off her skirt and pants. Then he seized her head, thrust her face down into the bath and held her under the perfumed water until she thought she would die. When he finally released her, retching, gasping for air, he threw her down on the tiled floor, crushed her with the bulk of his body and straddled her.

He hissed in her ear, 'Think I don't know what you've been up to? That I don't know what's in the cupboard in here? You stupid bitch. I know exactly what you do.'

'Pretending to be such a lady, Julia, when you're really just a common fucking thief ...'

At the end of it, he'd stood up and stared down at her as she lay crumpled on the floor.

'You're not even a good fuck, Julia. Be ready by eight. We're dining with the Russian tonight.'

She crawled to the bathroom cupboard and looked again at all the things she had taken. They shimmered with memories of her close shaves, little triumphs and moments of pure exhilaration. She'd risked everything to take these things and this was the result. This was the raw, warped core of her life.

She'd lain on the bathmat, exhausted, staring blankly at the windowpane rinsed with unseasonal rain.

*\*\*\**

Julia closed her eyes against the memory of Magnus's silence in the car on the way to Mama Ruby's. Only as they had been walking in to the restaurant had he spoken. 'Don't think this is over, Julia,' he'd said quietly. 'You've played me for a fool. Every mouthful you take tonight, every sip of wine. They'll all be bringing you closer to the end of the evening. To coming back home with me.' Then he'd laughed. She shuddered at the memory of that empty, frightening sound.

What a fool she'd been to spend all these years with a man she loathed. After today's attack, she was determined to find a way to leave him ... if she survived this.

She must have dozed off, because she didn't hear the footsteps, but she was wide awake when the door opened. The light from the doorway blinded her. The woman approached, pulled the gag out of her mouth and unlocked the handcuffs.

Julia massaged her sore wrists and stood. 'I need to go to the bathroom,' she whispered.

The woman indicated that she could leave the room.

Directly opposite, a door stood open and Julia glimpsed a washbasin. She stumbled inside, opened the taps and plunged her face into cold water. As she glanced up, the bathroom mirrors caught the reflections of a terrified woman. She looked more like a corpse than a human being. One eye was closed, her hair matted with congealed blood, her mouth bruised.

Suddenly, shockingly, a telephone rang. Julia listened to urgent conversation just outside the door. Although she strained to hear, she couldn't make sense of anything.

The woman wrenched open the bathroom door.

'Wash,' she commanded. 'Get the blood off, we're leaving.'

Julia didn't move for a moment.

'Where are we going?'

The woman ignored her.

'I'll get you as much money as you want,' Julia said. 'Nobody will ever know about you.'

'Do you think I'm mad?' The woman was restless, jumpy. 'You'd go straight to the police. The alternative is to kill you here. Like I've been told to do.'

Terror swept through Julia. Who had 'told' this woman to kill her? Why? She remembered television footage of hostages in Iraq just before they were beheaded, desperately pleading for their lives. She remembered herself on the bathroom floor. Trying to writhe away from Magnus. She hadn't begged. And she wasn't going to beg now. She wouldn't do that, whatever happened.

'I don't know why you want to kill me, but if you're going to do it, for God's sake, do it quickly,' she said before turning back into the cloakroom and shutting the door on the woman's surprised face.

What did it matter anyway? She had nothing of value in her life. In the past twenty-four hours, she had been arrested for shop-lifting, brutally assaulted by her husband and kidnapped. Death would be a sweet escape from this nightmare. After a few minutes, Julia walked out and faced the woman. She surveyed her dispassionately. She still wore the black hooded tracksuit, her long hair scraped into a ponytail. She was beautiful in a pale, Eastern-European way, lean and strong with delicate features and cold, pale eyes under straight, dark brows.

'Move,' said the woman. She waved a gun in Julia's face. Her voice had an accent of some sort, perhaps from London.

'I'm not going to tie your hands. I expect absolute obedience. When we get to the parking floor, if you make any attempt to escape, I'll shoot you.'

Julia believed her.

'There'll be a car parked near the lift. When I open the door, get onto the back seat and lie down. One false move and you're dead. Get it?'

'Yes.'

They left the apartment and descended in the lift. The woman pushed Julia with the muzzle of the gun. They moved towards a white Toyota parked nearby. Julia got in and lay down on the back seat. The woman fiddled in the boot of the car, then opened the door again and threw a heavy rug over her. It was dusty and scratchy. Julia tried not to cough. As they drove out of the underground parking she heard a shout. The woman braked and pulled over; her window hissed down.

'Hi,' she said.

'Everything okay, sisi?' a male voice asked.

'It's fine,' the woman said. 'I'm going to the office.' There was a metallic click as she cocked the gun.

'Ah, it's very early for work.'

'Yes, I get overseas phone calls. Any trouble? I heard police sirens in the night. See anything?'

'There was a hold up at Mama Ruby's restaurant,' the voice said. 'I only came on duty afterwards. I didn't see anything.'

'Jo'burg's a dangerous place for us all. Bye now. Take care.'

She accelerated out of the parking lot and made a sharp right. After a while Julia worked out that they were going south. The regular, distinctive bumps felt like the concrete highway, the N1 that snaked around Soweto, then ran due south to Bloemfontein and beyond. The woman drove fast and said nothing. She slowed for the tollgates, then sped on the open road for about forty minutes.

Julia was sweating, her breath restricted by the blanket. Tiny fibres found their way to the back of her throat, making her gag. Her blood roared in her ears. The car slowed down. The woman pulled over, drew the car to the side of the road and stopped.

This is it. Julia felt surprisingly calm. She sat up, pulling the blanket away. She's going to kill me.

It was still dark, but she could see the first streaks of dawn fingering the eastern sky.

The driver's door clicked open. A foot hit the gravel at the side of the road. 'Get out.' The pistol's cold muzzle pressed into her neck. 'Walk ahead of me across the field,' the woman hissed.

As Julia's feet touched the ground, she was struck by a moment of blinding clarity. She wanted to live. The thought surprised her; she had contemplated suicide so many times. The air was cold but fresh. Through the quiet night Julia felt the whisper of a breeze. The maize field they walked in was scratchy, the dry mealie stalks murmuring sweet sounds as they passed. She tried to turn, face the woman. She knew it was harder to kill someone if they were facing you, breathing on you. Even the most deadly assassin asked his victims to turn away.

'Kneel,' the woman commanded.

Julia fell on her knees, jerking with nerves, gasping. This was where she was going to die, in a maize field off a national highway. As she gulped her last breath, dropping her head forward, Julia felt an ache of regret for what life could have been. She heard the woman making a call on her mobile, talking to someone, but she couldn't catch the words.

The cold metal crack of the pistol shot ripped the thick night air.

The sound echoed across the fields.

Julia looked around.

Her ears were ringing.

There was no blood.

The woman had fired into the ground beside her.

Julia fell forward, twitching with terror and relief. She was alive. She could hear distant noises over the veld: the sound of cars on the highway. A plane droned overhead. The world was still turning.

'Get up,' said the woman. She strode away from Julia, heading back to the car.

Julia tried to stand but her legs wouldn't support her. She lay for a moment, gasping, tendrils of panic uncurling in her stomach. Then she dragged herself up and staggered towards the car. The woman was talking on her mobile, her back to Julia.

'Yes, of course she's dead. You heard me shoot her. In a field off the N1. In a gully. Deep bush; nobody's going to find her for weeks.'

Julia fell back into the car. The woman returned and sat silently. Julia tried to analyse why she hadn't tried to escape, run screaming for the highway, but she couldn't. Her mind wouldn't work. All she could do was remember the hostages rescued in Iraq, talking on television.

*We established a connection with our captors. We knew that if we spoke to them they would see us, as people, not as victims.*

'Why didn't you kill me?'

'Perhaps I've got a use for you.'

'Thank you for sparing my life.'

'There's plenty of time. I plan to kill you later.'

'Why?'

Silence. A huge vehicle flashed past, lights blazing. It lit up the woman's face.

'Why are you doing this?' Julia asked. For a moment, she was the interrogator. 'You've kidnapped me, beaten me, and tried to kill me. Why? You don't even know me.'

'Collateral damage. You served a purpose. Call it bad timing.'

'So this is not about me? Then just let me out. Drive off. I'll never speak about it. I promise. I'm a rich woman; I'll give you anything you want.'

The woman clutched the steering wheel for a moment before answering.

'It's gone too far. You're coming with me to a place I know, and then I'll decide what to do. If you make any attempt to escape, I'll kill you. Get it?'

'Yes,' Julia answered. After a long silence she said, 'Please tell me who you are. What's your name?'

'Why?'

'I just want to know.'

'It makes no difference. I'm dead already.' The woman glanced at her in the rear view mirror. 'And so are you.'

Julia lay back on the seat as they sped into a waking world. They stopped once for fuel. When Julia went to the cloakroom the woman walked behind, the gun at her back. Nobody took any notice of them. The fuel attendants looked away from her stained, bloodied clothes and bruised face.

They drove east after Colesberg, into the Karoo, with its wraparound blue skies, strange little towns with windmills for trees, red earth and horizons full of puffy cumulus clouds. When she saw the signs to Cradock, the historical Karoo town, Julia tried to make another connection.

'Why would a woman like you do something like this?'

There was silence.

'The robbery at Mama Ruby's was life-threatening.' Julia pressed on. 'You could have been killed.'

'Perhaps I don't give a shit.'

Julia saw a chance to relate. Hostages always say you must try to relate to your captor. 'I know what you mean,' Julia said. 'I feel like that most of the time.'

The woman smiled tightly. 'Really? I would say your biggest problem is whether to put pink or blue candles on the table at your dinner parties.'

'Is that how I seem?'

'The most dangerous thing you've ever done is water the roses when your gardener is off-duty on Sunday.'

'Appearances are deceptive,' Julia said, carefully feeling her split lip with her tongue. 'I was arrested yesterday for shoplifting.'

'I don't believe you.'

'It's true. It feels like it was a thousand years ago, in another life, but it happened.'

For the second time Julia had managed to surprise her.

'What's your name?' the woman asked.

'Julia McEwen.'

*They started calling us by name. That made it harder for them to kill us.*

'Is this for real?' the woman asked.

'Yes, I spent yesterday afternoon at a police station, before going to that restaurant last night.'

'Are you married?'

'Yes.'

'Does your husband know you're a shoplifter?'

'He suspected, now he knows for sure.'

'So he finally realised the prissy lady he married, the one who talks with a plum in her mouth, is a criminal. Not even a clever one. Just a common little shoplifter?'

'Yes.' Julia sat back in the seat.

*We never argued with them; we submitted to everything.*

They drove in silence, until at sunset they arrived at a tiny coastal village. A jumble of shuttered beach cottages scrambled down enormous dunes and scrubby bush, protecting them from prying eyes.

The woman knew how to get into a shabby, clapboard cottage. It smelled of mould and salt, and was furnished with dilapidated chairs and scrubbed wooden surfaces. The woman flung open the windows. Sea tides hissed and crashed at the doorstep.

'Take that room,' said the woman, pointing to a door on the left. 'Remember what I said. Don't try anything stupid.' Her voice was flat, machine-like.

Julia nodded wordlessly. The woman's eyes scared her. She walked into a small, musty bedroom. The window was barred. The key turned as the woman locked her in. She tried to take off her filthy clothes but somehow her hands wouldn't work properly; she fumbled with buttons, but then just gave up. She slumped onto a stained mattress that smelled of dust and salt. She gazed at the cracked wooden ceiling, listening to the wind skimming sand off the dunes.

Although she was desperate for sleep, her brain fizzed with a kaleidoscope of events. What was she doing there with a woman who pretended to be a man, who wanted to kill her, but hadn't, who had been 'told' to kill her, but hadn't?

A brilliant light turned on in Julia's head – the light she had first glimpsed in the veld. She visualised herself free again. She would make changes, leave Magnus, live differently.

She sat up and stared out of the barred window. A wave, like thousands of metres of navy blue silk, unfurled on the beach. The sea hissed and slid.

She wanted to survive this. The trick was to stay alive, whatever it took.

# 6

I woke with a start and sat bolt upright in bed, my heart pounding. Sun streamed through a crack in the bedroom curtains. A loud crashing downstairs had woken me from a deep sleep. My mind cleared and I realised somebody was banging on a door, yelling my name.

Immediately I was on my feet, weapon in my hand. I looked at the bedside clock. Nine. I'd overslept. I had spent the whole night tossing and turning, twisted up in the sheets, the events of last night galloping through my brain. I hadn't closed my eyes until daybreak.

Half slipping on my black leather boots, I shuffled down the stairs into the narrow hall. I stood still, watching the doorknob turning, and for a gut-churning moment my heart almost stopped. Then, gripping the gun with one hand, I flung open the door.

Zak Khumalo leaned against the door frame, smiling at me.

'Good morning, Detective Inspector Tswane.' His tone was silky.

He was wearing the usual: sleeveless black T-shirt and black fatigue pants. A black leather jacket was draped across one shoulder, hiding the gun at his hip.

'Do you always sleep in those boots?' He raised his eyes, giving me a long, slow look.

'What the hell are you doing here?'

'Not the warm welcome I'd hoped for after driving all night to offer you my protection,' he said.

'Protection? Excuse me? That's ridiculous. I don't need your protection. Who said anything about protection?'

'Looking at your hand, I think you do,' he smiled. 'Commissioner Matatu has assigned me the job of being your bodyguard.'

I shot him a nasty look and turned away. I put my weapon down on the hall table and almost gasped as I saw my reflection in the hall mirror: no make-up, bags under my eyes and hair all over the place.

'Do you ever think of knocking like a normal person?' I asked.

'I did knock, but you didn't answer. Your cell phone is off. I was just getting ready to kick the door down.'

'Thank God you didn't.' I turned my back on him and marched down the hall into the kitchen. It's not easy to march in a dignified fashion with boots half-on, half-off.

Zak followed behind, holstering the gun.

'Coffee?' I asked in the most unfriendly way I could muster.

'What exactly happened?' he asked. 'Matatu was concerned after a phone call from the Grahamstown station director last night. He tried to contact you, but your phone was switched off, DI Tswane.' He looked at me reproachfully. 'Not proper police procedure at all. Remember Matatu's golden rules?'

'Oh, please! Don't go there ...' I could just imagine the conversation.

'Just tell me what happened,' he insisted.

I described the events of the previous evening, leaving out the smell that had clung to me all night. I wanted to mull over that by myself.

'Why didn't you use your gun?' he asked.

I felt my cheeks grow warm. 'I didn't get to it in time.'

The contours of his face hardened. 'You shouldn't carry a gun unless you're willing to use it. What the hell did you think you were doing, walking unarmed into a strange house?'

His attitude was really beginning to irritate me. 'Thanks, Zak. I'm fully aware that I was off-guard. Stupid, really to think that a safe house would be – you guessed it – *safe*.' I slammed a mug down onto the table and coffee splashed onto my hand. I yelped. 'Only the police use this house. Right? No one else knows about it. That's what I was told.'

'Well, congratulations, Thabisa, now you know not to believe everything you're told.'

I stepped up close to him. I had to stand on tip-toe to meet his eyes. They were dark and secretive eyes and they were staring at me with ... could it be amusement, lurking in their depths? Were the corners of his mouth twitching?

'You want me to admit I've screwed up? What is this anyway, Zak? An interrogation?'

My hand and arm burnt like a furnace. My head throbbed. I wanted to go upstairs and stand in a boiling hot shower for eight hours non-stop, until I felt clean and strong again. Instead, I had to put up with Zak Khumalo.

Zak rocked back on his heels and laughed out loud. His laugh was deep and infectious. If I hadn't been so distraught I might even have laughed with him.

'Lucky for you I'm a good interrogator. You want to give it a try, right now?' he asked, a cool note of warning in his voice. Now his eyes were the colour of iced cola. Thank God I only liked mineral water.

I was suddenly aware how big he was, not heavy, but broad. Strong and tall. He had to duck his head to go through the kitchen doorway.

'Come on, we both know you've been careless, Detective Inspector Tswane. Big title for a little woman.'

Little? Hardly the first word that comes to mind when I think of adjectives to describe myself. I'm five foot eight, a strong girl from rural stock. I run and work out to keep fit and to keep the fat at bay, but there's an on-going battle between my curves and me.

'You patronising jerk,' I said. 'You know I'm a good police officer. There's no need for this. You're being a pain, as usual.'

Zak clutched at his chest. 'I can't believe you said that, DI Tswane.'

I grinned reluctantly. 'You'd better believe it, Khumalo.'

'Joking, Thabisa. Just joking. It's got nothing to do with you being a good cop. Calm down.' And then, his tone became serious. 'Look, it's worrying. You've been attacked, yet you stayed in the house, alone, overnight. The guy might have come back. Did you think about that? You've switched your phone off, which is crazy. Have you looked at your messages?'

I glanced down at my phone. There were several missed calls and two messages from the boss. I needed to focus. I couldn't let personal issues from my past compromise my professional life. I had worked too long and too hard to get where I was. The valley wasn't going to jeopardise that. I'd been foolish, and I deserved Matatu's censure. No point in being defensive about it. I turned away from Zak, clutching the phone, feeling at a distinct disadvantage.

'Better hurry, Thabisa.' Zak's voice was amused. 'Fetching as your outfit is, I don't think it's suited to long-distance travel.' As well as my leather boots, I was wearing short, cotton pyjama bottoms and a tight white T-shirt. Zak was clearly enjoying the whole outfit, especially the T-shirt. I swallowed my annoyance, marched out of the kitchen and went upstairs, trying to subdue my desire to have the last word. I just couldn't think of a bad enough one.

I took a shower, scrubbed my teeth, dried my hair and dressed in my heavy black jeans, and a thick black sweater. A stun gun clipped to my belt, just in case of trouble ... from Khumalo, and my toughest walking boots.

When I returned to the kitchen, Zak was washing up the coffee cups. I almost laughed out loud at the sight.

'You look good, washing the dishes', I said. 'Never thought I'd see the day.'

'I'm a secure guy, DI Tswane, I can cook too. Let me cook for you one day. You might be surprised.'

'Cool it, Khumalo,' I said.

He turned, his eyes grazing all my curves. 'Wow,' he said. 'Very professional.'

'I didn't want to look like a cop,' I said.

He gave me a cool, appraising look.

'You never look like a cop,' he said. 'Now, tell me, how long will it take us to get to this valley of yours?'

'It's not necessary for you to come with me. I can do it on my own,' I said.

It was bad enough having to go back there, let alone having Zak Khumalo witness it.

'I've been instructed by the boss, he insists I go with you. Not negotiable, DJ Tswane.'

I was never going to tell Khumalo what had happened to me the last time I was in the valley. I hated the thought of him knowing about my humiliation. His being there when I met up with my grandfather and his wives again was just going to make everything worse. But, once again, matters seemed to be out of my control.

'It's four hours by four-wheel drive, then six kilometres over a mountain on foot. There's only one way in. Are you up to it?'

He turned and grinned at me. 'I should ask you that,' he said. 'Do you think you can make it with that injured hand?'

I ignored him.

'There's a four-wheel drive at the station. We're using it, whether Director Mandile wants us to or not.' Zak opened his mouth and I put up a hand to stop him. 'Don't even discuss the director, he's a desk-bound wimp. With attitude.'

Zak raised an eyebrow. 'It's going to take around seven hours to get there, right?' he asked. 'We won't make it there and back in one day. Can we spend the night in the valley?'

'We'll have to,' I said. 'Though I doubt you'll be able to cope with rural life.' He laughed out loud. 'I'm a rural boy myself,' he said. 'My mother was Matabele from Zimbabwe. My dad was Zulu. I know all about villages, believe me.' He looked straight into my eyes until I flushed and looked away.

Zak Khumalo was smooth alright. Smooth and confident. Good thing he wasn't my type.

***

In the car, driving north, Zak glanced at me expectantly. 'You all right with this?'

'With what?'

'Having me on the case with you?'

I didn't answer for a minute. 'We've worked together, we make a good team. I suppose it's okay you're here.'

After a short silence he asked: 'Thabisa, who knew you were at the Hill Street house last night?'

'Director Mandile, Bea – his assistant. I've known her for years, we worked together at Mossel Bay. No one else.'

'Are you sure?'

'Nobody knew about it. Hang on.' An image of Don Jacobs, leaning too close for comfort flashed into my mind. 'I did talk to an ex-cop who was on the plane coming down from Johannesburg. He mentioned the safe house. Remembered it from when he was stationed in Grahamstown. But I didn't say anything specific to him.'

'Who was it?'

'Don Jacobs, one of Ollis Sando's bodyguards. He left the force a couple of years ago.'

'Hmm ... what did he ask you?'

'What I was doing in Grahamstown, that sort of thing.'

'How long have you known him?'

'I knew him at Pretoria, a few years ago ... Afrikaans guy. No threat.'

'Ja ... right,' he said slowly. 'But things can change.'

I watched his profile. Dangerous and attractive. Mostly dangerous.

'There's something odd about this case,' I said. 'It doesn't add up. These guys use helium to change their voices and they are ... well, they're polite to their victims.'

'They weren't so polite to the old man they shot at Kenton.'

'No,' I said slowly. 'Something went wrong that time. And what's with the way they escape? Nobody sees them after they attack and leave the crime scene. Ever. They melt away, disappear, or so all the witnesses say.'

I paused for a moment, running through everything I had learned so far. Ending with the memory of flames flickering, the smell of skin scorching.

'Zak, why would somebody warn me off this case and attack me? The guy knew my name. That's creepy.'

He shook his head but made no comment.

We drove through hills and valleys, ruled lines of pineapple plants, rocky cliffs and the occasional blaze of aloes. The sky was chrome, the winter air crisp; the trees the colour of rust and blood. The mountains ahead were so clear they could have been on a film set.

'Still got your bank-teller boyfriend?'

'I don't wish to discuss my private life,' I said.

'That means it's over then.' He laughed. 'This is what happens to us, Thabisa. Police officers make lousy partners. I've been there, believe me, I know. If you want a relationship it has to be with a fellow cop.'

'Zak, just shut up, will you?'

'So you grew up in this ancient, remote valley?' he asked after a few minutes. 'How come you ended up as a police officer?'

'Long story.' I turned away from him, irritated.

'Well, we've got a long time ahead of us. Do we drive all the way in silence?'

*What shall I tell you, Khumalo? That my grandfather is a chief both by blood and custom, whose bloodline dates back to the ancient Thembu clan? Although he can't read or write, he captivates his audiences with his brilliant stories. Of long-ago battles, defeats and victories. The sound of his voice hushes a room.*

*And when you are related to someone like him, the demands of your birth lie heavy. His only daughter, my mother, suckled me until I was strong enough to drink from a cow. I remember being rocked in the sun with a gentle song. A skirt flapping in the breeze and bare brown feet skipping over stones.*

*Maybe you'd like to know that I grew to look like my grandfather? My complexion as light as his; the colour of warm honey. It wasn't the dark chocolate of my mother and the other villagers.*

*Shall I tell you, Khumalo, what a bad kid I was, after my mother died and my grandfather's face had set like a stone, because now he mourned his entire family? I wasn't supposed to behave like a boy and run wild. Perhaps that's why he sent me to school, Khumalo, to stop me behaving like a wild child.*

*Shall I tell you about when I was seven years old, Khumalo? When the cattle were brought down to the valley where the grass lay succulent and ripe, and my grandfather took me to the valley trading post.*

*'A yard of trobald for the skirt, petticoat and bloomers for the school,' my grandfather said in isiXhosa to the white lady in the store.*

*She smiled at me. Told me that my eyes were beautiful. 'What about her slate and chalk?' she asked my grandfather.*

*'No,' said Chief Solenkosi Tswane. 'It's enough.'*

*So the kind trader lady gave me a slate and chalk and wrote my name for me.*

*My grandfather was the one who said 'no missionaries' and 'no churches'. He even said 'no schools', but he sent me. My grandfather was not somebody to question. He was noble in all the ways that made him a chief. He was the one who wielded the spear of authority. Proud to be amaQaba and worship the ancestors. Stubborn, proud, noble, but absolutely impossible.*

Plenty to tell Zak Khumalo, but I said nothing. There was a long pause. 'I was the only kid in the valley to go to school,' I said cautiously.

'Was that difficult?'

'I walked up the cliff path every day to the farm school for three years,' I said.

'What was it like?'

'In summer it was easier, but you had to watch out for leopards and baboons. Winter was hard, we had snow often.'

'So you climbed alone?'

'Yes.'

'Tough kid.'

'Yes, but I wasn't a valley kid any more. The last time I was there I couldn't even carry the water up from the river on my head. My old friends had a good laugh. "Is this what schooling does for you?" they asked. "Have you forgotten everything? *Tyho, Tyho, Lomfazi!* – Look at that girl!"'

Zak threw back his head and laughed. 'So you couldn't carry the water, but you could read and write, eh?'

I looked out of the window, biting my lip.

'Come on, Thabisa, people like you and me, we all have issues with this. We all wonder if we're too busy and proud of ourselves to appreciate the people at home.'

Never forget where you come from. That way you'll always be sure not to go back.

*At eleven I was a clever little girl, Khumalo. The chief's only living blood relative. Pretty, and quick witted. At the little farm school at Engcobo, where I went at seven years old, there were few resources, but Mrs Talbot, my teacher, said I had my own inner resources. She encouraged me in every way, said I was special. And then, Khumalo, Mrs Talbot, her husband, John, and our valley trader, discovered a scholarship for a famous girls' school in Grahamstown. The scholarship was aimed at educating rural kids. The whole idea was that they would return to their homes and contribute to the education of everyone else.*

*I won the scholarship.*

*Sounds good doesn't it? Not in the valley, though. The villagers feared for my family. 'Chief Solenkosi Tswane has gone mad,' they lamented. 'With wide-open eyes he is bringing destruction on his household.' The gogos, washing clothes in the river, called to each other that the ancestors were turning in their graves. We were summoning evil spirits by this education. Their chief had dared to break a timeless chain. Retribution would follow.*

*There was nothing they could do or say to change his mind. They had to get used to the idea.*

*So I left the valley.*

'You finished school.' Zak prompted. 'And then?'

'After school, first the Hammanskraal Police College, then Mossel Bay, New Brighton Station in Port Elizabeth, Pretoria and now Johannesburg. The real world. Gritty, dirty, exciting. I loved city life. As far as I was concerned, the valley could stay buried at the foot of the Drakensberg Mountains.' I smiled wryly. 'I felt like a kid in a candy store. In Johannesburg everything was possible. It was the big picture. Everything advanced; opportunities for everyone. It was where I belonged.' I stopped. What was it about Zak Khumalo that made me shoot off at the mouth like this? Sharing confidences, learning nothing about him in return.

*One thing I will never tell you, Khumalo, is the way I was punished. How I swore on all that I held holy that I would never go back.*

*How on that night I left the valley, bleeding, humiliated, shattered. I crawled to my hut with blood running down my back, sticking my clothes onto the raw wounds. I collapsed on the straw matting and lay for a few minutes, gasping with pain. I heard footsteps approaching and shrank back; surely they weren't coming for me again? 'Thabisa,' a voice whispered, and a hand pushed a jar of herbal ointment around the door. The women made this salve from the wild herbs that grew in the valley. I never knew who offered this small kindness. I applied the ointment gingerly and it helped. My mind was made up. As soon as dawn broke I packed a few possessions into a plastic bag and left the valley without a backward glance. I walked painfully up the mountain to the Talbot's farm and asked for help. They took me in, nursed me back to health and arranged for me to get to the police college. They never asked me what happened. I never told. I just swore that I would never go back to the valley. Never.*

And now, here I was, on police business. On my way back.

I stared out of the window at the empty sky, the flat tops of thorn trees. A swirl of dust as a distant farm truck made its way across a dirt track.

Zak broke the silence. 'Between your oversleeping and my sweet talking Mandile into giving us the four-wheel drive, we're running late, especially if we have to hike down to the valley. We'll have to overnight in Queenstown. We'll leave for the valley first thing in the morning. Okay?'

I nodded.

'Good news is you get to spend the night with me. A single, perfect night.'

I stared ahead, stony faced. 'A warped sense of humour you've got, Khumalo. Any more sexist remarks and I'll report you to Divisional Commissioner Matatu.'

'Lighten up Thabisa. It was a joke.'

'No, Zak.' I turned to face him and spoke seriously. 'It wasn't. We're colleagues. Treat me like another police officer. Give me some respect.'

'Impossible. I can't treat you like any other colleague.'

'Try,' I said shortly. 'Think of me as the perfect police partner on this case.'

'Now, why would I want the perfect partner when I have you?'

'Does everything have to be a joke with you?'

He moved his shoulders away, laughing, as I punched out at him. 'Not everything, Thabisa. But for most things humour isn't the worst solution. You should try it some time.'

There was silence for a while.

'You don't give much away, do you, Khumalo?' I said finally.

'I'll tell you anything you wish to know.' He glanced at me out the corner of his eye.

'That would be nothing,' I said smoothly.

'I think you're scared.'

'Scared? Of you?' I laughed.

'Only you can answer that, Thabisa.'

'You've got to be joking. Every time you see me we have this sort of conversation – loaded with innuendo. It all gets so tired, Khumalo ...' I rolled my eyes 'I can't believe girls fall for it. And yet, judging by your track record, they do.'

'How would you know about my personal life? You've been checking up on me, admit it, DI Tswane.'

'You know as well as I do that there are no secrets in a group who work as closely as we do. Your love life is common knowledge.'

'Well, then, it should be common knowledge that I am the hunted rather than the hunter.'

'Oh, come on, that is so not true. So you can stop preening. But I do have one question.'

'Please,' he smiled, 'ask me anything.'

'When do you intend to be quiet and let me sleep?'

'I won't interrupt your beauty sleep. But be warned, Thabisa Tswane, I never fail when I really want a woman. In this case, I predict that one day you will come to me.'

'In your dreams, Khumalo,' I whispered, as I reclined the seat and lay back.

Space and winter sun crashed through the window as the four-wheel drive hummed along, following the ribbon of road. The day enveloped us. Zak reached into his jacket pocket and chucked a pouch of CDs into my lap. I looked in surprise at his choice. I thought he'd be more of a hip-hop, heavy metal guy. Cool, happening music to match his image. I chose some light classical music, it floated round the car, relaxing me for the first time that day.

My eyes drifted closed. I forced them open and looked at my watch. Three hours to go, more or less.

'If you get tired, just let me know,' I said.

He laughed. 'I'll remember that,' he said softly. 'Thanks, Thabisa.'

I looked at him narrowly. For once in his life Zak Khumalo sounded as if he was being serious.

I leaned back in the seat. This was so out of character. A few minutes before he'd been all macho and muscle-bound. Now he seemed gentler, kinder.

I closed my eyes, letting sleep fall on me like snowflakes, drifting down on my eyelids, carrying me away ...

'You don't by any chance have a split personality do you?' I yawned.

'No,' he said quietly. 'There's only one version of me.'

# 7

## 20 June 2006

We checked into a run-down little guest house just south of Queenstown. Then we went out and found a nearby restaurant and shared a curry. The place was full of chattering locals and tourists.

I watched Zak collecting plates from the buffet table.

He looked like a leopard among a flock of unsuspecting sheep, content to let them graze, but with the power to change direction at any minute. There was a dangerous quality about him that I found unnerving, He was the mystery man in the unit. I'd joked with him about his love-life, but really, how much did any of us know about Zak Khumalo? He wasn't such an open book after all. And he liked it that way.

Enough Thabisa! I shook my head. Just because I'd been stuck with the guy in a car for a few hours didn't mean I was interested in him. He was a work colleague, that was all. It was all so irritating being in such close contact with a man like him. I was annoyed that Matatu had inflicted this on me.

When we returned to the guest house, Zak opened my door, switched on the light and scanned the room. 'No madmen lurking in darkened corners with lighters in their pockets,' he said. 'I'll be banging on your door at five.'

'I'll be ready.'

Zak leaned against the door frame. 'You'll need to move now,' I said. 'Otherwise I won't be able to lock my door.' He looked at me steadily, then smiled.

'In case there are any more weirdos lurking around,' I said crossly. 'Not because of you!'

He bent his head and brushed my cheek with his lips. I scowled at him.

He stepped back and a small smile pulled at the corner of his mouth. 'Good night, Thabisa,' he said softly.

He strode off and soon I heard his door opening. Much as I hated to admit it, it was good to know he was sleeping close by.

I brushed my teeth and had a quick shower, then stretched out on the bed, fully clothed. I'd sleep in my clothes and be ready to leave the moment he knocked on my door. I lay there, light on, eyes wide open. This had been a long day, but I wasn't tired. I would never be able to sleep. My hand still throbbed. But it wasn't only that that kept me awake.

I was disturbed by Zak. Why was he such a tough person to read? One minute all street swagger and muscle, the next kind and understanding. Unpredictable. I didn't like it. I like people up-front and direct. And he was a strange mixture: cool and kind. I had interpreted enough of the looks he gave to other females to know he was trouble in human form. And he obviously thought I was as easy and gullible as they were; ready to fall for his looks and a great body. 'Well, think again, Zak Khumalo,' I muttered, leaning over to switch off the bedside light. 'You're just a shallow, sad, empty shell.' On that happy thought I fell asleep.

***

When Zak knocked on my door, I was ready. I'd washed my face and tied my braids up into a ponytail. I watched as he brought the four-wheel drive to the door. It was still dark but dawn light soon broke across the sky in every shade of red. A winter sunrise. It all seemed so much bigger out here, a massive canvas covered in great splashes of colour.

The distant mountains were beautiful, dusted with early snow. When we reached the red cliffs, we left the four-wheel drive parked under thorn trees, shouldered knapsacks and started walking. Ahead of us lay a wasteland: stones, rocks, thorn bushes and dust. Peak after peak of rugged mountains stretched to the horizon, shivering in the haze rising from the barren rock.

'Tough country,' said Zak. 'So this is where you grew up to be a tough kid?'

'Everyone round here has to be tough. It's a hard life. Shame, Zulu boy, is this walk proving too much for you?'

He laughed softly as I drew ahead on the path. 'The view is good from where I am.'

I tugged my sweatshirt down so that it covered my bum. 'Don't you take anything seriously?' I said.

'Like I said, Thabisa, life is serious enough already.'

I ignored him.

It was hard, steep and dangerous on the cliff path. Great flanks of mountains reared up around us. Valleys plunged below, perilously close to the path. The mist charged down on us like dragon's breath. The whole country was painted in shades of terracotta, as if it had been burnt with a blowtorch in some macabre workshop, then left to rust.

'This was all caused by a volcanic eruption millions of years ago,' Zak remarked as we walked. 'What we're looking at was once the shores and bottom of an ancient lake.'

'How come *you* know that, Khumalo?' I teased.

'I'm a man of hidden depths,' Zak said. 'Or it could be because I did some geology at college. Look at those rocks.' He pointed above them. The rocks rose like gigantic teeth, set in a lop-sided grin. 'That's where there's been more recent volcanic activity.'

I could only see the horizon dominated by rock, mountains, sun and heat.

'Perhaps you're right about the lake,' I said. 'These old paths are thousands of years old, made by the San. I often used to find sea shells embedded in the rock when I climbed to the farm school.'

'You must have been a real tomboy,' he said.

'I went to school on paths like this every day. Climbing up those footholds wasn't easy.'

'Where was the school?' Zak asked.

'It's to the north of here, quite a long climb. You can't see it from this angle because of the mountain. It's an old farmhouse, or it used to be.'

'It's left you with good muscles,' he grinned. 'I enjoy watching the Thabisa Tswane show.'

I turned, annoyed, and almost slipped. Zak put out his hand to steady me. His touch was light and his hand warm. It brushed against my breast as he held my arm. I pushed him away. He gave a low, mocking laugh.

'So, what was it like for you when you went to that fancy girls' school in Grahamstown?'

'Hard at first, but I got used to it. Everything was good, the sport, the teachers, the other girls, but the food was horrible. I missed our home food.'

'What's the school like?'

'Old buildings, sports fields, lots of interesting things to do.'

'Why did you join the police force; why not go on to university? Did you pass matric?'

'*Of course* I passed matric, what a stupid question. I got an A for matric. I could have gone to UCT or Rhodes.'

'Then why the police force?'

'I wanted to do something practical for my country and I had a friend who ... encouraged me.'

'A boy friend?'

'Nothing to do with you, Zak. Anyway, I like police work. I'm glad I trained at Hammanskraal. I don't think I'd be happy in an office job, sitting at a desk all day.'

'Funny, I can see you at a boardroom table, dressed in your navy blue power suit, directing Anglo American strategies.'

'Thanks for the thought. Now let's talk about you.'

There was a long pause before he spoke. 'I'm just a simple sort-of Zulu, sort-of-Matabele boy. Nothing to tell. Just a boring guy from the bush. And then from nowhere in particular.'

After that we walked in silence. But even in that short interchange Zak had learnt much more about me than I had about him.

We passed a place where I had played as a child. A stream bubbled out of the mountainside, before it became the river that flowed into the valley. On a sheltered ridge it had formed a chain of small, clear pools. Their banks shelved gently and over the centuries beaches had formed, washed white by the gushing water.

I sank down beside the biggest pool, pulling off my heavy knapsack. 'Let's have a rest,' I said. 'It's a good place.'

I pulled off my walking boots and waded into the water, watching the dirt wash off my feet in cinnamon swirls. It felt good. Zak followed. He threw himself down on one of the little beaches, looking around appreciatively.

'This is great.'

'I came here as a kid with my friends; I'd tell them stories and write their names in the sand. They liked that.' I smiled as I remembered. My friends' laughter, the joy of kids playing around together. No complications ...

'What did they think about you going to school?'

'They thought I was the unlucky one. They got to play here every day.'

'Did you feel like the unlucky one?'

'No. I always felt fortunate. This was my favourite place when I was a kid.'

'I can see you here, jumping from rock to rock, bossing all your village friends around, smart little kid.' His dark eyes rested on me.

Time to end this conversation. Once again, Zak had managed to get too close, too familiar. What was with all his questions anyway? Wasn't someone as vain as Zak Khumalo supposed to be too self-involved to be interested in someone else's life? Besides, I had enough to think about. Meeting my grandfather wasn't something I was looking forward to.

I got out of the water and pulled on my boots again. 'Come on, Zak, now you've rested, let's get going. Or do you want me to carry your knapsack for you?'

Zak threw back his head and laughed. He looked wholesome, sitting in the sun, so relaxed that I almost liked him. What a pity appearances are so deceptive.

We continued in silence. As we walked, we heard the sound of surging water. To the right, a river leapt at us between high banks. It rushed over shining boulders, crashing around our legs as we jumped across slippery stepping-stones. I led the way, balancing precariously, jumping from rock to rock.

'How did you get over this, when it was in flood, to go to school?' Zak asked.

'Put my school uniform on my head and waded.'

'That must have looked good.'

I ignored him.

***

Nobody arrived in the ancient valley by accident. Lying at the foot of the massive Drakensberg Mountains, it was a daunting climb down. Twisted sandstone ridges cradled the valley, hid it from the world.

At first sight, the village seemed buried in silver grass as tall as a man. Down through a dry gully we found a dusty track. The village lay ahead. With every step I took, I travelled back into the past.

The first thing that hit me was the smell. The potent mix of wood fires, pungent cooking smells, animals and people who lived close to the earth. A smell I had forgotten in the city. I had to stop and catch my breath.

We attracted immediate attention. Like a chink in a dam, the first trickle of villagers approached us. Then the entire population poured out of nowhere. Dozens of them dressed in deep red blankets, their faces, hands, hair and clothes a rusty, dusty ochre. Most stopped, staring in open-mouthed amazement at Zak and me. Children ran in front of us kicking up the dust, calling out. Chickens ran squawking among goats, old ladies washing clothes in the river waved, shouting out greetings.

Looking at this village scene, so familiar, yet so alien to me now, I thought how Zak and I upset the balance, so perfectly first-world in our designer jeans and tops.

Cows mooed, women walked past, water buckets on their heads, to collect water from the river; some smiled and burst out laughing, others lowered their eyes, reluctant to stare. One bare-breasted girl stared provocatively at Zak as she walked past. I glanced at him. He didn't move a muscle.

Old men, smoking clay pipes outside their beehive-shaped mud huts, stood to see this modern couple walk past, a quickening mood descending on the valley. With our noisy entourage swirling around us, we walked up the dusty track to the chief's homestead. My grandfather stood at the door, a blanket around his skinny shoulders.

'Now I see you. So, you have returned to the valley at last, Thabisa Tswane?'

Tall, imposing, he had hardly changed since I had last seen him.

I looked straight ahead. My hands behind my back. I stared at him, although this showed him no respect. This man who had betrayed me, abandoned me, allowed me to be punished. He had tempted me with the promise of a better life through education, only to snatch it away from me. How could I still feel anything for him, this stubborn, intolerant old man? And yet ... there was something of him in me. Blood ties are the worst ties of all. They're also the strongest. I wanted to reach out my hand to him. But I didn't. I couldn't.

I glanced around, his wives and some village elders had gathered beside my grandfather and I noticed familiar faces and embarrassed smiles as they watched me. Not from Ngosi, his chief wife, she curled her lip when she looked at me. I stared back at them all. I wanted them to know that I remembered what they had done to me. And I wanted them to know I was a police officer doing my job. Not the chief's granddaughter running back when he summoned me.

'So you've come to find these city criminals in the valley?' my grandfather asked, as I finally knelt in traditional greeting. Zak knelt too I noticed. Zulu customs were similar to ours.

I felt a rush of conflicting emotions as I wondered how far back I had to go to straighten things out with my grandfather. It would take years.

During the traditional greetings, which took longer and seemed more tedious than ever before, I gazed over my grandfather's shoulder, watching the mottled white and brown cattle standing in the shining water of the river. Cattle meant everything in the valley. Cattle meant power; money, food, medicine. You could rise up and hit out as you wished if you had cattle. My grandfather had wanted to sell me for 50 cattle a few years ago. What was I worth now?

Chief Solenkosi Tswane indicated that we should enter his homestead. It was just as dark, smoky and depressing as I remembered.

'So you've come home at last.' My grandfather's eyes searched my face. 'Are you ready to marry and have children? You're getting old now, Thabisa, this might be hard to achieve.'

Zak subdued a smile.

'No, Grandfather. As you know, I have come to speak to you about the bank robbery you witnessed a few days ago.'

'Ah, the mystery criminals?' He turned away scornfully. 'So my granddaughter only comes to ask me questions about small matters after so many years away.'

He had asked me to come here. My boss told me to come here. I wouldn't have come if I hadn't been forced to, by him. What was he playing at?

'A man was killed in this robbery. This is a serious crime. Please tell me what you saw.'

'There are many things a police officer needs to know, Thabisa. These are mostly the practical rules we teach in the valley every day. We have our own laws here. But even an important police woman like you needs to know that sometimes things are not what they seem to be.'

'Yes, but what did you see?' I insisted.

'I see you still have a lot to learn.'

'Listen, you have asked for me, and only me, to come to interview you about this murder.' I stopped and drew a deep breath. He was not going to goad me into losing my temper and looking like a petulant child. 'So please cooperate and answer my question. What did you see? What happened?'

There was a long silence, while Solenkosi Tswane stared hard into my eyes. I stared back, refusing to drop my eyes like all valley women did whenever a man was around.

'Well, smart police officer Thabisa, who has forgotten her people, I will tell you. First I saw two tall men go into the bank. They were dressed in masks, dark coats and gloves. These are the men everyone saw. The black men they tell us who have been robbing many banks.'

'And then?'

'When they came out they were different.'

'In what way?'

My grandfather sucked on his clay pipe. He moved away and turned his back on me. There was silence for some minutes, before he turned back to face me. 'In this valley, the law is different,' he said. 'I am the law here. I am the Chief. No man questions me. What I am about to tell you is the truth, I will not be questioned by my own child.'

I knew that it would be pointless to argue. I waited.

'When they came out, one of them had a white hand,' her grandfather announced.

'A white hand?' I asked.

'They went in black, but they came out white.'

I glanced at Zak. He was staring at my grandfather intently. Over the years, Chief Solenkosi Tswane had acquired a fearsome reputation for his dramatic speeches and his mask-like expression. He hadn't changed.

'What do you mean?' I asked.

'You're the clever police officer. You tell me what this means.'

Zak stepped forward and gave the formal, tribal greeting to a chief, in perfect isiXhosa: 'I am Zulu. I acknowledge you, Chief Tswane. May I speak?' he asked with downcast eyes, the correct way to address an elder. My grandfather nodded.

Zak was playing the good boy here. I wasn't going to go that route. But I had to admit he might get the better results.

'Do you believe these men were white?' Zak asked.

'I have told you already about the white hand. What other explanation could there be?' Chief Tswane asked.

'Did you hear the gun shot?' Zak asked.

'Yes, I saw the gun, but there is more.'

'Who was carrying the gun?' I asked.

'The tallest one with the white hand. But there is more to tell. To the Zulu boy I will tell the secret. This is not a woman's matter.'

'What secret?' I persisted.

'Only to the Zulu,' my grandfather said.

I moved back, fuming. It hadn't taken long for my grandfather to belittle me and put me in my place. I tried to hang on to my self-respect. It would have been so easy under these circumstances to slide back into village ways. This was going nowhere. After all the trouble of getting here, Solenkosi Tswane wasn't going to tell us anything useful.

Zak stepped close to the chief while he whispered to him. He and Zak looked at each other for a moment, before my grandfather turned and moved away into a back room.

'Well?' I asked. 'What is this about?'

'You're not going to believe this.'

'Try me.'

'He says our criminal with the white hand likes red nail polish. He thinks it's a woman, a white woman.'

I shook my head. 'What did you say?'

Zak grinned. 'Your grandfather is very impressive, Thabisa,' he said. 'Very impressive.'

I turned on my heel and walked away.

No comment.

# 8

## 20 April 2006

'I'm cutting your hair. It's a dead giveaway,' said Sue.

'Okay,' said Julia. 'Do it.'

Sue took a pair of scissors and hacked into Julia's hair. Julia smiled, remembering the loving care and attention Carlton Hair had lavished on it over the years. 'Cut it really short, like a boy,' she said.

Long strands of red hair fell to the kitchen floor.

'We'll dye it,' Sue said. 'Dark hair isn't such a giveaway.'

Julia looked at herself in the mirror, her thoughts scattered like spilt marbles on a travertine floor, the sort of floor she had in her Johannesburg house, in another time, another place, another planet. Just a few weeks ago she had been living in a gracious house, with servants and gardeners to fulfil her every need and whim. How had she got here, living in this beach shack with a captor who might kill her at any moment? It was surreal. But then again Magnus was just as dangerous as this woman, in his own way. The only way to survive this was to adapt. And she would adapt whatever it took. Because one day she was going to have her revenge on Magnus. That was what drove her now, kept her going. The thought of Magnus suffering. Held in a dangerous place. Helpless to fight back. The thought of him dying. Slowly. Painfully.

'When will you show me how to handle a gun?' she asked.

'Later.'

***

Julia had made some progress. Sue was still in charge and Julia was her humble servant, her captive, but the threats to kill her seemed to have stopped.

After the first day, she'd said: 'Call me Sue, and don't ask any questions.'

Sue had nightmares, bad ones. She received regular phone calls that always upset her. She was obsessively tidy, forever checking her watch, exercising twice a day. She was driven, by something or somebody who wouldn't let up. Apart from that, Julia knew nothing about her. She wanted to understand her strange captor. She longed to ask a dozen questions. It was obvious that Sue was in genuine distress, unable to throw off whatever was tormenting her, but who Sue was and why she was doing this remained a mystery.

All Julia could do was watch quietly, wait and learn.

Sue was beautiful, feline. Tall, thin and graceful with long legs, muscular thighs and a luxuriant mane of blonde hair. Her cold blue eyes were as intense as searchlights, and Julia was caught in their beam.

Julia pretended to admire her, said she wanted to be like her, asked Sue to show her how. At first Sue refused, but after a while, the idea seemed to appeal to her. The more Julia grovelled, the more Sue accepted her.

Julia was submissive, never challenged Sue, or questioned her, never looked at her directly, but inside her mind new ideas were forming. She was coming to life again. Ideas were working their way to the surface, all concerning the new life she was living. It was odd, considering the precarious situation she was in, but she felt a sense of renewal.

The road to the cottage led through a steep bumpy incline of coastal forest, the house completely invisible through a thick and tangled wall of milk woods. Their branches formed such a low arch over the driveway that the car was only just able to pass beneath.

The cottage was nothing more than a shack. But there was something basic about the shabby furniture and cracked surfaces that Julia found oddly comforting. She compared it with her Johannesburg home and its silk curtains, Persian carpets and upholstered furniture. The cottage stripped everything back to barest essentials. This new no-frills life tugged at her; it seemed appropriate for someone who had lost everything and didn't even know whether she would survive another day.

She had her own bedroom in the cottage, but what a poor bedroom it was. A stained mattress, an iron bed frame, an old blanket that smelt of salt and dust, a washbasin in one corner. But at least Sue didn't come near it. She just locked Julia's door every night.

Julia didn't try to escape, or beg help from the few coloured fishermen who passed by in the early winter mornings. All she wanted was to live. Escaping meant Sue would try to kill her. And if she did manage to escape, what would be waiting for her? Police stations, endless questions, explanations and – finally – Magnus. She didn't want that. She never wanted him in her life again. Unless it was at his funeral.

After two weeks, Sue had allowed Julia to take short walks along the beach. It was an undisturbed bow of soft, white sand with rocky outcrops at either end. All along the beach were trails that led her through waist-high ferns, past thickly clustered yellowwood trees draped in mossy vines. When the sun came out she sometimes swam. The water was so cold it numbed her entire body. There were tricky currents and often Julia felt like giving in to them, letting them carry her away. But she never did.

Her life had become slow and simple, lived only in the present. It wouldn't last, she knew that, but for now she was happy to be alive, breathe the tangy sea air, walk in the sand with bare feet, listen to the tides. Compared to living with Magnus, being on tenterhooks all the time, only coming to life when she conducted her forays into the shopping malls, it wasn't a bad alternative.

Two days after the hair cut, Sue pushed open Julia's bedroom door and strode into the room holding a gun.

So this is it, Julia thought. She's going to kill me. She stood up from the old wicker chair where she had been sitting, and faced Sue.

She wasn't going to cower, if this was it, she would bloody well stand up straight and look her in the eye. Julia couldn't move. It was as if time had fallen away. They faced each other for a long moment. Then Sue dropped the gun onto the stained mattress.

'Okay,' she said, I am going to show you how to use this. Time for you to pull your own weight around here.'

Julia's hands were shaking and her heart was hammering, but she played along. She became familiar with loading and unloading guns, 9mm Glocks and Z88s.

Naturally neat, precise and cerebral, she quickly learnt to read maps, plan strategic attacks and getaway routes. She learnt how to suck helium in a special way from the small portable flasks Sue provided. The slow sucking technique turned her voice into a Donald Duck squeak for more than fifteen minutes. She recoiled for a moment, shocked with the memory of her kidnap, when she first heard Sue's voice, distorted and tinny. The cartoon characters of her childhood with their friendly grins, flapping ears and fluffy yellow coats turned into grotesque monsters. Now Bugs Bunny and Donald Duck were caricatures you'd never want to meet on a dark night. Nursery room nightmares. And she was part of it.

# 9

My grandfather played host that evening. His newest wife, Nomvula, a plump, buttery girl, younger than me, served us a rich soup, a moat of broth around a castle of mealie-pap. As globules of golden fat slid down my throat, I counted the calories in horror. There was mutton steam in my hair, the smell of charcoal in my clothes. My French painted nails had worn off during the mountain climb and were encrusted with dirt.

I glanced at the wives. Several of them were new, and young, but not one was pregnant. Solenkosi Tswane might be tribal chief of the valley, but he was over eighty. I was still his only blood relative and likely to remain so.

The suffocation of the valley had set in. My grandfather gestured to me to stand or sit, his wives signalled where I should be, moving around me as if I was a child again. I was used to looking after myself, making my own decisions, and now, in the space of a few hours, it felt as if I had never left. There was something about the way my grandfather and his older wives issued orders, no matter how simple, that made me prickle with annoyance.

It was hard for me to even look at Ngosi, Chief Tswane's oldest wife and the ringleader in my ritual punishment so many years ago. She was an old woman now, small and frail with grey hair and narrow eyes. Yet I still felt a nervous knife-stab in my chest when I looked at her. I stood impassive while she inspected my face and clothes in an insulting way. 'Eh-eh, and now you are getting older, you still don't look anything like your father,' she said, sucking her teeth and curling her lip defiantly.

What the hell was that supposed to mean?

Ngosi stared at me disapprovingly. There was a message here. I remembered her face during the punishment; I had never liked her, but she had turned into a monster that night. I would never trust her again.

Zak was enjoying himself. He slipped into the family scene, almost like a son. Never mind that he was Zulu and not even pure Zulu, at that. This super-smug highly irritating police colleague of mine fitted in perfectly, posturing, hand-slapping, hip-swaying. Bursts of male laughter, loud men's talk. My grandfather and Zak were unbearable.

Before the meal, an elder slit a chicken's neck open and, mumbling a brief prayer, allowed its blood to seep into the soil. I closed my eyes so I didn't have to watch. Zak led the loud noises of approval at this barbaric behaviour. The men laughed, slapped each other on the back and pretended to kick one another.

I was the only woman seated on the woven grass mat near my grandfather – an unheard-of concession, one ordered by my grandfather, to the obvious irritation of the wives, especially Ngosi. Reluctantly, the wives served me. They didn't sit with the men and kept their eyes downcast most of the time, except when they shot inquisitive glances at me. My braids seemed to intrigue them and they gazed at my hairstyle in ill-concealed envy. If only they knew how long I'd had to sit at 'Black Like Me', the salon I went to in Sandton. It took a lot of hard work to create the hundreds of thin braids adorning my head. I wanted to tell them how painful it was, that I gritted my teeth and held my breath at every pull. It was worth it at the end, when I swung the braids around my head and over my shoulders, but sometimes I wondered why I put myself through the agony.

The women were wearing traditional dress: a leather skirt, beaded top, and a head turban twisted into complicated patterns covering their hair. The standard dress for married woman. I saw them looking at my jeans, giggling, whispering to one another.

Zak completely ignored me. I might as well have been any of the other women in the room – invisible. Certainly not his police partner.

It was like a Soweto shebeen, all beer, brandy and men showing off. A far cry from eating out in Melrose Arch, with tablecloths and wine glasses, where men and women actually talked to one another.

When I couldn't bear the atmosphere any longer, I got up from the table. There was a sudden silence. Conversation died and all eyes followed me as I left the hut.

I walked down to the river. Johannesburg was so far away. I closed my eyes and tried to remember city sounds. The constant background noise of traffic, industry, police sirens. I missed it. Especially the smell. There's something about the smell of a city; the smartly dressed people, the brightly lit stores, the perfumed air of the shopping malls. But then, as I remembered breathing in the teeming air of Johannesburg, I remembered another scent. The smell of my attacker came back to haunt me. It was a perfume I knew from my school days in Grahamstown. The headmistress wore it. Sweet, almost cloying, I could conjure up the memory of that smell as she walked past at assembly.

Dammit. Chanel No. 5. The name clicked into place in my mind. That was what my attacker smelled of. How weird was that? French perfume at the scene of a heist? Add that to the red nail varnish and it looked like my grandfather might be right. A woman was involved. And a white one at that if his description was anything to go by. I needed to think about this.

***

When I walked back and joined the others, I announced: 'I'm going to bed. Good night.'

The wives gasped again. No valley woman would ever dare behave like this.

To my surprise, my grandfather put down his pipe and stood.

'I wish to speak to you,' he said. 'Follow me.'

Immediately Ngosi stood, glaring at me. She turned to my grandfather, shaking her head, whispering to him angrily, her eyes on me. He drew back, frowning.

'That is enough, wife,' he said. 'Know your place. You dare to question me?' Ngosi stood aside, casting angry looks at me. She had always been a meddler, her nose in everyone's business. Now she was twitching to get into mine. What the hell was all this about anyway?

Moving quickly for an old man, he led me past the huts reserved for his wives. As his great wife, Ngosi occupied the largest of these and hers was situated to the right of my grandfather's hut. To the left was his second wife's hut, flanked by the three smaller huts kept for the others. Behind these was a larger hut in an area of the homestead I had never ventured into. This hut didn't have an open entrance. A sheet of corrugated iron filled the doorway, secured by a heavy padlock. A young man stood guard at the entrance and my grandfather rapped out a command that sent him scurrying off. He took a long leather thong from around his neck and inserted a key into the lock. The young man returned, carrying a paraffin lamp.

'Give it to her,' my grandfather said, then waited until he was out of earshot. He put his shoulder to the door and it scraped open. I followed him inside, and we faced one another in the flickering light of the paraffin lamp.

The hut was empty, apart from four large rush screens which hid the circular walls from view.

'I wish to show you something,' he said. 'This is why you are here, Thabisa. You think it was because of the murder that I witnessed. That murder was predicted by the ancestors so that the police would send you back here to me.'

I shook my head and turned away. This was ridiculous. My grandfather seized my arm and shook it. He pulled me towards him;, his narrow brown eyes scanned my face. His strength was amazing considering his age. His grip was like an iron band.

'Look at me!' he commanded. 'I am your blood. You are mine. I wanted you to come home to me. I have something important to show you. I need to know if you can understand. If the spirit is in your eyes to see this thing I will show you.

He stepped away from me and rolled back the first of the rush covers. He took the lamp from me and held it high.

I gasped. It takes a lot to amaze me. But this did.

# 10

One month earlier

## 25 May 2006

They never took more than they could carry in four plastic shopping bags. They dressed in black from top to toe, voices charged with helium and armed with Glocks. They always fired into the ceiling when they surged into the banks, stores or filling stations. Nothing big, just small country places to start with. It distracted attention, terrifying people. Then they locked up their victims, in cupboards, back-rooms, or safes, before they made their getaway. As they left, they ripped off their masks and unzipped their hoodies to expose colourful T-shirts. Then they walked away slowly from the scene. It amazed Julia to see what happened after that. People only saw what they expected to see. And nobody expected two white women, strolling calmly along, carrying shopping bags, to be armed robbers.

Their first heist as a couple was a small service station, just north of East London. They arrived as it was growing dark. The owners, a middle-aged Indian couple, ran the shop, serviced the forecourt and filled the petrol tanks of the heavy lorries that motored down the coastal road towards Port Elizabeth. They fell back, terrified, as Sue and Julia confronted them.

'Don't shoot, don't shoot. We're only a small business ... we don't have much money. Don't shoot! We've got four children,' they wailed.

If she hadn't been so high on adrenaline, Julia might have felt sorry for them.

Sue spoke in her cartoon voice: 'Good evening. This is a robbery. Put the cash into these shopping bags. Don't try to stop us. This is a good story to tell your kids tonight. Don't try to be clever, or we'll shoot.'

The Indian man led them down a dark passage and opened the door to his office. The entire floor was covered in banknotes. Sue and Julia stood knee-deep in money.

'What the ... What's this?' squeaked Sue in her Donald Duck voice.

'Our life savings,' the service station owner said softly. 'We don't trust the banks. Please. Please, I beg you. Don't take it all.'

'Only as much as we can carry,' Sue said.

They piled notes into the shopping bags until they were full. Then, keeping their guns trained on the cowering couple, they backed out of the service station, moving towards their stolen car with its false number plates.

'Thanks for your cooperation. Better trust the banks from now on, yes?' Sue shouted in her tinny voice.

They drove off, with a screeching of tyres.

'What about that?' Sue said, 'Imagine all that money floating around on your floor, I mean, it's crazy. What happens when you want to vacuum?'

Julia glanced at her, feeling laughter welling up in her chest. 'Can you believe it?' she said.

Sue suddenly exploded with laughter. Julia joined in. They drove along, howling with hysterical mirth, fuelled by the adrenaline rush of the heist.

Getaways were easy. They were just two white women out shopping. They pinpointed vehicles before they executed a job, in quiet streets or parking lots. Julia learned how to change number plates. She was amazed that so many people in the Eastern Cape left their keys in the ignition.

Julia learned quickly. Something in her had crossed over and she didn't want to stop.

The phone calls came twice daily. Sue shut herself into her room to take them. Julia felt sure she was talking to a man. Once she heard her cry: 'No, I can't do that! I won't do that!'

Although Sue ended these calls looking calm, her fingers gripped the cell phone so hard her knuckles were white. Sometimes she went out afterwards and didn't return for hours. These were the only times that she locked Julia in her room. Apart from that her freedom was increasing daily. She walked alone along the lonely beaches and Sue never questioned where she had been. She seemed quite sure that Julia would always return to the cottage.

They spent the money they took on food, drink and not much else. Sue stashed the rest away somewhere in the cottage. When Julia asked why they were doing these heists, Sue said: 'Practising. Savouring the thrill. Learning to survive.'

'What for?'

'The big one.'

'What big one?'

'Wait and see.'

Julia would have to chip away at Sue's armour plating for years if she wanted to reach the person underneath. Sue was damaged. No amount of friendly glue would ever mend her. She talked in bald, clipped sentences. Her tough, uncompromising attitude was more than skin deep. Her eyes were often unnerving, curiously flat and expressionless, almost inhumanly blue. Julia often saw a tiger crouched behind those eyes, eager to bite.

There were times when Julia genuinely admired her. She was chillingly competent in dangerous situations. Never nervous. She went about her business with the cool efficiency of an expert. Julia wanted to be exactly like her. She wanted to be brave and fearless too.

And then – Sue shot the old man at Kenton-on-Sea.

Julia tried not to vomit in the car when she saw the globules of brain and blood on her tracksuit. She saw the man's body sliding down, flopping about on the floor of the bank. The image played in her mind, over and over.

Julia expected a flicker of ... *something* from Sue. But all she said was, 'He had it coming.'

Julia dropped her guard. 'Couldn't you have just shot his kneecaps or something?' she screamed. 'Did you have to kill him?'

'Yes.' Sue said it calmly. 'Shoot when you have to, remember? He had a gun. He was going to use it. It was self-defence.'

Hot tears ran down Julia's face. 'Then it was an accident. We can tell them. We can turn around and tell them. It was just an accident.'

'Shut up!'

'This makes us murderers.'

'Stop being a bloody idiot!'

They were on the highway. Sue slowed a little, her eyes darting between the road ahead and the rear-view mirror. There were sirens, flashing lights ahead; two police cars approached them, fast. They whipped past without slowing. 'For fuck's sake, stop snivelling!' Sue said.

But Julia couldn't. She was gasping for breath, bile rising in her throat. 'Please stop the car; I'm going to throw up.' She fell out of the car and vomited at the side of the road.

'Toughen up Julia, you stupid bitch!' Sue shouted. 'You might have to do that yourself one day. Kill someone, so *you* don't get killed. Just remember that.'

*Never*, Julia thought. *I could never kill anyone.*

But she was wrong. Everything changed after that. Shortly after the bank there was the jewellery shop heist and Julia saw the full extent of the change in Sue's attitude. She seemed filled with a reckless desire to take more chances, increase the risks. She abandoned the tried and true; now she wanted to go further, the more dangerous and difficult the better. Julia went along with it, infected by this new spirit of recklessness. She loved the adrenaline surges, the spirit of adventure, being so good at something so dangerous. Being part of a team, a team that could do anything – risk anything.

They were in Port Elizabeth at the Walmer Park shopping mall in the early hours of the morning. The security guards weren't around. She and Julia smashed through the glass doors and helped themselves, stuffing Kruger Rands and jewellery into their bags.

Julia saw him first – a heavily built guard, brandishing a truncheon. He aimed at Sue, lining up a straight drive at her head. He would have smashed her whole face in. Before he swung, Julia was behind him. She dropped low and fired the Z88 into his left kneecap. He screamed, writhed in agony as his patella shattered. Julia imagined broken bone, ripped ligaments and torn cartilage exploding around his leg.

Sue and Julia ran through the sound of sirens, threw themselves into the pick-up truck they'd stolen earlier and drove quietly away. Nobody followed.

Neither of them spoke.

Once they hit the main road, Sue pulled into a rest area. 'Thank you,' she said. 'You saved my life. I misjudged you, I apologise.'

Julia didn't answer. She was shaking so much she couldn't speak, but Sue's praise made the heat rise in her face. The pleasure was a rush, better than anything she'd experienced.

'I can't believe I did that,' she said.

'You were brilliant. You kept your cool and did it.'

Sue's face was more relaxed, not so tight and angry. Her voice was softer too, not hectoring and threatening.

Julia shook her head. 'It was reflex. Pure luck. I didn't like it.'

'You don't have to like it,' Sue said, 'as long as you can do it. Now let's go home and make breakfast.'

As they drank coffee and ate croissants, Sue started talking. She told Julia about a man. He was manipulating her. He thought Sue was alone at the beach shack and she, Julia, was dead. There was also a job. She had promised him she'd do it. If she didn't, he would expose her to the police, or he would kill her.

As Sue spoke Julia's eyes didn't leave her face. She stared at her with fierce concentration. 'Who is he?' she asked.

'I can't tell you, but I can tell you how it all started.'

# 11

The room shifted and swam in front of my eyes. It was hung with bead-work, every wall covered in intricate hieroglyphics. The work of hundreds of years displayed in front of me. The history of the valley.

The past came rushing back. I was a little girl again. I smelled the dark brown smell of wood-smoke, heard the river rushing by, and felt the clay floor of our homestead under my bare feet.

My mother explaining to me in her gentle voice, teaching me the way of the beads. I felt the hard glass slipping through my baby fingers, as she taught me the meanings.

Then she was gone. Ngosi was there pushing at me, pulling at me, demanding that I listen and understand. I didn't want to have Ngosi telling me about the beads. Where was my mother?

I heard Ngosi's voice saying, 'I must teach her, she has the gift, and she has the eye to see. The beads speak to her.'

I was running away, going to the river, crying. Blocking out the meaning of the beads, comparing my mother's gentle hands with the leathery hands of Ngosi.

Now, as I looked, the symbols swam and shifted in front of me, it was like a song that had always lived in my mind but now all the meanings came flooding back. I understood everything.

Although the women of the valley made the beadwork, they worked in fragments. Not one of them ever saw the assembled pieces. In elaborate rituals, only the paramount chief, *sangomas* and diviners of the valley constructed the records.

The only people who saw the completed work were the senior wife of the chief and his own daughter. Ngosi and my mother. And now me. One of the only women to see this room.

I stepped forward, gazing at the glistening walls, my eyes flying across the history of the valley. The secret language returned as I concentrated on the dots, zigzags and stripes. The meaning of the beads slipped into my mind. I could read everything.

And, as I read, part of me wished I could go back to the room where the women sat, eyes averted, heads bowed. It would be safer sitting there with them, ignorant of the history unfolding in front of my eyes.

My grandfather held the lamp higher, and in the flickering light, I read of bloody executions. My father, my two uncles, murdered during the struggle. They had been betrayed by an *inyoka* – a snake, the beads told me.

I stepped back. 'Why didn't I know this before?' I asked my grandfather.

'The time was not right,' he answered.

My eyes flicked beyond the story of blood and betrayal to a gentler tale. In the swathes of coloured beading, embedded in the symbols and emblems, I read of an ancient ancestor, the survivor of a shipwreck, a white woman with eyes like crystals, who had come to the valley. Was she the answer to my grey eyes? I stepped in towards the beads again, trying to bring everything into focus. The scope was much larger than I thought at first. I needed to see more.

As I stepped forward, Solenkosi Tswane lowered the lamp.

His leathery skin, folded into hundreds of deep lines, made it difficult to read his emotions. His narrow, dark eyes were fixed on my face. I noticed how straight his back was for a man of his age.

'You see your history? I know you do. The ancestors have been talking to me, Thabisa. They have spoken. They tell me there is a truth to be told. A truth about the three murdered members of our family line. Those men who died. Those men the snake betrayed.'

'Let me see more,' I said, trying to take the lamp. He drew back.

'No. This is all you need to see for now. If you want to see more you must return to the valley.'

Proud, I thought. Royal. For a moment I felt close to him. I was shocked to feel it, believe me. I suppose it was something to do with blood ties. But the moment didn't last. This man had conned me before … me, his granddaughter, and his only relative. His only hope for his line to continue. I struggled to get back into my own comfort zone, the place where I hated him without reservation.

'So my child, the beads still speak to you?'

I bowed my head.

'I show you this so that you will see that you are mine. That my blood runs in your veins. I look at the clothes you wear, the way you walk and talk. It tells me you have outgrown this village and your family. Have you also outgrown your black skin?'

'Of course not, *Tat'omkhulu*,' I said. 'I'm proud of my black skin.'

'I listen to you talking English to this Zulu man. Have you forgotten your language? Are you now so modern that you no longer know where you come from? Have you forgotten the red soil, the wattle huts, the talking beads of your village?'

'Of course not,' I said. 'I speak isiXhosa all the time.'

'But you have chosen to work with men and carry a weapon?'

'I am a police officer, *Tat'omkhulu*. This is what we do.'

'And who is this man? This Zulu? Is this a man who will marry you? Pay *lobola* for you?'

'He's a colleague, *Tat'omkhulu*. Not a prospective husband.'

'You speak English, you ornament your hair, your hands, your face. Why is this?'

'There is nothing wrong with what I do, Grandfather. I'm a modern South African, a working woman. You educated me. It was your choice to send me to school.'

He turned away angrily, jerking the red blanket around his body.

'It was to have one, just one, in the valley to read and write for us all,' he said. 'I want our line to continue, the line of the chieftain. When my sons died, and then my daughter, your mother, there was only one hope. That hope was you. *Ungumzukulwana wam* – you are my grandchild.'

'You can't keep looking backwards, *Tat'omkhulu*. You need to look forward. Times have changed.'

'Hmmm,' he threw his hands up at me dismissively. 'We need to keep the traditions of this valley. Our ancestors speak to us here. We will not leave. We will never leave this place.'

'You don't need to leave the valley. You only need to allow the young people to go to school. Find a teacher. Let them learn.'

'And have them go away like you, and never return?'

I sighed wearily. Being shouted at and bullied doesn't exactly make a girl keen to come home, I wanted to say. But what was the point? His ways were as deeply engraved as the dust creased into the wrinkles on his face. My mind was a jumbled mess. The bead room, the news of my father's death. The whole valley atmosphere. It was impossible to argue with him. I was weary, I needed to lie down somewhere and get my head together. The revelations of the bead room had been a massive shock. I had never seen or heard of it in all the years I spent in the valley. Now I really needed time to think, I wanted to recharge my batteries. Fat chance of that when I had to share a room with one of his young wives. I wondered what his motive was in showing me the bead room. And why now? Why not before?

My grandfather lowered the lamp, and gestured to the entrance. We walked back to the main room. Back to the real world where everything seemed so normal. But what was normal? Life was becoming more complicated by the minute. The bead room flashed and glistened in my head, all its mysteries swirling in front of my eyes.

*** 

I spent a restless night, tossing and turning on a thin straw mattress in a room with some of the young wives. I longed for my orthopaedic mattress and crisp cotton sheets, a loo that flushed, running water. Sleep was impossible. From nearby homesteads, I could hear faint titters of laughter that every now and again became raucous howls. Rhythmic clapping, men's voices, dogs' piercing barks, laughing. I needed earplugs. Whoever said town life was noisy hadn't tried to sleep in my grandfather's village. I could smell my mint toothpaste wafting past the wood smoke. There was a buzzing in my left ear. A valley mosquito had found me and was rubbing its hands together and licking its lips.

Just as I finally dozed off, a cockerel roused me and I struggled grumpily out of bed. Why would I ever want to come back here, to live in a place where I was uncomfortable, miserable and misunderstood?

# 12

I walked down to the river at first light. The bank was lined with *gogos* washing clothes. '*Wena*!' they called out, leather-worn hands squeezing waterfalls from the washing. 'The disobedient girl is back.'

I ignored them, watching the children playing in the water. They floated paper boats, splashing and giggling. It reminded me vividly of my own childhood.

I was aware of a young woman approaching, and realised that it was Pinda, my old friend, one of the reluctant attackers on the night of my punishment. She was all grown up, dressed as a married woman, with her leather skirt and swathed head-dress. A little girl appeared beside her, clinging to her hand, standing close and watching me. Pinda's daughter? Surely not. But she obviously was. Her hair was pulled into little bunches, sprouting all over her head at different angles, tied with ribbons and beads. Hair adornment had obviously found its way into the valley, but only for children and unmarried women. The married women still wore *iqhiya* – traditional headscarves.

'I like your hair,' I said to the child. She blinked slowly, and parted her lips, but didn't say a word.

I smiled at Pinda, the new grown-up Pinda, with her chocolate skin. She smiled back, her cheeks creaseless and smooth as toffee.

'Hello, *ntang'am* – my age mate,' I said. 'Is this your daughter? So now you're a mother? What's her name?'

Pinda kept her eyes downcast.

'Zindzi,' she said, 'she's four years now.'

'She's cute,' I said. 'How are you, Pinda?'

'I'm well, thank you,' she replied. Then she reached out her hand, and touched my braids. She fixed me with a look, a little tilt of the head, and a tiny smile. She knew everything about the old me, but nothing about the new me.

I took a deep breath. 'My life has changed, Pinda, but it is a good life.'

'I'm glad,' she replied quietly.

I wondered how Pinda had felt the night of the cutting. How hard it must have been for her, to be forced to hurt a friend.

I reached out my hand and took hers.

'I am happy to see you again, Pinda,' I said. 'I am happy you are a mother, and have such a sweet daughter.'

Her eyes filled with tears. 'And I am sorry,' she whispered. 'So sorry.' She shot a nervous glance at the river, where all action had ceased, and all eyes were focused on us. Then she turned away, taking her little girl with her. They both turned back to look at me and wave.

I tried to imagine little Zindzi in years to come. Would she still be happy to live in the valley, or would she make a break, get out and away? How long could the valley contain its children?

***

As soon as we could, Zak and I left the valley. Zak appeared unfairly sprightly after all the drinking and smoking of the night before. He could at least have been slightly hung-over.

As we climbed up the steep mountain pass I decided to tell him about the bead room. My grandfather had told me not to speak to anyone else about it, but I needed to talk to somebody I could trust. And much to my surprise, I realised that Zak was that person. Not that I was going to divulge anything more about my personal life, I wasn't too sure how far I could trust him on that score. But this was evidence. Pieces in a jigsaw puzzle. He might be able to help me sort out my feelings over it.

'I only saw it for a few minutes,' I said. 'If only he'd let me see more. I wanted to ask him so many questions.'

'Did you know about any of this?'

'Only rumours. I was told that my father and two uncles had died in an accident. I asked many times, but never got an answer. My mother died soon afterwards. When I lived in the valley I was always asking, but it was never discussed with me. Now it's clear they were murdered.'

'Why?'

'Probably because of anti-apartheid activity during the struggle,' I said. 'They were betrayed. I don't know the details. Didn't, that is. Until last night. The beads said they were betrayed by a snake man.'

'A snake man?'

'That's what the beads said.'

'What else did you see?' he asked.

'The beads go back centuries. It seems I had a white great-great-great-great *gogo* about three hundred years back.'

Zak laughed. 'So that's where those eyes come from. There's a whole clan of people descended from white castaways living near the Xara River, not far from Umtata. Ever heard of them?'

'No.'

'Black skin and pale eyes, apparently. Remarkable. Perhaps your long-ago *gogo* came from there. Some powerful young chieftain sees a beautiful castaway girl with big grey eyes, buys her from his neighbouring tribe with an unheard-of amount of cattle. It's not impossible, is it?'

'No,' I said slowly. 'I guess not, but I think you've got an over-developed imagination, Khumalo.' Nearly as over developed as your muscles, I nearly said, but stopped the words before they slipped out. Not before I did a quick scan of his body though. Good scenery in this part of the world on a cool Wednesday morning.

'Imagination?' He laughed softly and shrugged. 'Perhaps I have.'

'How come you knelt to my grandfather?'

'I knelt to him because I respect him, Thabisa. He's a remarkable man. I miss my own grandfather, he was a great guy. These elders have a lot to teach us, you know. I actually envy you having this link to your village life. I miss all the friendliness, all the connections, don't you?'

I could see he was sincere. It amused me. He was usually so cool. 'Oh please, spare me. Are you trying to tell me that the oh-so-modern Mr Khumalo likes all the traditional stuff?' I enjoyed the chance to get under his skin for a change.

'Was it easy to read the hieroglyphics of the beads?' he asked, neatly changing the subject.

I had a flashback to the night before, the bead patterns swimming and forming in front of my eyes. I felt it again and closed my eyes briefly.

'It's an odd feeling. Like dancing, you always know how. I was taught when I was very young. I remember lessons with my mother and then Ngosi. It's crazy. The valley people have kept bead records for hundreds of years. Another way of writing. They use the beads to record history. When I saw the bead room I realised that I'm probably the only one who can bead-read and read conventionally. I wonder why the other girls didn't get the chance to learn the beads? It seems unfair that I was the only one.'

'Well, you are the tribal chief's granddaughter; you would have been groomed for that reason alone, surely?'

'Don't remind me,' I said.

'Who else can read them?' Zak asked.

'My grandfather, his chief wife, the *sangomas* probably, my mother when she was alive and now me.'

'In Zulu culture most beadwork relates to love and marriage,' he said. 'It's an indication that you're available in the marriage market.'

'Valley rituals aren't like that. Obviously you Zulus have a different agenda.'

Zak ignored me. 'Let's get back to business,' he said. 'Our criminals are not as simple as we thought, right? We need to know what we're dealing with. It looks like one of them could be a white female. If so, that's highly unusual.

Thelma and Louise – remember that movie? – Bonny and Clyde and Patty Hearst – that girl who was kidnapped and ended up being a bank robber. There are probably others, but not many that I've heard of.'

'Have you ever dealt with white female criminals?'

He hesitated. 'Never in a situation like this. Who has? It's probably a first for all of us. We need to think hard about who she is and why she's doing this.'

'I smelt perfume on the guy who attacked me at the safe house. It wasn't any old perfume, either. It was Chanel. No. 5.'

Zak stopped so suddenly, I nearly cannoned into him. He turned to face me, shot me a look of cool assessment. 'Thanks for finally letting me in on that vital piece of information,' he said dryly.

I concentrated on the bird song, looked at the great white clouds drifting above us while I tried to keep my temper.

'I wasn't keeping *anything* back from you,' I said calmly. 'It only dawned on me last night, when I was trying to get to sleep; I remembered that the headmistress of my Grahamstown school wore it. We were all in awe, and wanted some too. It's a very distinctive smell, you don't forget it. In fact, isn't smell the sense that stays with us throughout our lives?'

Zak stopped. 'Come, sit down here, Thabisa,' he said. 'Let's go through this carefully, close your eyes, pretend you're a witness. Let me ask you what you remember, every word, every twitch. If this is stacking up the way I think it is, you're the only person who's had any contact with her.'

I sat on a rocky ledge and closed my eyes.

'I really thought it was a man. He was so strong and violent. It was only afterwards that I realised there was something seriously odd. The perfume. And now, with what my grandfather said about the nail polish, everything's been thrown out of kilter.' I bit my lip and frowned. 'How could I not have recognised the smell? And if I missed that, was there anything else I should have noticed?'

'Exactly my point. Come on, Thabisa.'

'Okay.' I closed my eyes. I willed myself back into that dark house. I felt the fear again. The horror of that squeaking voice, the strong hands on my neck, the flames on my hand. The feeling of helplessness ... 'I wasn't thinking straight, my mind-set wasn't right. How could I have mistaken a woman for a man?'

'What did she say?'

'"Get the hell off the case!" But most of the time he – she? – was completely silent. That was the most frightening part. And the voice, it was right out of a cartoon, it was Bugs Bunny shrieking in my ear. It made my flesh creep.'

'It's possible we're dealing with a pair of crazies. They could be getting their kicks from crime and avoiding being captured,' Zak suggested. 'It happens.'

'But it doesn't fit in with warning me off and knowing my name, does it?'

'No,' he agreed. 'It doesn't. We haven't got any answers yet, just a few facts that can't be explained, but –'

Whatever Zak was about to say was lost. I looked up at the jagged rock face and what I saw there made me thrust myself violently back, pushing against him.

'This is very friendly, DI Tswane ...'

'Oh my God,' I breathed. 'Keep still.'

We had clambered along a precipitous rock face, going from foothold to foothold across a steep, tumbling rock fall. I flicked my eyes upwards. A leopard stood on the rocks just above us.

We drew back, hardly breathing.

The leopard was right above us. It was big, with a stocky body and powerful limbs. Brown rosettes stood out sharply against its golden fur. It was stretching in the sun, twitching its tail and powerful neck muscles.

Zak's hand was in the middle of my back, pushing me flat against the rock. He stood in front of me, his body protecting me.

Cold sweat trickled down my back. Mountain leopards were dangerous, secretive and stealthy. I had seen them before, but never as close as this.

We shifted around and braced ourselves, pressing as far back into the rock as we could get. The great cat looked down and slowly turned its head. The golden eyes stared straight at us. I almost stopped breathing, caught in the headlight beam of the cat's eyes. I sensed Zak moving his hand towards his gun. Even the smallest movement focused the leopard's intense stare. For several long moments the creature looked at us, then gave a lazy yawn and ambled off.

'Oh my God,' my voice was shaking. 'Do you think it's gone, properly?'

'Don't know, I'm going to look,' Zak said.

I heard him unholster his gun. He motioned me to stay where I was. I pulled my own gun out and muscled my way in front of him.

'I'll go, it's my territory,' I said.

Zak grabbed me by the back of my jacket and yanked me back.

'Stay here,' he said, as he climbed up and disappeared over the lip of the rock face above us.

I waited. The silence was deafening. My heart was beating triple time and my palms were slick with sweat. I told myself I had to think clearly, but my mind was clouded with emotion. Emotion? About Zak? I must be mad. I was so angry with him. I knew how dangerous leopards could be, what they could do. Why did he have to rush off like that? Like a typical alpha male.

There was a sudden thump behind me. I whirled round to find Zak right there.

'No sign of our feline friend,' he said. 'There are a few caves above us. He's probably in there, so let's get the hell off this mountain. I don't know how you survived as a kid around here.'

I couldn't speak. Relief flooded my body and I dug my broken nails into my hands to stop myself crying. I tried to turn away. What was the matter with me? This was ridiculous. Zak took hold of my shoulders. His knuckles brushed my neck and his eyes lingered on my mouth.

'What's this? Feelings, DI Tswane? Surely not for me?'

'Of course not. It's just an adrenaline rush,' I managed to say.

'You must have seen a few leopards up here when you were a youngster?'

'Yes, but they are dangerous. Thanks for checking.'

'Not at all,' he said. His eyes focused on me, but although I tried to read what was in those dark eyes, I couldn't. As our eyes met, my body flooded with warmth. His eyes moved to my mouth and stayed there. Then he took hold of my shoulders and pulled me against him. His big hands covered both sides of my head. He kissed me as if he was biting into fruit. It was sweet, hot, and dangerous. He kissed me with his whole mouth. I felt tingling and alive. I wanted it to go on, forever –

It was he who broke away. He held me at arm's length.

'Forgive me,' he said, with a wry smile. '*That* must have been an adrenaline rush too.'

When he let me go, I nearly fell over, my legs like jelly. It was all I could do to clamber up the cliff path.

We climbed the rocky way back to the dirt road where we had left the four-wheel drive. When I looked back down into the valley the huts looked like toys, drifts of smoke rose slowly in the lazy afternoon air.

We hardly spoke on the journey back to Grahamstown.

Okay, okay, so I did find Zak Khumalo attractive. But it was more in a moth-to-a-flame sort of way. When it came to looking for a partner – a proper life partner that is – he wasn't my type. At all. He was just another colleague – with a really bad reputation around women.

When we arrived at the Grahamstown police station, although it was late, Bea was standing in the office, dressed in a yellow suit with enormous shoulder pads and impossible zebra-print heels. She was clutching a huge lemon meringue pie from the home industries shop nearby. When she saw Zak her mouth dropped open.

'Wow!' she said, clutching the pie as if it was a life jacket in a storm. She swallowed visibly and dragged her eyes away.

Okay again, so Zak was definitely a 'wow'. Half a head taller than me, perfectly toned muscle, dressed in his usual black. His T-shirt looked like it had been painted onto his biceps. His skin was dark. His eyes were dark. His hair was dark. And apart from now knowing he could kiss like Jude Law kissed Nicole Kidman in *Cold Mountain*, I knew nothing else about him. His life was a pretty dark secret too.

Zak walked into the director's office. Bea rolled her eyes at me.

'It's a work relationship,' I said.

'Are you *kidding*? If he'd been here any longer I would have melted,' Bea said. 'And this *has* melted,' she said, slamming the lemon meringue pie down on the desk. 'Now tell me all about it – and I mean all!'

'He's a player, Bea, that's all. It's quite sad really,' I said.

'I'll play with him,' Bea said. She turned and looked back at me over one of her padded, yellow shoulders. 'Oh, by the way, that Australian doctor, Tom Winter, has phoned here a few times, looking for you. Some girls have all the luck!'

# 13

22 June 2006

Sue leaned forward, her shoulders hunched.

'I got a job. I met a man. I got involved. He persuaded me to do things, not that I needed much persuasion after the first time. I didn't know much about thrills and violence, until he exposed me to them. Then I loved it all. It appealed to my screwed-up personality. I loved the adrenaline rushes. I loved living on the edge. It was so exciting.'

Julia didn't say anything. But she knew exactly what Sue was talking about because she had felt it too. She sat at the scrubbed wooden table in the kitchen resting her chin in her hand and straining her body and her eyes towards Sue. Outside the wind howled as a storm moved up the coast, whipping the ocean into great, rolling waves that smashed down onto the beach outside the cottage.

'Go on,' she urged.

'I had a choice. I could stay home and be safe, or get out and live dangerously.'

'Don't you think armed hold-ups are a bit extreme?'

'You mean shop-lifting would have been more acceptable?'

'It isn't life-threatening.'

'Maybe I didn't care about life-threatening.'

'How could a man persuade you into this sort of crime? Was he blackmailing you?'

'I was mad for him. I would have done anything for him.'

Sue was speaking in the past tense. Was she having second thoughts? Was it over?

'Go on ...'

'An ad in the newspaper started it,' Sue said. 'Just what I was looking for, an overseas job to get me away from England, out of the rut of living in bloody Essex. I was working for boring idiots, earning peanuts. No life at all.'

'So you got the job?'

'I applied and they phoned me, told me they wanted to meet with me. So I went up to London for an interview. When I walked in, there was this big black guy in an Italian suit. The office was enormous, with pictures of animals all over the walls. Lots of deep cream carpet, a huge walnut desk, it was all rather like I imagined the President of the United States' office would be. As soon as I walked into the room I was captivated by the sheer power of the man. The way he moved to greet me, his cool confidence, immaculate clothes, long tapering fingers, half-mocking smile. He had so much more magnetism than my current boyfriend, Freddie, a computer nerd with a Porsche. This man would need nothing but his own presence to excite women. He would just have to stand there and look at a woman, like he was looking at me. I ran my eyes over him and imagined him naked. I'd never fucked a black man. I was intrigued. I'd always wondered if the rumours about them were true.'

Julia didn't blink. 'And are they?'

'All true.' Sue smiled slowly and rolled her neck on her shoulders.

'What happened?' Julia asked.

'Well, long story short, he made a play for me, I got involved, came to South Africa and everything changed. There must be something in my makeup, some adrenalin-junkie streak that he picked up on. I knew he was newly married, and his wife was some amazing beauty queen, she was Miss Ethiopia or something, but I didn't care. He wanted me. I wanted him. We were like animals on heat. A big part of the excitement was the discovery that in the lying and deception stakes I'd met my match. He was a man after my own heart.'

'So he's somebody important?'

'You don't need to know.' Sue paced the room. Her eyes were doll's eyes, blue glass, blank.

'It was like being a drug addict. I couldn't do without it. Him, the sex, the power, the rush. Once we did it in his office, on his desk, with his secretary knocking on the door. Another time I sent him an SMS when he was in an evening business meeting. I pictured his face when he read it. I could almost hear him say, "Excuse me for a moment. I have to take an urgent phone call." I waited for him, naked, in the ladies' cloakroom. The risk was knife-edge, my heart was beating so fast I thought I'd have a heart attack, but he was ready, willing and able. I unzipped him, straddled him on a toilet seat and fucked him stupid. Afterward he zipped up and went back to the meeting. Mr Cool.'

Julia said nothing.

'I've heard that stuff about people who drink love potions and turn into sex zombies,' Sue said, 'and that's what I became. Have you ever felt like that?'

'No,' said Julia. 'Never.' She felt as if she'd been split into two separate women: one practical, un-shockable, listening to these unimaginable things; the other looking at everything from a distant place, through a strange, detached lens. Weighing the evidence, storing facts away for when she might need them.

'I've always loved shocking people. I wore combat boots with my school uniform, dyed my hair purple with pink stripes, and pierced my tongue. I had tattoos before anyone else did, in the weirdest places. Took drugs. I didn't give a shit what people thought of me. Not like you, Julia, with your dignified airs, your cucumber-sandwiches-with-the-queen voice. I suppose you were head girl at school and all that crap?'

'Don't worry about me. What did your parents think about all this?'

'Parents? There weren't any parents. My mother ran away with hippy freaks when I was about three. She didn't even know who my dad was. My grandmother tried to bring me up. But in the end, she gave up on me. I don't blame her. I was a nightmare.'

Sue began to laugh, but it wasn't a real laugh, just an empty cut-out sound, dark, like something hurtful was choking her. She sat forward quickly and fixed Julia's eyes with a stare.

'After all the sex tricks, he wanted me to go further.'

'In what way?'

'More adrenaline rushes. Petty crimes, to start with. It escalated pretty rapidly. He said that what he liked best about me was that I was brave. I was wild. I'd do anything.'

Julia felt she was in a dream, sitting at the kitchen table talking about crime, as if it was a shopping list, or they were discussing the weather.

'Like what?'

'First we held up an Indian restaurant and stole naan bread for a curry party, just for fun. And so that he could test me I suppose. See if I could keep my nerve for the big stuff. Because the next thing we did was scary. We broke into a high-security town-house complex in Sandhurst, right under the noses of the security guards and stole jewellery and gold bars. We did a few more like that and then, the next job was insane. We broke into a cabinet minister's apartment and took some photographs. Political leverage, he said. Always very useful. It was terrifying. We had to climb up a fire escape in the dark and break a window. I nearly fell off the roof and killed myself. But somehow, when I was with him I felt electrically charged and the fear just added spice to the thrill.'

Sue stared into middle distance, a faint smile on her lips. 'Being with him in a posh bedroom was the best; smelling the scent of rich women – women like you, Julia. I loved inhaling their perfumes, looking at their expensive clothes, rifling through their underwear, trying their clothes on. That was the exciting part, that's what gave me the biggest rush.'

'And he was with you all the time?' Julia asked.

'Yes,' Sue said. 'He got a huge kick out of it. When we had sex afterward, rolling round on the rich people's beds, it was incredible. I would have done anything for him. Anything.'

'Was it just for kicks, or something else?'

'He was grooming me.' Sue blinked. 'It hit me one day. Like a ton of bricks. I realised suddenly that he had ulterior motives. I should have cottoned on sooner, but I was too blinded by lust and need and want to pick up on it.'

Julia watched the emotions play across Sue's face. 'What was he preparing you for?' she asked.

'He moves in certain circles, politics, judges, cabinet ministers. It allows him to see things coming and prepare for them. He'd taken many years to get his spider web in place. Then, just as he had everything set up the way he wanted it, and his career was set to go through the roof, he heard there were incriminating documents concerning him which the press might get hold of.'

'What sort of documents?' Julia imagined hot fingers prodding her along, forcing her to ask these questions, while Sue just kept talking, a torrent of words tumbling from her lips. It seemed like a relief for her to tell Julia these things.

'A crime he had committed in his youth. It would be twisted to make him look bad, once the police and the press got hold of it, it would destroy his whole life, his future would be blown out of the water. It's something really bad, but he won't tell me what it is. He swears he was framed, that he's not guilty.'

'And he wants you to get these documents?'

'First he wanted me to do a heist on my own at Mama Ruby's restaurant, just to prove I could go it alone.'

'So, that's why ...?'

'Yes. He told me he'd organise the getaway car. He also said he'd be there. In the restaurant. Watching me.'

'So he was there that night?'

'Yes, so was his wife.'

Julia leaned forward. 'What did you think about that?'

'I never asked questions about his wife, but I was surprised to see her in the restaurant, of course. I was angry but tried to stay cool – he hates scenes.'

'What sort of man is he?' Julia whispered.

'Powerful, self-made, complicated. He hates weakness of any sort. He thinks most people are idiots. "There's so much opportunity out there, why don't people realise they've got to grab it?" That's what he says.'

'He particularly hates beggars, "How can they stoop so low," he says. "Why don't they go out and find something useful to do?" When they unfold those cardboard messages, "Retrenched, four children, thank you, God bless", he wants to unfold his own message: "Fuck off and get a job".'

'He also despises most women; he's a complete chauvinist, even about his own wife.'

'And did that include you?' Julia asked.

'No, he said I was his partner, his brave, wild partner. But underneath, yes, he probably did despise me. He was always in charge, he always did the planning, he was the director of everything we did.'

'Why do you think he was like that?'

'I don't know. He was just totally fucked-up about women. He spent five years at university in England. It made him question his culture, which often treated women like second-class citizens. But in the long run, instead of changing his attitudes, helping him see women as equals, being in England entrenched his feelings. Made him want to dominate and humiliate women even more. The old ways were the best he'd say. Women knew their place then. None of this trying to be as good as men, or better, even. That used to make him really mad, thinking about women being in control. I think he must have had some damaging experiences with women at Oxford. It was as if he wanted revenge to get back at them, at all women. He sought out the wild, liberated ones and then crushed them. There was something in me that made me stand up to him and fight back ... for a while anyway.'

'What would he do if he knew about me?' Julia asked.

'He'd come down here and kill us both.'

'I know him, don't I?' Julia's eyes didn't leave Sue's face. Inside she was shaking. For a precious moment she was the interrogator. But how long before Sue's tiger swung round and bit her?

'Who is he, Sue?'

'I can't tell you.'

'It's Ollis, isn't it? Ollis Sando? He was in the restaurant that night.' Julia's shoulder blades tensed under her sweater. She leaned forward and touched Sue's arm. 'Sue, let me help you. I know Ollis and Sitina Sando.'

Sue got up from the table, her arms crossed defensively in front of her chest. She bit her lip and paced the floor of the kitchen. It was as if the scales had fallen from Sue's eyes, and she realised that she may have gone too far. Crossed a dangerous line. She glanced at Julia, 'I'm not telling you anything more,' she said.

But Julia saw the uncertainty in her face. 'Why do you still want to do this for him?' she asked. 'Why do you let him manipulate you?'

There was a long pause. It was the first time Julia had seen Sue unsure, vulnerable. 'He's got too much information on me. He could get me arrested; I don't fancy a South African jail. And I still ... care about him.'

'If it is Ollis, and I believe it is, I've got to tell you about Sitina, his wife. He's married to a powerful woman. She's well connected in top political circles; her father is the Ethiopian ambassador.'

'She's very beautiful,' Sue said.

'Very beautiful. But it's not just her beauty. She's a force to be reckoned with.'

'Fuck you!' Sue rounded on Julia. She turned from her restless pacing, dragging a hand through her tangled hair. 'Of course it's Ollie. Next you'll be telling me how happily married he is. Right?'

'I was at their wedding. I didn't get the impression that it was a convenience thing.'

Sue pressed her lips together. 'I don't want to hear this, okay? Just shut up about it.'

'Okay.' Julia shrugged. 'But Ollis didn't marry Sitina only because –'

'Okay, I get the message. She's beautiful. Well-connected. She's also a cold controlling bitch.'

'Sue, what can I gain by lying about this?' asked Julia. 'Sitina's lovely. An incredibly warm person. Everyone was amazed when she married Ollis Sando. He's the cold, controlling one. He might be in line for the presidency, but he's an arrogant, devious shit.'

The angry tiger pounced. 'Shut the hell up!' Sue swallowed hard. 'Remember who you are. Remember what I can do to you!'

Julia cursed herself for relaxing her guard. She had treated Sue as if she was a friend who needed support and advice. Bad mistake. This woman could kill her. She was a hostage. She had to behave like one.

'I don't want to upset you, I'd do anything to help you, Sue, you know that,' she said quietly.

Sue relaxed for a moment, her shoulders slumped. She looked tired and drawn. She turned on her heel and walked out of the kitchen and into her bedroom, slamming the door behind her.

Julia stared after her. Sue was still in command, but the scales were tipping.

# 14

Every year Grahamstown's streets explode with pulsing energy during the annual arts festival fortnight. Every possible venue buzzes. Schools, churches, theatres and halls sizzle with plays, symphonies, ballets, recitals and dance events. While I was at school in Grahamstown, I was aware of the build-up to the festival, but most of it happened during the holidays, when I was back in the valley. So I loved the vibe now.

The streets flooded with people: crazy clowns tumbled or walked on stilts; fire eaters blazed; students wandered about dressed in wild clothes; guitar and drum players busked at every corner. Despite the cold, restaurants spilled onto the pavements, exploding delicious smells out into the night air. Asian mixed with Italian, mixed with boerewors, sizzling on a braai. The air was rich with aromas that made my mouth water. Strangers smiled and nodded to each other as they passed.

Tom Winter gripped my arm as we emerged from the cathedral and walked up toward the restaurant. We stopped for a moment to warm our hands at an open brazier where a group of young men performed an energetic gumboot dance.

'Thanks, that was great, Tom,' I said. 'I loved it. I used to sing in the school choir. I'd forgotten how much I liked classical music.'

'Good,' he said. 'I'm glad you braved coming out with me. You look beautiful, by the way. I haven't seen you dressed up before.'

Grahamstown in June was freezing. I was wrapped up in Bea's red, fake-fur coat and hippy black skirt. I'd added a long purple scarf. I wasn't sure whether this was suitable for dining out so I was relieved that I looked exactly like all the other festival goers.

I glanced up at Doctor Tom Winter. His stories about growing up in Sydney, surfing on Bondi beach and his adventures with sharks had made me laugh.

'He's a serious babe,' Bea had said earlier. 'All the nurses and staff at the hospital are mad for him. He's single and available.'

'Hungry, Thabisa?' Tom asked, sliding his arm around my shoulders.

Too fast, I thought, pulling away. Just because I'm single doesn't mean I'm instantly available.

Tom smiled, 'I'm just trying to keep you warm, Thabisa,' he said softly. 'It's a cold night.'

'Let's go. I'm starving,' I said, relenting and putting my arm through his. He was strong and solid to lean on. I liked the way he strode along, full of determination. He kept looking down at me to see if I was alright. I liked that too. I couldn't help but compare him to Zak, who would have suggested 'warming up' of a completely different variety.

As we walked toward the restaurant, passing dozens of people clutching festival programmes, I noticed two women moving through the crowds toward me. There was something different about them. They didn't look like holiday makers, having a good time, but walked with purpose, like they were late for an appointment. They didn't look like theatre goers either. There was something business-like about them. They moved with synchronised steps, like soldiers. Both tall, they wore long, dark coats. One was blonde; the other had short dark hair. They walked swiftly, talking intently to one another.

As they passed us the dark one turned her head and looked at me. Our eyes met for a moment. Then the two of them were gone. I stopped and looked back, but they had been swallowed by the crowd. I was sure I'd met the dark one before. Something about her tugged at my mind. I knew the woman's face. It nagged at the corners of my mind, like a half-forgotten tune, as we walked into the restaurant.

Tom's eyes lit up when the waiter took Bea's red coat from me.

'I can't believe you're a police officer,' he said.

'Why?'

'You're such a feminine woman; I can't see you arresting people or shooting anyone. Not wearing that sweater, anyway.' Tom looked straight into my eyes.

To my annoyance, my cheeks flamed. The black sweater with the low-scooped neckline was rather clinging, but it was all I had with me.

'Well, I usually do the shooting and arresting wearing a bulletproof vest,' I said.

'What about you, Tom? You still haven't told me what an Aussie doctor is doing in the Eastern Cape.'

'I'm here for the next two years, as part of an Australian government support scheme,' he said. 'I'm usually based in Sydney at the Royal North Shore hospital. I'm supposed to be doing research on HIV-related diseases, but I keep getting seconded into the system, and end up being on the wards for hours when I should really be in a lab. There's so much to do.'

'Were you born in Sydney?'

'Born and bred. It's a great city.'

'I'd like to visit Australia someday,' I said.

'It's a great country. A fantastic place. Beautiful scenery, friendly people and a good attitude to life.'

He sounded like a representative for the Australian tourist board. I smiled to myself. He also looked very tired. I imagined what being a young doctor working in a government hospital was like. Run off his feet most of the time and overwhelmed by the hundreds of people he had to deal with every day, instead of doing what he came to do.

'If you ever come to Australia, I'll show you what Sydney has to offer.' His face lit up with enthusiasm. 'I'll take you round the harbour. We'll go to lunch by water taxi to Doyles at Watsons Bay. Greatest fish and chips on the planet.'

He talked about himself easily, determined to tell me his whole history. Maybe it was an Australian thing, this quick-fire delivery of all the facts. I sat back in my chair, amused by his boyish enthusiasm. It sounded like he'd had a trouble-free life, full of holidays in the sun, the best schools, lots of family support. Even being hit by the enormous challenges of an understaffed, poorly resourced Eastern Cape hospital hadn't dampened his enthusiasm. I felt much older by comparison. Older and more cynical. But there was a kindness about him that I liked.

'Sounds good,' I said when he finally petered out. 'I've got friends in Sydney. They emigrated to Australia a few years ago. They live in a suburb called Manly.'

'Really?' Tom's eyes widened. 'That's a coincidence. My brother lives in Manly. It's a great suburb. People mostly get there by ferry from the city. It's a pretty trip.'

'One day I might go and see them,' I said. 'They were very good to me when I first came to school in Grahamstown, Doctor White and his family. I stayed with them. They "westernised" me. I had to learn how to turn on taps, eat with a knife and fork, sleep in a proper bed, that sort of thing. They had three naughty little boys, who must be quite grown up by now.'

'Tell me about you,' Tom said. 'I know you're Xhosa. Are you from somewhere around here?'

I smiled, looking around the restaurant with its shines and clinks, its fanned napkins and resplendent cutlery. I rubbed the stem of my wine glass between my thumb and forefinger before I spoke. 'I come from a seriously remote valley at the foot of the Drakensberg Mountains. When I left, fourteen years ago, I was the only person who could read and write. Nowadays there are a few others who have left the valley and gone to the cities. Maybe when they come back, they have picked up some schooling, but not many of them, believe me.'

He raised his eyebrows. 'That's amazing.'

'Well, it's true, even my grandfather, the tribal chief, can't write, but he can certainly add up. He knows the value of money. He was the one who decided that I must be educated.'

'How come?'

'It's a long story. I was the chosen one, went to a farm school, then won a scholarship to high school, then on to police college. The finished product is sitting in front of you.'

'The finished product is wonderful,' he said. 'Do you speak with clicks?'

'Of course,' I said, and gave him an example. *'Iqaqa liqikaqikeka kuqaqaqa!* – The wild cat is rolling on the turf. It uses one of the isiXhosa clicks, the *q*. Neat, eh?'

He laughed. 'You reckon you could teach me to do that?'

I shook my head, laughing. 'Easier said than done. We inherited this language from our San ancestors. Thousands of years ago they developed click sounds to communicate while they hunted. We still use them, every day. Stick around and I'll show you the *c* and the *x* clicks.'

'It's fascinating,' Tom said. 'The aboriginal people in Australia have special sounds too, they call them Songlines.'

'Songlines? What are they?'

Tom smiled. 'It's really complicated to explain. Songlines are the way people navigated during the Dreaming, which they believe marked the beginning of everything. They believe their ancestors sang the world into existence ... began it all with their special songs and stories, dance and paintings. It helped early people to travel the deserts, and communicate with each other.'

'Oh, that does sound pretty complicated.'

'It is. There are dozens of books and ancient records about it. I wish I had time to learn more about it.'

'IsiXhosa's very descriptive: good for swearing,' I said. 'We're also great at making music.'

'I bet,' said Tom. He searched my face. 'May I ask you a personal question?'

'You can ask.'

'You've never been married?'

'That's right. Why, does that surprise you?'

'It certainly does.' He smiled. 'Not many women who look like you make it past twenty-five without getting married at least once.'

'I'm thirty-three. Is that a nice way of asking what's wrong with me?'

Tom laughed. 'Do you think I'm being nosy?'

'You think I'd be a prize catch?'

'Yes, I do.'

'Well I'm not. Definitely not. A few guys might think it, from a distance.'

'What's wrong up close?'

'I'm not like most women.'

'Why's that?'

The waiter appeared and hovered over us as he served our drinks.

Tom raised his eyebrows the moment the waiter disappeared. 'Go on, I want to know why you're not like most women.'

'I seem to be doing all the talking here, Tom, it's your turn next. But if you really want to know ... I'm reasonable looking, successful, independent. I meet a guy. He wants to go out with me. The first few dates, he shows me off to his friends. We like each other. We get intimate. Then, in a month or so, I get a new assignment. I have to go away, sometimes for weeks. I work around the clock. I come home in the early hours. Now, this guy wants a partner for a dinner, to go to the bush, or fly to Cape Town for the weekend. I can't do it. So, eventually, he decides that the relationship isn't working out after all. He leaves.'

I surprised myself, telling Tom all this. He was a good listener. I looked at his handsome, blue-eyed, pale-cheeked face, and a sudden vision of Zak flew into my mind. His dark eyes skimming over my face, his sudden grin when he caught me looking.

'So he couldn't cope with your job?' Tom prompted me. The waiter appeared with our food. He took a long time to serve us. I felt Tom's impatience. It amused me. I sliced my steak, grinning at him, deliberately not rushing to continue.

Finally I said: 'Some men like to be in the superior position. They love the *idea* of being with someone like me, but the reality is far from what they want. It sounds fun to have a detective for a girlfriend, especially one who works in the Violent Crimes Unit. And then there's the salary. I'm pretty well paid for what I do. Some guys don't like a woman making more money than they do. The ones who do make more money don't want a woman whose job is more important than her love life. They can't handle the fact that my work takes priority. I'm not complaining. I'm just explaining how it works.'

I stopped, took a sip of wine. I was more relaxed than I'd been for days.

'What about the cultural side of this?'

Now he was getting onto tricky ground. A little too tricky for a first date. I answered slowly, 'I'm a bitter disappointment. As the chief's only blood relative, I'm supposed to be living in the village, doing beadwork, having kids. I'm right off the planet as far as they're concerned.'

'And haven't you ever wanted to settle down, have kids, the whole thing?'

'Every woman I've ever known wants that in some way.'

'And you?'

I shrugged. Answered lightly. 'Maybe someday, when I find the right man. It's not easy to find someone who you'd like to grow old with, believe me.'

He nodded slowly and smiled at me. 'Tell me more about your valley. I know you're amaQaba, but what does that mean?'

'Among other things, it means we worship the ancestors.'

'How do you do that?'

'Well, it's not exactly Christianity. Ancestors are our link to God. Every African has to keep in touch with his ancestors throughout his whole life.'

'Like guardian angels?'

I laughed. 'Ja, that's a good way of describing it. That's what my grandfather believes. What I used to believe too.' I felt sad for a moment, remembering things which used to mean so much to me.

We laughed, drank several glasses of good wine, and chatted. I liked Tom Winter. He was attractive, charming and fun, but at the edge of my mind, a face kept dragging at me. I tried to push it to the back of my mind, and concentrate on Tom, but I guess a police officer is never off the job. The tall, dark-haired woman. Who was she?

After dinner, we returned to the safe house on Hill Street, and I asked him to come in for a nightcap. There was a security guard outside on the pavement. Thanks Bea.

Tom opened a bottle of wine. I filled his glass and we stood in the kitchen while the kettle boiled for my coffee.

'Thabisa, what happened the other night?'

'What do you mean?'

'Who attacked you?'

'I honestly don't know.'

'Are you on a special assignment?'

'All assignments are special when you work in my department,' I said.

He took the milk jug out of my hand and placed it on the table. Then he wrapped his arms around me, bent his head and kissed me, gently, on the lips. 'You're lovely, Thabisa,' he whispered.

It was a quiet, tender sort of kiss, not half as dangerous or exciting as the one yesterday on the mountain path. But, what the hell, it was still a pretty good kiss from an attractive man, and he wasn't pushy, arrogant Zak Khumalo, A-grade kisser. With Tom though, I was determined to keep it cool. I pulled away, smiling.

My cell phone message alert bleeped. I glanced down and saw three missed calls from Zak Khumalo. Damn. I hadn't switched my phone on to 'ring' after the concert. It was still on 'silent', but the reception in Grahamstown was so erratic, I had been careless. Damn, damn. Khumalo had the uncanny knack of turning up where he wasn't wanted at exactly the wrong moment.

Unwillingly, I called him back.

'Yes?' I asked.

'Don't you ever answer your phone?' he demanded. 'Are you alone?'

I hesitated. 'Not exactly.'

'Well, get rid of whoever it is. I need to talk to you. I'll be there in twenty minutes.'

Impatience surged through me, but I turned back to Tom, smiling ruefully. 'Tom, I'm sorry, I've got to ask you to go. I've got a colleague coming over to brief me on something.'

He smiled. 'Okay. But don't think you're getting rid of me as easily as that, Thabisa. I'll be in touch with you tomorrow.'

'Thanks for a great evening, Tom, I've really enjoyed it.' I kissed him on the cheek as I saw him out.

Nice guy, bad timing. The story of my life.

Ten minutes later Zak knocked on the door. He was wearing a black T-shirt and jeans under his black leather jacket. As he hung the jacket up, I saw the gun stuck into his jeans in the small of his back. His mouth was hard and unsmiling.

'Your cell. Turned off ... again?' he said shortly. 'You know better than to do this, DI Tswane.' I watched his eyes scan the room, taking in the empty wine glasses, the open bottle, and finally me, and what I was wearing.

'Sorry Khumalo. I didn't realise that leaving the house had become a crime. And anyway, why are you interrogating me? What are you doing here?'

'I'm watching over you, like I've been instructed.'

'I don't want to be "watched over". You're harassing me, Khumalo.'

'Most women would be happy to have me follow them around.'

'I'm not most women.'

'Don't I know it!'

'What do you want?'

'Where were you?'

'That's got nothing to do with you. I'm off-duty. And what I do with my social life has nothing to do with you, so why this attitude?'

'You're not off-duty, Thabisa. You know the way we work. You've been assigned to a murder enquiry. There's no such thing as off-duty. We socialise when it's over.'

'Great speech, Khumalo. It might even work on somebody else. But don't try pulling the high-and-mighty with me. Just remind yourself of the women you screw around with when you're "on-duty". Besides, you're not even supposed to be on this case. It's mine.'

'Well, stay on it then.'

I fought to keep my voice cold and unemotional. 'Look at the facts. We've been into the valley to interview a witness. Job done. Am I supposed to stay in uniform all night, waiting for something to happen?'

'You were attacked the other night, remember? In this house. Don't you think there's a connection?'

'Cut it out, Khumalo. You just want everyone to think you're the best police officer around.'

'You're wrong,' he said flatly.

'No, you're just Zak Khumalo, mystery man. Off on your own missions. Keeping your own secrets. Why don't you spill some beans, Zak? Tell me what exactly it is that makes you so mysterious? I'm sure all the girls in Jozi would love me to give them some more details about their pin-up man.'

I fell quiet, took a deep breath and tried to scrape Zak Khumalo out from under my skin before he set up permanent residence there.

I looked up at him, expecting to see the usual smirk playing around his mouth, but for once Zak wasn't smiling.

'Okay, DI Tswane. Here's the reason I would have liked to be able to contact you. There's been another heist. Just like the others. Money Sure guards were delivering a night cash transfer to Birches – a department store here. The perps came out of the shadows and shot one of them.'

'Is he okay?'

'Well, he's not dead, but he's in hospital.'

'How do you know it was them?'

'They wore alien masks; spoke with the same cartoon voices, so the other guard told us. This happened two hours ago, Thabisa. While you were having some "time off".' He narrowed his eyes and stared at me with a frown. 'I needed you to be there, Thabisa. This is your case, right? I thought I'd have to go and see him. On my own. Because your cell phone –'

I'd screwed up. I was in the wrong and I knew it, but I was damned if I'd admit it to Khumalo. I stared at him angrily. 'I don't want a lecture from you, okay? I'm entitled to some time off occasionally. Having a date with a nice, polite man isn't a punishable offence.'

He crossed the room in a second. Then he was standing next to me, his face inches from mine.

'I'm not a nice, polite man. I don't play by the rules,' he said. 'But you know what, Thabisa? You don't need a nice, polite man in your life. You need somebody who knows who you really are – someone like me.'

He gripped my shoulders. It was a bad idea to be alone with this man; he had a frightening energy at his core. I should ring the police.

But he *was* the police.

He pushed me back against the kitchen table and leaned into me. His leg slid between mine, his lips brushing lightly across my neck.

'I don't like your attitude, Khumalo.' I wriggled away from his grasp.

'You think I believe that shit?' he murmured. He pulled me close again.

His hands moved slowly, deliberately across my body; I could feel his warm palms and the determined pressure of his fingers.

There were a thousand reasons why this was a bad idea but I struggled to remember what they were, as he pulled me toward him.

His eyes were dark and slumberous, watching my face for a long moment before he brushed his mouth on mine, then deepened the kiss.

He broke away and smiled as he bent, pushed my braids back with his big hands, and kissed my ear, running his tongue along my neck. The pleasure was so intense, so unexpected, that I moaned out loud and moved against him.

Then he pushed me away, so suddenly that I nearly fell. 'Sorry, DI Tswane, but this will have to wait, we've got to get back to the hospital, talk to these guys properly and write a report. But I'm so glad you seem so ... receptive. Yes, I think that's the word. Hell, I'm flattered, really flattered.'

I struggled to pull myself together. My mind was a storm field of conflicting emotions: anger and passion, irritation and desire. He stared down at me with a smug certainty that infuriated me.

'Coming along, DI Tswane? Or do you want to go up to bed and wait for me to come back?'

He had me at a total disadvantage. And that was exactly what he wanted. I'd fallen into his trap, like an idiot. I drew myself up to my full height. I was embarrassed, humiliated. And so furious I could hardly get the words out. 'I'll go with you to the hospital, Khumalo, and talk to these men,' I hissed. 'But don't even *think* about coming back here. If you do I'll ... I'll shoot you.'

He laughed. 'And yet, only a minute ago you were so friendly. What happened?'

'You really are a bastard, Khumalo. Don't you ever lay hands on me again.'

'Okay,' he grinned and moved away. 'The next time I lay my hands on you Thabisa, you'll be asking me to.'

'Let's get out of here!' I grabbed my jacket and headed for the door.

'I'm delighted to discover that the icy DI Tswane has a hot side,' Khumalo said, as we got into the car. 'There's fire in your blood. That's good for a man to know.'

'Be careful, Khumalo, remember too much fire can kill,' I said through clenched teeth.

We drove in arctic silence through the quiet streets of Grahamstown.

When we got to the hospital, I strode ahead of Khumalo down the corridor to the ICU where Jan van Rensberg was recovering, wearing an oxygen mask. His hair was reddish, his complexion ruddy and his watery green eyes tinged with red.

'They *mos* came out of nowhere, man. I tried to go for the taller one, but the shorter *oke*, the one with the gun, kicked me in the balls and shot me. My shoulder was numb, but I knew there was blood pouring out of it. I fell down. I couldn't *fokken* take my eyes off the gun, it was like a horror movie, you know? You don't expect it. They were wearing those alien masks and talking in cartoon voices, like Donald Duck, or Bugs Bunny. *Jislaaik*, it was creepy, man, really creepy.'

'Did you get a look at them?'

'No, they were dressed in black, with those masks things, you know? They were quite tall buggers, thin, and ... no, it was all too *blerrie* quick. I told you, man, those *ous* were like something from a horror movie. I didn't see them properly. Not up close so I could make like a proper ID.'

We couldn't get much more from him. I left Zak getting his signature on the report and walked into the corridor. I heard quick footsteps behind me, and turned to see Zak following. He caught me by the arm and pulled me into a deserted room full of file trolleys and manila folders. Zak walked in behind me and closed the door behind him. He stood so close I could feel the heat from his body seeping into mine. He put his hands on my shoulders and turned me round to face him. I tried to stay calm but his touch was humming through me, all the way down to my toes.

'About tonight,' Zak said. 'I'm sorry, I apologise. I shouldn't have behaved like that.'

I stared at him, dumbfounded. Zak? Apologising? I was tempted to ask him to pinch me, to make sure I wasn't dreaming, but then I saw that for the second time that night, Zak Khumalo actually looked as if he was taking life seriously. Maybe he'd respond to me doing the same.

'Why are you so secretive?' I asked. 'What's with you and me, anyway? I'm just a colleague, I don't want anything else, far from it.'

'I'm not what you think, Thabisa.'

'I know *that!*'

'It's more complicated. I'm not just a police officer.'

'What do you mean?'

Zak turned away from me. He gazed out of the window for a full minute, before replying.

'This is confidential. Nobody knows about it except Matatu. I run surveillance operations for a special government agency. I'm attached to the Violent Crimes Unit at the moment, but I'm not doing just police work.'

I rocked back on my heels. 'What are you investigating?'

'Don't grill me on this, okay? You don't want the details and I couldn't tell you anyway.'

'So what you're saying is, that you're some sort of double agent?'

'It's too difficult to explain. I'm a loner, I can't afford emotional ties. Let's just leave it at that for now. I'm never going to be the conventional, let's-get-married-and-have-kids type.'

I couldn't believe Khumalo imagined I was actually looking for somebody with that description to come into my life.

'You patronising jerk.' I hissed. 'Do you really think that's what I'm looking for? Don't picture yourself in that role in my life. Don't worry, you are so definitely not what I want, Khumalo. Don't kid yourself you ever could be.'

He smiled. 'I don't want to get emotionally involved and I'm sure you don't. I'm very attracted to you. I might get to like you too much. I don't want you in my space. It wouldn't be good for either of us. Not right now.'

'As far as I'm concerned, all you are, is someone I have to work with. You might be a good kisser, Zak, but I prefer men who are less shallow ...'

I turned my back on him, and walked out. I heard him laughing all the way down the corridor.

Then I had to get into the car with him and drive back to the safe house. There was a frosty silence all the way back too.

When we got back to the house, Khumalo jumped out of the car and opened my door.

'Right,' he said, 'you want me to come in? Are you worried about the intruder? Let me go in first and check it out for you.'

I pushed him away, and opened the front door.

'Go away,' I said, 'just go away.'

He laughed as I slammed the front door shut. I nearly opened it, and went out after him, I don't know why. I just wanted to kill him, hit him and hurt him in some way. But when I opened the door he was gone. For a few minutes I remained standing in the doorway staring at the space where he'd been, feeling the night air close around where he had stood.

I ran up the stairs and got into the shower. How humiliating. How dare this womanising colleague behave like this? It was sexual harassment; I would report him to Matatu in the morning. But when I remembered his mouth, his hands, his powerful body pressed against mine, I shivered, even though the water was hot.

It was then that I remembered. Funny how the mind works, it's like a filing system, teasing its way through information, sifting and sorting and burrowing down to the answer. Spitting it up at the weirdest times, like now, wiping all thoughts of Zak Khumalo from my mind.

The woman in the street? Julia McEwen, wife of the mining magnate, Magnus McEwen. She had been missing, presumed dead for the last four months.

# 15

## 27 June 2006

The house was perfect, a furnished cottage in a pan-handle off Graham Street. Surrounded by school playing fields and cricket pitches, nobody could see it from the street. The back garden was walled.

While Sue talked to the agent and signed forms, Julia had looked out, her eyes skimming the garden. She'd spent so much time in her Johannesburg garden, involved in all the planning, pruning, weeding, and planting, as well as the enormous pleasure of the results. An acknowledged orchid expert, she had been chair of the Sandton Gardening Club for three years running, the youngest woman ever to hold the post. Her garden was her sanctuary, her escape from Magnus.

Closing her eyes, she'd visualised her Johannesburg rose gardens: the orchid house, the lush lawns sweeping down to the pool, the jacaranda tree in full bloom, flower beds overflowing with day lilies and agapanthus.

Now she barely glanced at the pretty cottage garden outside the window. Gardens didn't matter anymore.

After Sue's confession, Ollis Sando hadn't been mentioned again. Julia had remained quiet and respectful until Sue relaxed. Their relationship returned to normal, but a slight shift had occurred.

Behind it an avalanche was building.

'We need another car,' Sue had said a few days before their next job. 'We'll keep the pick-up truck, but we need a back-up.'

They'd driven to Port Elizabeth and bought a second-hand white Toyota van.

'The most anonymous car in the world,' Sue said.

They made their way to a Mr Price warehouse and bought a big supply of sheets, blankets, pillows, duvets, towels, crockery, pots and pans, a starter pack of stainless-steel cutlery and three big rugs. At Pick 'n Pay they stocked up on mops, detergents, buckets, and an ironing board. At Truworths and Woolworths they bought jeans, sweaters, underwear and shirts. It was a shopping frenzy. They had so much cash, it was fun.

They'd stocked up separately on small helium cans, to avoid attention. Julia told a talkative assistant at Frolics Party Shop that they were for her child's birthday party balloons.

'Why don't you get the large cylinder?' the sales assistant had asked. 'Most people do that. They return the cylinder afterwards and get their deposit back.'

'I prefer the small disposable ones,' Julia said. She was beginning to feel uncomfortable. She wasn't good at lying. 'You have got that type haven't you?'

'Yes, but they're much more expensive, people don't ...'

'I'll take six of them,' Julia interrupted. 'And give me a hundred assorted balloons, please.'

The sales assistant stared at her.

'You want six disposables? Where are you having the party?'

'Um, well, we're not sure yet, not sure of the venue that is ... here, just give them to me, please, don't bother about a bag, I've got a box in the car.'

The sales assistant watched Julia through the shop window as she bundled the packages into the boot of her car and drove off.

Sue went in two days later and bought more disposable containers.

'This must be a popular time of the year for parties,' the chatty assistant had remarked. 'I had another lady in here this week, buying up big.'

Sue smiled. 'These are for a school concert.'

'Which school is that?' the assistant asked.

But the customer left before she got an answer. She didn't even wait for her change.

When they got back to Grahamstown, Sue had paced around the cottage, saying nothing.

'I'm going to talk to the bank manager at Bank of the Eastern Cape,' she finally said. 'The safety deposit boxes are in the vault. The documents were kept at the High Court, but they've been moved. I thought I might drop by and get to know him. I've got a healthy bank balance at his branch.'

Julia nodded. 'Do you want me to come?'

'No. I want you to stay inside. The Arts Festival has started. I don't want you bumping into anyone you know.'

'They won't recognise me.'

'They might.'

'Never,' said Julia. 'I'm a different person now.'

And she was.

'I've heard there's to be a night cash delivery at Birches tomorrow. I think we'll pitch up,' said Sue. 'We've made a big hole in our savings.'

'Okay,' said Julia. She loved the thrill of a heist, the moment when they surged in and pulled out their guns. She loved to see the guards turn pale, and raise their hands, sweating with fear. It felt so good. She'd learned so many skills. What a waste not to show them off. It was scary, it was risky, but there was an eerie feeling of familiarity about it. She had uncovered an insatiable appetite that had nothing to do with money.

The next day, dressed in black from head to toe, with their alien masks and helium packs in their pockets, guns holstered on their hips, they were ready. They parked the Toyota, number plates covered in black masking tape, near an alley that cut through from the High Street to Carlisle Road. They could run through the alley and make a quick getaway through Fiddlers Green. Easy. They strolled back to the high street, mingling with crowds of festival goers.

As they walked up toward the cathedral, Julia saw an interesting couple approaching. The man was tall and blonde, the woman dark-skinned with braided hair, wearing a bright red coat and purple scarf. They were talking and laughing together. As they drew close, Julia noted that the woman had pale eyes. They were almost silver, like gun metal, but there was something even more unsettling about her; a confident, alert look, a look of recognition. Their eyes met.

*Oh, my God. She recognises me.* She waited for a shout, running feet, a hand on her shoulder, but nothing happened. She turned. The crowd gathered them up. Julia's heart pounded uncomfortably. So what if the woman recognised her? Called the police? Then she could be released from Sue. But – Julia turned and looked at the clean profile of the woman walking beside her – she didn't want to be released.

***

It was after midnight when they saw the Money Sure security van arrive at Birches. As the guards opened the back door of the armoured vehicle, Julia saw they were unarmed. Unbelievable. Money Sure guards were usually armed to the teeth. Julia and Sue put on their alien masks, inhaled helium from their packs and surged forward.

'Stand back!' Sue squeaked.

The guards, two red-faced guys reeking of alcohol, were caught like rabbits in a trap. They'd obviously decided that quiet little Grahamstown was a crime-free zone, then been caught up in the festival's warm, fuzzy atmosphere. Julia moved forward, ripping open packets of cash, stuffing money into grocery bags. Sue held the guards at gunpoint. They were speechless with shock.

'Keep still,' Sue squeaked in her Donald Duck voice. 'Don't move, boys. You can go back and have a few more drinks when we're finished.'

As she spoke, one of them dived at Julia.

Sue leapt forward, slammed a vicious kick into his groin, then shot him in the shoulder. He fell back, screaming, eyes wide, one hand pressed against his chest. His colleague knelt beside him, trying to stem the blood already staining his shirt. Julia and Sue took their chance. Grabbing the grocery bags, they walked steadily back down the alley where they had been waiting, toward Carlisle Street. Once out of sight they tore off their masks. The secret was to look normal. No panic. No running. As they emerged from the alley into Carlisle Street, a crowd of rowdy university students was weaving toward them on the other side of the street, coming up from Fiddlers Green. They shouted out: 'What's happening? Was that a gun shot?'

'No way,' said Sue. 'Just a car back-firing.' Her voice was almost normal; the helium had worn off.

The students slowed down. They were drunk, pushing and jostling each other. One was wearing a crown, the others dressed in cloaks and witches' hats.

Julia and Sue turned up their coat collars, hiding their faces as they walked past. They fell into the car. The adrenaline was pumping. They began to laugh. They couldn't stop. With tears pouring down their faces, they clutched each other, shrieking with laughter. When they got back to the house and parked the car in the garage, Julia turned to Sue in the darkness.

'Brilliant,' she said. 'You saved us. We've got away with it!'

Fizzing with joy, with relief, with pleasure, Julia turned her face. Their lips connected. It was the easiest thing in the world. Sue's lips were soft. It was so different from kissing a man. A deep flush, like hot, red wine rose up and surged through Julia's body. Taboos of a lifetime were swept away as Sue laughed softly and pulled Julia closer.

# 16

## 28 June 2006

'You look different,' Bea said as I walked into the police station. 'Why are you looking so twitchy this morning?'

*Damn Khumalo.*

'It's got something to do with that sexy doctor, right?' Bea asked.

'There was a heist, and then we had to go to the hospital and interview the guards. They were unarmed, big problem. I'm not exactly smiling this morning,' I said.

Bea rolled her eyes.

'Ja, right,' she said. 'But I bet you got some time with that sexy doctor. What happened?'

Today Bea was packed into tight poison-green trousers and jacket. Her pink T-shirt had 'Foxy Lady' spelled out in sequins across her boobs. With her arms and legs crossed, and her foot jiggling impatiently in pink stiletto-heeled boots, she looked ... well, eye-boggling was the word that sprang to mind.

'Come on, Thabisa, how was the date?'

'Good, he's a cool guy.'

Before Bea could continue her interrogation, Zak walked in. He looked at me, giving nothing away. His eyes held mine for a moment before he turned away. I was still furious with him – and myself– for last night. It had shaken me that I could have been almost ready to – no, I wasn't going there. And what about his big secret, his hidden world? I wondered who he could be working for. What was his connection to the Eagles? I wanted some answers about my colleague, Zak Khumalo.

Bea's eyes widened. She missed nothing. As I walked past her desk, toward the director's office, Bea hissed: 'That guy's so hot. If I were ten years younger ...'

'Bea!' I warned. I made the zipped-mouth sign.

'Okay. No talking. My lips are sealed. Look at me, I'm locking my lips and throwing the key away.'

'If only ...' I said.

As I passed the desk, I caught sight of myself in the make-up mirror on Bea's desk. I noticed my embarrassed expression. It wouldn't go away.

*Damn Khumalo. Damn him.*

The only interview room at the police station was small and stuffy. It held the body odours of dozens of previous guests. The windows were high on the wall. They didn't open. On a small table sat a twin-tape deck, with a panic button behind it. A video camera was trained on the room from a bracket above the door. There would be no recording today. The five student interviews were informal. The first three had told exactly the same story in quiet, frightened voices. Now Zak, Mandile and I were about to interview the last two.

'Take a seat please,' I said.

The girl, Anna Silvers, was short and blonde with a studded tongue and a semi-permanent scowl. The boy, Andrew Dent, looked as if he was always top of his class. Clever-looking guy. His intelligent face was framed by long hair and a smarter-than-you expression. His skin was pale, his eyes hidden behind round-rimmed glasses – a nerd with a tight mouth.

I had dozens of questions on my list; they all had to be answered.

The girl did most of the talking. 'Look, I'm happy to help, but we were all pissed, returning from the festival.'

'What time was that?' I asked.

'I dunno, after midnight I guess.'

'What did you see?'

'Well, nothing really. We heard a shot, thought it was a gun, but the guy said it was a car back-firing.'

'What man was this?'

'There were two of them, on the other side of the street. I don't know which one. It looked like two guys wearing beanies.'

'Tell me exactly what you saw.'

'We were fooling around, there were five of us. We'd been to this party, you see, with the actors from *Red Mamba*. Have you seen it, it's great?'

'Let's stick to the facts. You were in Carlisle Street and you heard a shot, and then saw two men approaching you?'

'They weren't approaching. They were just strolling, quite slowly.'

'Go on.'

'Andrew shouted, "Was that a gunshot?" didn't you, Andrew? The man said, "It's a car back-firing", something like that.'

'Did you notice anything about his voice?'

'It was quite high. I thought it sounded a bit odd.'

'What do you mean by odd?'

'Like he'd got a sore throat or something.'

Andrew Dent spoke for the first time: 'It sounded like a woman's voice.'

'That's crazy, Andrew, it couldn't have been a woman,' said Anna.

'Thank you, Andrew. Do you remember anything else about this man?'

I asked, deliberately casual. *Never make them think it's important. If you do they'll want to please, and their imagination will start filling in the gaps.* 'When you passed them what did you see?'

'We were on the other side of the street,' said Anna. 'They were just two guys, in beanies, okay? We couldn't see whether they were black, white or sky-blue pink.'

'Were they carrying anything?'

'I told you, we were pissed. We weren't looking. Maybe one of them was carrying a bag ... I dunno.'

'What happened next?'

Andrew Dent took over. 'We walked along Cawood, came out at the side of Birches store. That's when we saw the van and two guards. One on the ground, the other kneeling beside him. It was like ... well, there was blood all over the place.'

'What did you do?'

'I sobered up fast. Tried to call Emergency Services on my cell phone, but there was no reception. So Peter – you talked to him earlier – he ran to the police station and that's when the police arrived on the scene. And the ambulance. We thought it was a heist. They must have driven off in a getaway car.'

'The guy was bleeding like a stuck pig. When the paramedics turned him over, the blood gushed out, like in the movies,' said Anna. 'It was obviously an armed hold-up and they got away before we got there. So why are you here, wasting time questioning us? Why aren't you out there, setting up roadblocks, or whatever it is you're supposed to do?'

'Thank you, that's all,' I said, standing up and closing the file. The two students left.

Zak and Mandile looked at each other, eyebrows raised. Mandile shook his head.

'These privileged students, think they rule the world,' said Mandile. 'Isn't that what all students think?' I asked, barely suppressing a smile. 'Isn't that the point of being a student?'

When we walked into the main office, it buzzed with activity, police officers working on computers and interviewees lining up to wait their turn.

Bea approached and stood next to me. 'Forensics just called in. They're looking to see whether the bullet from Birches is the same as the one that came from Kenton-on-Sea. They've examined blood splatter and powder residues, ballistic angles, all that. They said that it was a clean shot, ripped through the flesh, missing bone and exiting again. This guard is one lucky fellow. They found the bullet lodged in the door of the armoured vehicle.'

'Thanks Bea,' I said.

'Oh, one more thing, Thabisa. I phoned round the party shops where they stock helium. Usually they hire the big cylinders out, but one place in Port Elizabeth, Frolics, in Walmer Park, sold small disposable cylinders last week. She says they're about the size of a smallish vacuum flask. Not very popular because they're expensive. It's unusual to sell them, especially so many. '

'Descriptions?'

'She said two separate women. Each bought six cylinders. One a mother, the other a teacher. She remembers them because the one seemed flustered and left quickly. The other one didn't even wait for her change and it was quite a big sum, she just left it on the counter and disappeared. It seemed a bit odd.'

'That's useful. Send someone to talk to Frolics. Thanks. Well done.'

I turned to Zak. 'Let's talk to the guard next.'

We returned to the interview room. Piet Kruger was a shattered man, trembling, pale and sweating profusely. 'Look you *ous*, I'm a bit tired, and my ears are still *fokken* ringing,' he said.

'Just tell us what happened, please,' I said.

'We opened the door of the van and they were just sommer there. They came out of *fokken* nowhere. There was this explosion and Jan ... he fell down. I'd been crouching down, opening the vehicle door, and when I looked up there was this *moerse fokken* weapon and two men.'

'Yes, just tell us what happened next.'

'The oke holding the gun was all in black. I kind of froze. Jan dived at one of them, but the *bliksem* shot him, and then, he just collapsed.'

'Did they say anything?'

'Just that we should *bly stil* and ...'

'Yes?'

'Well, that we could *mos* go back to the ... well, the pub ... later ...'

'Had you been drinking?'

Silence.

'Please answer the question.'

'Ja.' Piet hung his head. His life as a security guard was over.

# 17

## 28 June 2006

'About last night. Don't read anything in to it, okay?' Sue said.

Julia smiled. 'Like what?'

'It was only sex. I've had sex with women before. I don't care about gender, but I prefer men. I like the apparatus better. With women it's a bit too mechanical.'

Julia said nothing. It hadn't been her. Julia McEwen hadn't been there last night. A new woman had taken over, an unbelievably sexy woman. A movie star. A porn star. Sue's hands had caressed every part of her. She had covered Julia with her hot mouth. And Julia had panted, thrust, bit and cried out. She was wild, messy, wet. At the height of it, she'd heard her own applause thundering through the bedroom, for this sexy woman who wasn't her at all. Who could have thought it could happen like that? That it could be so amazing?

'Didn't you enjoy sex with your rich husband?' Sue asked.

'No.'

'Have you had lovers?'

'No.'

'Nobody else?'

'No.'

'Bloody hell, Julia, what have you been doing all these years? Well, just remember, this thing now was only sex, it doesn't mean much to me. Just the means to an end.'

'Yes,' said Julia. 'I know.'

They were having breakfast in the kitchen. Julia chopped fruit, percolated coffee and buttered toast. She felt light, weightless and energised. Last night had liberated her in some profound way. She was on a different path. After last night there was no going back. She hummed as she juiced oranges, scrambled eggs, sizzled bacon. The crossover had happened.

\*\*\*

Sue watched Julia through narrowed eyes. She had managed to destroy everything about Julia that reminded her of the British royal family. Now

Julia was refugee-thin, her long red hair razored and dyed into black spikes, the cut-glass voice the only thing left of what she had been. To start with, Julia used to slide her eyes away when Sue spoke to her, but that nervous habit had disappeared.

When they did a job, Julia was good. Really good, a natural. When the nervous energy slid into place and she was high on adrenaline, she was hot. It was only occasionally now that Julia's cool façade slipped, showing how fragile and wounded she really was.

Last night had surprised Sue. The ice queen had melted. The aloof, unattainable Julia had turned into a wild woman.

Sue looked around the cottage kitchen. It wasn't Buckingham Palace, but it was better than the beach shack and a lot better than the block of council flats where she'd lived in Middlesex. Rose Garden Close. Somebody had a sense of humour.

She smiled as she thought how easy the heists were compared with working in the accounts department at Planet Cell. There her brain had been suspended for eight hours a day in a boring little office processing customer accounts. It was supposed to be trendy; everyone wore casual gear and went to the pub after work. Not that she gave a fuck. She had never stayed anywhere long. She was always restless, waiting for the next thing, whatever that might be.

The next thing was the newspaper advertisement.

*Computer software-training expert required for South African company. Twelve-month contract. All relocation expenses paid. Bonuses.*

She wasn't exactly a software-training expert, but she had grand ambitions. She was always writing off for jobs and usually didn't get as far as an interview, but that day Sue had a feeling. She had emailed her details.

Shortly after that her cell phone rang. A man with a foreign accent had asked to speak to her. He invited her for an interview the following day in the city. Sometimes, when she spoke to men on the phone, Sue would end up saying something cheeky, provocative, like, 'Pity you can't see me, because I'm really pretty'. It usually got a reaction. So she tried it out on him.

There was a long silence before he replied. 'Well, I'm certainly looking forward to meeting *you*, Miss Kellon.'

She hugged herself. She knew she'd get the job if he did the interview. Blokes loved her. *I'll soon be out of here. I'm bright, I'll get by.*

Back then Sue always felt she was about to go on stage and act out a part where she was the star. It was the same feeling that she got when she went into a club and pinpointed the bloke she was going to take home and fuck that night. They didn't know who she was. They hadn't even met her, but she had picked them out. It was her power game, just waiting to be played.

She always did the choosing. They were the co-stars.

Her wits, face and body were her means of escape. She knew that life throbbed more powerfully somewhere else. All she needed was nerve and confidence.

Something should be happening. Something big. Time was passing; she was already thirty-two. She was ready for the big adventure. The days were whirling by. There was breathlessness in her life. She was standing on the edge of something. She just knew it.

The offices of Phoenix Empowerment Investments were up-market and luxurious. She was looking good – not just good, bloody fantastic – in her black power suit and killer heels. A group of workmen watched her, their eyes following her with a slow burn as she walked past a construction site near Canary Wharf. She felt like a high-stepping racehorse, pawing the ground, while she waited for the starting pistol.

'Come in,' said a man.

She opened the door and walked in. When she had told Julia about it, she hadn't mentioned the sheer, physical impact of that first meeting, the melting sensation in her gut when she saw Sando for the first time. Huge black-and-white photographs hung all around the room, showing buffalos snorting, elephant charging, lions tearing little deer apart, but the most dangerous animal in the room was him.

He was a tall, powerfully built, black man, dressed in a tailor-made dark suit, dazzling white shirt and silk tie. She had felt a sharp and thrilling lust just looking at him.

'You are quite correct,' he said gravely, his eyes travelling over Sue's face and body like road drills.

'What about?' she asked.

*My God, was he a mind reader?*

'You *are* very pretty,' he said.

'Oh, that ... Thank you,' she said.

She knew this wasn't the way to open an interview, but it was all in her favour. She felt he sensed the real Sue, the restless, up-to-mischief, vibrant Sue. Bugger the qualifications, but they'd gone through them anyway, spinning out the moment between them. She was the actress again, preparing to step into the spotlight. She couldn't stop wondering about him.

While he described the job, telling her about South Africa and Johannesburg, where she would be based, what Phoenix was all about, she ran her eyes over him: full lips, shaved head, glossy eyebrows, brilliant teeth, hooded, sexy eyes. She looked at a wedding photo displayed on the desk. The bride was so young; Sue thought she must be his daughter, hanging on his arm, gazing up at him: 'Daddy ... buy me a wedding, Daddy'.

'Yes, I'm fully qualified in all those skills,' she assured him. She answered the questions with all the things he wanted to hear. Only a moment and Sue believed her own lies. She was good at that. She was descended from a long line of manipulators. Only problem was, she suspected she had met her match here. Sue watched his eyes move up and down her body, flicking over her breasts, skimming down her hips to her legs. Her skirt had ridden up, exposing her thighs. His eyes met hers. She smiled very slowly, and licked her lips. She knew how to turn men on.

Later, in his hotel room, she had to admit he was a remarkable lover. He went through his paces to show her what he was capable of. First the deep sucking kisses, the nipple licking, his lizard tongue sipping at her, then the swift, practiced undressing. When he finally slid inside her she was astonished at the pleasure. Even when he'd whispered smugly, 'Am I too big for you?' she didn't care how arrogant he sounded. He gave her the licence to be herself. However outrageous she was, she knew he would match her.

Well, naturally, she got the job. What she'd told Julia was true; he was like a drug. She was mad for him, drugged with love, lust – who the fuck knew – but it was all madness. She discovered as soon as she arrived in South Africa that the girl in the wedding photo was his wife. They were newly married. She didn't care. She never questioned his motives. She was enthralled by him. It was as if he had slid open her mind and climbed inside.

For a while he was satisfied with all the sex tricks at which she was so skilled. But he wanted to heighten the sexual excitement and soon he suggested more dangerous activities, hooking her in from the start. The reality of breaking into a heavily alarmed and guarded apartment and stealing documents gave her the strongest rush of adrenaline she'd ever known. They had sex afterward, standing on the open veranda, in full view of the security guards – if they'd looked up.

She had learned that altitude gave people a false sense of security. The higher they lived, they more secure they felt and the fewer security measures they took. She and Sando exploited this belief time and time again. She took most of the risks, climbing up the side of buildings, hanging from ledges and crawling up walls. Then she'd let him into the apartments and they'd take what they wanted. Sando was an expert safe combination breaker. They were usually so hyped up, they'd have sex then and there, wrestling on the silken bed covers of Johannesburg's rich and famous. It was complete abandonment. She loved it.

They were almost caught one night, when the owners of a penthouse they had broken into returned early. Sando stepped coolly onto a fire escape and Sue dived into a cleaning cupboard beside the lift. When the couple walked out of the lift, she rode down to the basement and walked away into the night, clutching a bag of exquisite diamonds.

'You got to love it, it's so easy,' Sando had laughed. 'It's like taking candy from a baby.'

Part of their haul was a huge pear-shaped diamond on a thick gold chain. Sue wanted it, but Sando had said no. It was his. She shrugged. There was so much to choose from, why quibble?

Mama Ruby's was to be the first time she operated alone, her opening night. Sando had promised he would be there to see her in her starring role. He explained everything and Sue agreed. She would hide in the ladies' cloakroom, dress in a black tracksuit and alien mask and inhale helium from a small canister to disguise her voice. Then she'd burst into the private dining room, fully armed, take as much as she could, then get out, while everyone was still in shock.

The getaway van would be waiting to take her around the block. She'd change in the back, then the van would drop her off and she'd coolly walk in to the basement parking at her Melrose Arch apartment. She could watch the action in the square from her seventh-storey hideout.

But it hadn't worked out like that.

The first shock was seeing Ollis and his wife. He hadn't mentioned that she would be there. Sitina Sando was a beauty, much younger and lovelier than Sue had thought. She could have been Sando's daughter. Sue saw at once that Sitina was wearing the large, pear-shaped diamond on the thick gold chain that she, Sue, had risked her life to steal.

Then the alarm system, which Sando assured her had been disarmed, started wailing like an air-raid siren. It was bedlam. Thinking quickly, she realised she had to get out fast. She needed a hostage to help her escape, so she grabbed the first person at hand, the woman with the red hair. Julia McEwen.

Sando had called her later, demanding that she kill Julia, then go immediately to the isolated beach house near Port Alfred where she would be safe. She had intended to kill Julia on the road, but when it came to it, she couldn't. She didn't want to be Sando's puppet, not after seeing him with his wife. In the restaurant he had been solicitous, even tender, with Sitina. He was so obviously a married man. It made her feel sick. It didn't match the image she had of him, the way he was with her and the wild sex they'd been sharing. But, of course, he always went home to his beautiful wife.

He called her every week with instructions emphasising his control over her. He never referred to the heists in the Eastern Cape. Sue made sure he didn't know she was involved, or, more importantly, that Julia was alive and helping her. If he ever learned that she hadn't killed Julia – that Julia was actually there, with her, sharing everything – he would definitely kill them both. He would be ruthless. So she played along.

A few weeks after Sue had abducted Julia, Sando called and told her it was time to plan the raid to recover the documents which would jeopardise his future. Now he told her where they were; what she must do to deliver them into his hands.

He told her to go to the Grahamstown police safe house and frighten a Violent Crimes detective, Thabisa Tswane, off the case. She had been seconded to Grahamstown to investigate a crime wave.

'Hurt her,' he said. 'Threaten her. She's too good at her job. Frighten her out of the area. She'll find something, and if she does, she'll implicate me.'

He told Sue about the bonus he would transfer to her overseas bank account the day she handed him those papers. Enough to set her up for life.

Part of her wanted to please him, but whenever she remembered his wife's neck, the diamond necklace hanging around it, a small voice somewhere in the back of her brain told her she didn't like the idea. Not one bit. Still, she had to risk her life for Sando. What option did she have?

She shuddered as she remembered what had happened with the Russian. The Russian who had committed suicide when he was visiting South Africa. Well, that's what everyone thought. But Sando knew what had happened to him, and he would use that information without a second thought if she rebelled. Who would believe her story against his? She would go to jail.

There was no way out, no going back. She had to do what Sando told her.

# 18

It took me most of a day to get back to Johannesburg after Commissioner Matatu's call.

'We want you back in the office as soon as possible,' he'd said. He gave no reason why.

I drove to East London, waited three hours for a delayed flight, landed at OR Tambo International Airport and drove to the office, arriving after five in the afternoon.

Matatu was waiting. He questioned me about the case. I laid out all the evidence, before voicing my suspicion that we were looking for a white couple, one of them a woman.

'This is not the normal profile of crime in South Africa, or anywhere else. Women rarely commit this sort of violent crime,' Matatu said.

'I've never heard of it, either,' I said.

'There's certainly an odd twist to this. What's happening in Grahamstown?'

'Forensics are on it. We've laid on extra security at all the banks.'

Matatu nodded.

'Is there any movement in the Julia McEwen case, sir?' I asked. 'I'd like to see the photographs again.'

'Nothing new. Yes, I can show you the photographs.' Matatu clicked on his laptop and Julia McEwen looked out at them. A fine-boned face, framed with long red hair, dark eyes under highly arched brows. The face of a well-maintained, elegant woman in her late thirties.

'Why do you want to look at these?'

'I believe I've seen her,' I said slowly.

'Where?' Matatu asked sharply.

'At the Grahamstown Arts Festival a few days ago.'

'My God. Are you sure?'

'The woman I saw had short, dark hair, but I'm certain it was her. She's got a distinctive face.'

'This is the first sighting since the kidnapping. The general opinion is, of course, that she's dead.'

'I believe she's alive. That's the woman I saw.'

Matatu rocked back on his heels and drew in his breath. He clicked the mouse again, opening more images of Julia McEwen: Julia at an orchid show receiving a cup; Julia with her husband, dressed in a ball gown, her hair swept up in a chignon; Julia receiving a cheque for her favourite charity from one of the big banks.

'Did you get the impression she was still a hostage?' Matatu asked.

'She didn't look like a hostage,' I said. 'She was with another woman. They looked like companions.'

'It's uncommon for a woman to be a hostage taker,' said Matatu. 'It's rarely happened as far as I know.'

'What about the husband?' I asked.

'Magnus McEwen offered a substantial reward when his wife was kidnapped. Nobody's come forward, but the reward still stands.'

'Has he kept in contact?'

'Not regularly.'

'Strange. Your wife disappears, she's missing for months and you don't hassle the police daily?'

'He's a strange man. He probably believes she's dead and there's no hope.'

'Could he have had anything to do with it?'

'We've interviewed him on several occasions, but never picked up on anything. They were married for over thirteen years, seemed settled enough on the surface. There was some talk of a girlfriend, but nothing conclusive. What we have discovered is that Mrs McEwen was a compulsive kleptomaniac. Classic impulse control disorder. Usually an indication of mental problems, particularly with affluent women. There have been seven reported incidents, but it was only after the last one that she was arrested and formally charged.'

'What's the husband like?'

'Self-opinionated, bombastic, wouldn't be easy to live with.'

'Anything else, sir?'

'We interviewed their domestic staff. They all liked Mrs McEwen, but they're not keen on him. They told us that the McEwens lived separate lives, slept in separate rooms, never spent much time together. She was a trophy wife, dusted off when she was needed. For the rest of the time, one of those society hostesses, always out raising money for charity.'

'Hmm, all rather sad isn't it? To be missing, presumed dead, but your rich husband isn't making any great effort to find you.'

'We don't know that that's strictly true, Thabisa, but he does seem rather detached about her disappearance. What else are the police in Grahamstown doing about the current crime wave? Have they found out anything more about these criminals with the cartoon voices?'

'They're knocking on doors, stopping people in the street and visiting all the hotels and guest houses in the area. We've put up posters and advertised the reward money more aggressively.'

There was a pause before Matatu continued: 'Let me tell you why we've asked you to come back at such short notice, Thabisa. Some people from the Truth and Reconciliation Commission Support Unit want to talk to you.'

'Really? Why?' I asked. 'I thought the TRC finished its work over a decade ago.'

'Did you follow the events?'

'Of course. It was compulsive viewing, sir.'

Matatu was silent.

'What has this got to do with me?' I asked.

'I think you'd better let them explain to you, Thabisa,' Matatu said.

A few minutes later, I was ushered into a large L-shaped room with broad windows overlooking the city. My heart sank when I saw who was there. Zak Khumalo. What the hell did he have to do with the TRC? What was all this about? Zak and a white man with silver hair sat at a large desk covered in files.

The two men stood when I entered. The older man stepped forward.

'Detective Inspector Tswane,' he said, offering his hand. 'I'm Richard Bowles of the Truth and Reconciliation Commission Task Force. Of course, you know Zak Khumalo. Please take a seat.'

He motioned toward a leather chair. I shot Zak a cold look as I sat down next to him. I was furious with myself for letting him know so much about my private self. I should never have confided in him. He smiled. I ignored him.

'Detective Inspector, are you aware of the work that the Task Force does?' Bowles asked.

'No, I'm not,' I said.

'We're part of the Crime Combating and Investigation Branch,' Bowles said. 'After the Truth and Reconciliation Commission hearings ended in the late nineties, there were loose ends to follow up. The Task Force was formed for that function.'

I had been fascinated by the TRC hearings, set up as a platform to hear confessions about offences committed in the name of either apartheid or liberation. Anyone who truthfully acknowledged their involvement and then apologised to the country, was exonerated. The proceedings, carried out live on national television and chaired by my hero, Archbishop Desmond Tutu, had proved extremely successful in defusing tensions and setting the country on the road to real peace.

'I thought the TRC had closed its books?' I said. I realised now that Zak Khumalo must be involved in this work. This was his secret life. Or part of it.

'There are lines of enquiry that still need to be investigated. One of them concerns a certain Lucas Makanda. Are you familiar with the name?'

'No,' I said.

'He was one of a gang who blew up the Blue Moon Cafe in East London in 1976, where two people were killed.'

'I'm sorry, Mr Bowles, I'm not familiar with the case.'

Bowles learnt back in his chair and steepled his fingers. His brusque, hard manner intimidated me. I supposed he was used to hearing terrible stories and it had hardened him. His thin face didn't have an inch of kindness in it.

'Let me tell you what happened. In 1975 and 1976, Lucas Makanda was known to be recruiting freedom fighters in the rural villages of the Transkei. On the evening of May 28, 1975, a bomb was thrown into the restaurant. It was a popular, family place, whites only, of course. The bomb exploded, killed two people and injured fifteen others, mostly children.'

'How terrible,' I said, imagining the carnage.

'Three young black men were seen running away from the scene. A reward of three million rand was offered for their arrest. A month later three men were taken into custody. They all confessed and were executed six weeks later.'

'Was Lucas Makanda one of them?' I asked. I glanced at Zak. He turned and looked at me. There was something like pity in his expression.

'No, but during the TRC, Lucas Makanda testified that he had planned the attack. He said the three young men had been betrayed by an unknown person who claimed the reward. We suspect that Makanda may have claimed it himself.'

'Is it possible to talk to him?'

'He died last year. Now his family has requested that the case be re-opened. This was refused originally when they asked, in 1998. There was no military presence in or near the Blue Moon Cafe. It was an attack on civilians, hardly a fight against the armed force of the regime. Now one of his grandsons, a lawyer, is pressing for another hearing. He has connections in high places and it has been decided to re-open this case. We want to learn more about whoever claimed that three million-rand reward and make sure it wasn't Makanda himself,' said Richard Bowles.

'Please tell me what this has got to do with me?'

Zak and Bowles glanced at each other. There was a chilly silence in the room.

Finally Zak spoke: 'Thabisa, your father and uncles bombed that restaurant. They confessed to it.'

My mouth was suddenly dry. I couldn't swallow. 'I didn't know that,' I whispered softly. 'Oh my God.'

'I'm surprised you never asked,' said Bowles curtly.

'Why would I have asked?' I said. 'I've never heard this information before. Who would have given it to me! Anyway, I come from a rural, superstitious village and I'm a woman. Even if you have questions ... nobody answers.'

I could feel a storm of anger building up inside me. I was angry and disappointed with Khumalo, Bowles was a pedantic, unsympathetic man. I was listening to some deeply shocking information about my own family. I had every right to feel furious and disturbed.

'No doubt your relatives were influenced by Makanda. He was a much older and very persuasive man,' said Bowles. 'Our concern is, having recruited and set them up, did he then go on to betray them and claim the reward money?'

'Where is the documentation? There's got to be a record somewhere?' I asked.

'Perhaps there was,' said Zak. 'But there's nothing now. It must have been lost or destroyed. All we know is that the reward was paid to a man from the Thembu area, near the valley where you were born.'

'I see,' I said.

'Khumalo tells me that he recently visited your valley. Apparently there are unique records which exist there that could help our investigation?'

I couldn't look at Zak. This was a real betrayal. Zak had discussed me with this man. Talked to him about the valley and the sacred bead room. I had told him about it in confidence, not as part of the investigation we were there for. All the more reason to mistrust Khumalo even more. I folded my hands on my lap to stop them trembling.

'My people keep records in beadwork.'

'Can you interpret the beads?'

'Yes.'

'We need photographs of the beadwork and a corroborative witness to authenticate your statement. Who can confirm what the beads say?'

'Only my grandfather, and he won't cooperate.' I leaned forward, looking at Richard Bowles.

'Why not?' he asked. 'Why can't you make him cooperate?'

'Mr Bowles, my grandfather is a representative in the House of Traditional Leaders. He has the right to be consulted at national and provincial levels of government about issues or legislation affecting him and the people in his area, under his authority. The beads are only seen by him and the *sangoma* in the valley. He would never agree to anybody else looking at them, let alone photographing them. In this matter in particular he will have the final say.'

'But you have seen them?' Bowles pressed. He reminded me of a persistent little dog, worrying at my answers. I wanted to get up and walk out.

'Only recently and just for a few minutes. I did see a reference to three sons of the valley who were betrayed in 1976. That's all.'

'What sort of sign led you to believe that?' asked Bowles.

'A symbol of treachery.' I resisted shooting a look at Zak. He knew the meaning of the word alright. 'My grandfather believes that to disturb the beads in any way will provoke the anger of the ancestors.'

'That's why we are approaching you. You are in a unique position to influence your grandfather. Working with traditional leaders can be, well ... a delicate matter.'

'I am not able to influence my grandfather, Mr Bowles. He's an exceedingly stubborn man. He is the custodian of the valley. The beads are part of our heritage. They are highly significant.'

'This is an important piece of police information,' said Bowles.

'I repeat, my grandfather will not cooperate.'

'You could try, DI Tswane. Surely you could make an effort?'

I ignored him. There was a long silence. Nobody said anything. They just stared at me.

'Did all three men confess?' I asked, finally.

'Yes,' said Bowles. 'They maintained that they were liberation fighters. They knew they were defying the law. They were fighting for their rights.'

'Did they mention Lucas Makanda?'

'No. He was never implicated. Not until he applied for amnesty.'

'The reward seems very large, especially for those days.'

'Most of it came from an East London businessman, whose daughter and granddaughter had been in the café. They were both killed.'

I couldn't speak. I turned away.

'Would you like to see some photographs?' asked Bowles.

'Yes,' I said.

It was a short walk to the conference room, which was twenty metres long, with a window running the length of it, giving a panoramic view of the city. In the dusk, car headlights were floating gold sequins sparkling on the highway. A large screen hanging from the ceiling at the end of the room came alive with white light. Four photographs appeared simultaneously on the screen. All were young black men wearing prison garb. None looked familiar. Bowles pointed to a hollow-eyed boy, unshaven and trying to look tough.

'That is your father,' he said.

Tears rushed behind my eyes. The other two looked similar. Just three frightened kids.

Then Bowles put up a photograph of an older man. He looked like an ex-convict, with a shaved head and scar on his forehead.

'Lucas Makanda,' he said. 'As you see, he's older than the others. He and his family lived in semi-poverty most of their lives. If he did claim the ransom money, he certainly didn't use it to improve his lifestyle.'

In the next photograph a young blonde mother and daughter smiled at the camera. I knew what was coming. I fought the lump rising in my throat.

'Sarie and Wendy Potgieter; they were killed in the bomb blast. Wendy was nine years old.'

I stared at the screen for a long time before Bowles walked to the wall and switched off the lights.

My head ached. I wanted to leave. Get up and walk away from them all.

'All we ask is that you have another look at the beads in your valley. See what they say about this incident. Then we need your grandfather to verify your statement.'

'You're asking the impossible,' I said. 'Ask your colleague, Khumalo. He's met my grandfather.'

Zak approached and stood next to me. 'Nothing is impossible, if you want it badly enough,' he said quietly.

'Yes,' I hissed through tight lips, so the others wouldn't hear. 'You certainly know how to get what you want, even if it means betraying a colleague's confidence.'

'What we're going to do now,' Bowles said in a conclusive tone, 'is let Detective Inspector Tswane go about her business. I know she's on a case in the Eastern Cape, and she's eager to get back. Will you give this some thought, please? Get back to me in a few days?'

'Yes,' I said. 'Thank you for telling me this.'

I walked out of the conference room and stared through the window into the embers of a fiery Johannesburg sunset.

I could feel Zak standing close behind me. He put his arm round me.

I shrugged him off. 'Don't touch me,' I said, trying to keep my voice level.

'Just a concerned colleague,' he said. 'Are you okay?'

'Should I be?' I asked. 'I've just heard that most of my family are murderers.'

'Freedom fighters, Thabisa. Idealistic young men who wanted to abolish apartheid.'

'They murdered innocent women and children.'

'Apartheid forced many people to act for the greater good, Thabisa,' Zak said. 'And sometimes innocent people paid the price for that.'

I flinched, thinking of my country's dark past.

We walked down windowed corridors, full of glassed-off cubicles with people working inside them.

'Come, let's get out of here, go and have something to eat,' Zak suggested.

I didn't answer him.

'Look, Thabisa, I'm sorry I told Bowles about the bead room, but it's vital to this case that he knows about it.'

'Maybe so,' I replied. 'But you've betrayed a confidence. It tells me a lot about you. I was an idiot to tell you anyway.'

'Let's discuss your feelings over this, Thabisa. Why are you so angry? It's going to help solve a crime. It's our job, remember?'

I stared rigidly at him. I didn't enjoy having my vulnerability on display. I had no intention of discussing my feelings with anyone, let alone Zak Khumalo. 'You might be good at interrogating people, but you're not extracting more confidences from me. I've had enough drama for one day.'

He smiled at me.

'Why the patronising grin, Khumalo?'

'It's the grin of a man who loves you, babe.'

My heart skipped and I struggled to reply nonchalantly. 'Who said anything about love?'

'There are all sorts of love,' Zak said. 'My kind doesn't come with the usual conventions.'

We turned into an office with four real walls and a proper door, which read: 'Zak Khumalo'. Zak closed it. His eyes softened as he looked at me. He put his arms tight around me and held me to him for a few seconds before I wriggled away from his grasp.

'I'm sorry about your father and uncles,' he said quietly. 'It's not good to learn about it like this, but I want to find out who betrayed them and walked off with the three million rand. I want your help, Thabisa. I need you to show me the beads.'

I pulled away from him. 'In your dreams, Khumalo.'

I walked out and slammed the door behind me.

# 19

Sue smiled to herself as she swept into the bank. She didn't often dress like this, but when she did every head turned in her direction. She wore a short, black skirt and stiletto heels and her tight red jacket followed the sinuous lines of her body, opening at the front to reveal the taut swell of her breasts under a silky camisole. She would have stopped the traffic in London wearing this outfit, and in sleepy Grahamstown on a cold winter morning, she was dazzling.

She smiled to herself, remembering Julia's comment about her appearance as she'd left the house that morning. She had put on a spectacular push-up bra, a complete contrast to the usual breast-flattening clothing she wore when they were going on a heist.

'Wow,' Julia had laughed, 'nobody would mistake you for a man wearing that.'

'That's the point,' Sue replied. 'Today I'm all woman!'

The power of sex. If Sue understood one thing, it was that.

She remembered the time she and Sando had gone to the game park. The day he changed the dynamics of their relationship.

They had encountered a breeding herd of elephant not far off the private road they were on. He stopped the car.

'Get out and walk towards them,' he'd commanded. She started to walk in front of him through the waist-high grass. She was wearing khaki shorts and a loose silk top, with nothing underneath. She knew how good she looked and she could feel Sando's eyes slipping their way between her legs. Everything around her seemed to reflect her hunger for him. The waterhole, the heavy sky, the heat. She stumbled and half-turned.

'Don't look at me.' His voice jerked her back to reality. 'Just walk, watch the elephant, they don't know we are so close ... yet.'

They arrived in a small clearing where a large borehole pump shot up through the trees, its windmill arms catching the light. The elephant were very close now.

'Up against the tower,' Sando had ordered. She obeyed him and leaned against the corrugated surface. He came up behind her and parted her thighs with his knee. Her face was pushed against the hot tin of the water tower as he thrust into her. She was on fire.

'A little fear is good, isn't it?' he'd whispered. Her mind exploded like a chorus of demented angels as he slowly worked his magic and the elephant came nearer and nearer. It was a mixture of pleasure and fear more intense than anything she had ever experienced.

'It's good to push yourself further,' he said. 'Pleasure and pain are the best bedfellows, don't you think?'

He turned her to face him and leaned into her, kissing her hot, flushed face, thrusting his tongue in her mouth.

'Why don't you steal a car? I'll tell you exactly how to do it. You'll find the adrenaline rush delicious. You'll never feel so alive. I'll be there to help you. You'll be safe with me.'

And he had been with her, all the way, until now. Now it was time for Sue to put the next part of her plan into action and she had to do it on her own. She walked up to the counter and handed her card to the receptionist who gazed at her in astonishment.

'I have an appointment with the manager,' she said coolly.

A few minutes later, she was ushered into the office of Mr James Wilmot.

Wilmot's eyebrows rose as Sue made her entrance. One look at him and Sue knew he was perfect for her plan. About sixty, with the disappointed look of a man who has known failure in just about every area of his life, James Wilmot's long top lip made him appear permanently sad and serious. At least their encounter would cheer him up, give him something to smile about – for a while.

Sue's eyes flicked around the room, assessing everything. About a dozen cardboard boxes filled with books and files rested on the floor. The desk was clear apart from depressing photographs of a fierce-looking woman and four overfed children. The pale winter sun pierced the window and painted a yellow pattern on the wall. Dust motes swirled in the air. It was all rather gloomy.

'Oh dear, are you moving offices?' Sue asked in the husky voice she used on special occasions.

'No. Actually, I'm retiring,' Wilmot scrambled up hastily and indicated that Sue should sit down opposite him.

'How can I help you, Miss –' he glanced at Sue's business card, '– Miss Kellon?'

Sue smiled sweetly. 'Retiring? Surely not? You can't possibly be old enough.'

'We can't stay in our jobs forever, not when there are youngsters coming up for promotion,' he said, bravely trying to smile. 'Now, how can I be of assistance?'

'I wanted to meet you to discuss the account I opened here two weeks ago.' Sue crossed her legs. She saw his eyes widen and smiled to herself.

Wilmot might have been quite good-looking about twenty years ago. Now, though, he was portly and his grey hair was thinning. With his fair skin, pale blue eyes and stout build, he gave the impression of squat solidity, the epitome of a reliable bank manager.

He dialled his receptionist and asked her to bring the file on Miss Kellon. When she entered the room, the woman frowned at Sue, her mouth pinched like a lemon as her eyes ran over Sue's long, slim legs and swelling breasts. Sue smiled sweetly and watched as she left the room.

Wilmot studied Sue's account details, which his receptionist had placed on the desk. He blinked. Sue licked her lips with a small pink tongue as she watched him discover she had deposited four million rand into a cheque account two weeks ago.

'Miss Kellon,' he said, 'we must transfer your funds into a higher-interest account immediately.'

'Thank you, Mr Wilmot,' Sue said in her throatiest voice. 'I appreciate your advice. I really need a man to help me with financial matters.'

'Are you living in Grahamstown?'

'I'm renting a house here while I decide what I'm going to do next.'

'Are you ... alone?' he ventured.

'Yes.' Sue kept her eyes downcast. 'I'm a widow.'

She watched from under her lashes as Wilmot moved uncomfortably in his chair. He looked hot and flushed.

'Are you English?' he asked.

'Yes, but I've fallen in love with South Africa. Particularly this part of South Africa.'

'I would have thought ... Johannesburg?'

'No, Mr Wilmot, I'm a country girl. I'm considering investing in a game farm.'

'We've got some excellent game farms in the Eastern Cape. Have you visited any?'

'Not yet.' Sue bent forward, deliberately showing off more of her impressive cleavage. Wilmot's eyes were fixed on her breasts.

'Perhaps you could arrange some introductions for me?' she suggested, playing with the tendrils of blonde hair that curled around her face. Wilmot's eyes followed her every move.

'Yes, yes, of course. Perhaps I could suggest – Would you consider – I could drive you to some of these places myself?'

Sue smiled and widened her eyes. 'Oh, that would be so kind. But I can't expect you to do that. You must be such a busy man?'

'No, it's part of my job to ... Well, it's a public relations function. I would be honoured to escort you.'

'We could make it a real day out, I could take you to lunch. Perhaps Mrs Wilmot might like to come along?' Sue said sweetly, gesturing toward the photograph of the iron-faced woman on his desk.

'No!' Wilmot cleared his throat. 'That is, Mrs Wilmot is in Australia at the moment.'

'Oh,' Sue whispered in her little-girl-lost voice, 'so it will just be you and me?'

Wilmot's gaze roamed over her body, his forehead glossy with sweat. A few seconds passed before he realised she was watching him. When he saw her eyes on him, a blush burnt his fair skin.

They arranged a time and place. Sue turned to leave. 'Thank you so much, I'm so looking forward to our next meeting.'

James Wilmot was reluctant to stand up and see her out of his office and Sue almost laughed out loud. It wouldn't do for a bank manager to be seen sporting an impressive erection under his sober suit. She gave herself a mental high five as she swept out of the bank.

***

At the end of a week of game farm visits, James Wilmot was bewitched. His favourite moments had been when Sue pretended to be frightened of elephants, hiding her face against his chest whenever they appeared.

'James,' she had whimpered, 'just hold me. I'm scared, they're just so ... so ... well, big ...'

When she re-enacted these scenes for Julia later, they both collapsed with laughter.

'The poor devil doesn't stand a hope with you in those khaki bush shorts,' Julia said. 'They look as if they've been painted on. Indecent! And as for this Wonder Bra, it's actually pornographic.'

Sue shrugged. 'Good. I'm taking him to dinner tomorrow night,' she said. 'I'm going a few steps further.'

'Be careful,' Julia warned.

'Don't be stupid. He's totally harmless. I'm going to give him a bit of excitement and get some information, that's all. Easy.'

Sue sprayed her body liberally with Chanel No. 5, straightened her hair and wore a revealing black dress. It worked. James Wilmot stood with proud excitement when she walked into the restaurant and planted a kiss on his cheek.

'This dinner is a big thank you for all your kindness this week,' she said softly. 'What would I have done without you?'

Wilmot swallowed audibly and blinked rapidly a few times. Were those tears in his eyes?

'It's truly been a pleasure. More than a pleasure.'

Sue worked her seduction act on Wilmot all evening. He was desperate for her. Lust rose from him in clouds every time he looked at her.

'Tell me about your children, James,' Sue asked, guiding the conversation onto a more personal level.

'I've got two daughters in Australia,' he said truthfully. He didn't mention his six grandchildren. Sue had counted them on the photographs on his desk.

'I've always wanted a family,' she said wistfully. 'I never had the opportunity.'

'You deserve one.' James Wilmot reached across the table and took her hand. 'I hope you don't mind me saying this, but I feel so close to you after this week. I find you so very attractive,' he said tentatively. 'I've never met a woman like you before.'

*I bet you haven't.*

'Thank you, James, I find you terribly attractive.' She leaned across the table and offered him her lips.

He pressed his mouth to hers reverently, then sat back in his chair with such a look of joy that Sue almost felt sorry for him.

But not quite sorry enough.

'Look,' she said, 'I've got a suggestion. I hope you don't think it's too bold, but why don't you come over for supper tomorrow night? I'll cook. We can relax and get to know each other better.'

For a few moments James Wilmot appeared to be struck dumb by her suggestion. Then he squared his shoulders, his eyes brightened and he smiled in total delight.

He was pitiful, putty in her hands.

The following evening Sue locked Julia into her bedroom at the back of the house. 'I can't afford anything to go wrong,' she said. 'Don't move around or make any more noise than you have to. He has to think I'm a poor little widow, all on my own. Understand?'

Julia nodded. Sue was still the boss.

At seven sharp, Sue met James at the door. She wore a clinging turquoise dress designed to stop a man dead in his tracks. Inside the warm cottage, was a smell of delicious food. Sue had arranged fragrant bowls of flowers, and deep white sofas invited James Wilmot to sink back and relax. Candles flickered on every surface and the music in the background was slow and romantic.

'We'll have dinner early shall we?' Sue said.

James nodded, speechless.

'After dinner, I thought we could play a game.'

'A game?'

'Yes, Twister, my favourite.'

'Is it a card game?'

'No, not cards. We give forfeits.'

Now James was perspiring. He loosened his tie. 'Forfeits?'

'Yes, you can ask anything of me if you win your round. I can do the same.'

The room seemed marinated in a warm apricot glow. James drank the whisky Sue gave him in one mouthful.

'Anything I want?' His voice was harsh.

'Anything.' Sue sank into the sofa and nestled close to him. Her chin touched his shoulder. 'You've been so kind to me. What would I do without you?' She wriggled against him, the turquoise dress riding up her long legs.

James drew her close and tried to kiss her, but she moved away at the last minute.

'Just going to serve dinner.'

She fetched a tray bearing steaming bowls of soup from the kitchen. James Wilmot looked around the room; Sue could see he was captivated by the scene. The stone fireplace full of blazing logs, the low-beamed ceiling, the magnificent woman who had chosen to share it all with him. She could see heaven in his eyes.

'Come and eat.' She smiled at him in her special, provocative way.

James swallowed hard. Sue watched his Adam's apple push against his neck like a metal spring in an old bed, trembling, rising and falling.

Before they sat down, Sue moved forward and offered him her lips. He responded boldly, taking her in his arms and kissing her with enthusiasm. Each kiss, like the oncoming tide, was an advance on its predecessor. As his hands roamed toward her breasts, Sue stepped back.

'Mmm, James, this is so exciting,' she said. 'But the soup's getting cold. Don't let's rush things. We've got all night.'

She moved away briskly and sat at the table, smiling up at him. With some difficulty, James pulled himself together and sank into a chair, flushed and panting. It was clear he was aroused. Very aroused.

'Twister comes next,' Sue said, 'and its success depends on you, James, it all depends on you.'

Then she laughed. Not the soft, sweet, self-effacing laugh that she always used around James Wilmot. This was a true Sue Kellon laugh – loud and uninhibited. A tiny speck of something – was it doubt? – crept into his eyes and his expression changed. He looked at her sharply.

Recovering quickly, Sue rose and walked around the table. She took his hand and guided it against her thighs. She let his fingers explore the taut, satin skin, and as he groaned with pleasure his doubts melted and disappeared.

# 20

It was after one in the morning when Sue opened the front door of her cottage and released the dishevelled figure of James Wilmot into the darkness of Graham Street. She closed the door and leaned back against it for a few minutes with her eyes closed. The evening had gone according to plan. She'd got what she wanted. So had James Wilmot. She had choreographed an experience he would remember for the rest of his life. During dinner she had teased and flirted with him, constantly tracing her upper lip with the tip of her tongue, whilst he stared fascinated.

'What's your daily routine like, James?' she purred. 'Tell me exactly what you do, so I can visualise it.'

He went through his daily routine – going for a walk, showering, dressing and going to the bank.

'This is boring,' he said, laughing.

'No, it's not, James. I want to know everything about you,' she said in the little-girl voice he loved. 'What happens when you get to the bank?'

'I open it all up, let the others in and we all start work,' he said.

'Oh James, that's really important. You're the one who holds the key to the bank?'

'Yes, well I *am* the – the manager.' Her long, slim legs were distracting him and he stumbled on the words. Now her hand was on his thigh: stroking, moving upward.

He swallowed. 'Actually, it's not a key, it's a card. Rather like a complicated credit card.'

'What does it look like?'

He fished in his pocket and brought out an access card, swinging on its silver chain.

'Oh, James,' she sighed. 'It's all so sexy, all these electronic devices, all that *responsibility*.'

He lay back on the sofa while she continued her stroking. Feathery fingers touched him delicately and he shuddered. Then Sue laid the Twister mat down on the floor. It was a silly game, but it opened doors to pleasure he'd never imagined.

When the Twister spinner was thrown, it demanded the player put two parts of his body on the Twister mat ... two new parts every turn. You had to be a contortionist to play. Falling over, trying to place an arm in one corner and a leg in another, resulted in a forfeit and Sue's rules demanded that the forfeit be a piece of clothing. James was clumsy, ungainly and with each turn he stumbled and slipped.

'This isn't fair,' he said laughing in embarrassment.

'It's all to do with trust, James. No holding back. I tell you what,' Sue said, slipping off one strappy sandal, 'you forfeit when you can't do it, I'll forfeit when I can.'

James held nothing back as she forfeited her other sandal and earrings and he scrambled out of his jacket and shirt. He grew bolder as she stripped off the clinging turquoise dress, standing before him in a revealing bra and tiny lace G-string. She was his slave and he was the master. He forfeited most of his clothes until they finally stood in front of each other, almost naked. From then on, it was a teasing mixture of pain and pleasure, forfeit after forfeit, as they tied one another up, and played outrageous games with silken ribbons. He ran his hands over her body; she stroked him through his shorts, whispering encouragement.

'Now comes the next part,' she murmured. 'Tell me your most secret thing.'

'My most secret thing?' he asked. 'Well, I haven't got any secrets really; the only secrets I've got are to do with my work at the bank.'

'That's fine, James. That will do perfectly. It's a trust thing.'

He stopped for a moment. 'I'm not sure that ... well, I can't really ...'

Sue moved away from him. She stood briskly, pulling the turquoise dress back over her head and smoothing it down her body in the most provocative way.

'This is the whole point of the game, James. We have to be able to trust each other totally. No secrets. Shall I tell you my biggest secret? What I've been thinking about since we met? It's quite shocking.' She smiled and bent to slip on her shoes. 'On second thoughts, perhaps I'd better not ...?'

'No, please tell me, tell me,' he begged.

'Well, you and I have such good sexual chemistry. I fantasise that we go away together ... maybe to Mauritius ... to a dark nightclub, somewhere on a beach, on a balmy night, a place where only men can go. Men who want me. Men who envy you because you're with me. I don't want to shock you; I'm going to be completely honest, just like you should be with me. I'm naked in an enclosed circle. Nobody can come inside the circle with me. Men watch while I dance for them. That's my secret. I want to drive them mad. They can't touch me. Only *you* are allowed to come inside the circle and touch me. Only you James ... but not straight away.'

Sue glanced at Wilmot under her lashes. He was panting and red faced.

'Do it, do it – dance for me,' he commanded, his voice so hoarse she hardly recognised it.

She laughed. 'Only if you promise to tell me your secrets, all your secrets.'

'Yes,' he groaned. 'I promise.'

Sue stood in the middle of the Twister mat and spun in a circle, her arms extended.

'This is the circle James. Can you see it? Now, remember I choose the conditions. I want you to promise that you won't cross into the circle until I say so.'

'I promise.'

She stood for a moment looking at him. She knew she looked like an angel, with her long blonde hair floating around her shoulders. Then she began to peel off the turquoise dress, very, very slowly.

He caught his breath as she stood naked, apart from the tiny G-string, lifting her arms above her head, pivoting like a ballerina. Her long, firm legs led up to the ripe cheeks of her buttocks, her nipples stood out darkly against the rosy skin of her breasts. He stumbled forward, reaching for her.

'One more step and you're out of the game,' she said in an angry voice that she could see frightened him. He fell back, watching her. She smiled her secret smile.

'Please,' he begged. 'Please ...'

Gazing into his eyes, Sue slowly slid off the G-string. 'Are you ready to tell me your secrets? We can't go on otherwise. It means you don't trust me. How can we go further if you don't trust me?'

Through dry lips he began to describe the combination of the vault locks, where the safety deposit boxes were lodged. But he wouldn't divulge the security code he used on entering the bank. He explained how he changed the combinations every night. He described how the new combinations were sent from Johannesburg each day to his cell phone. Nobody knew the combination but him. He couldn't ... mustn't ... give those combinations away. He had signed confidentiality agreements that couldn't be broken. Not under any circumstances. He had said too much already.

'You don't have to tell me the combinations, James,' Sue whispered. 'You could just show me the cell phone; you don't have to say anything.'

He shook his head. 'I can't,' he said. 'I just can't.'

She stepped out of the chalk circle and pressed her naked body against him.

'Don't worry, James. Come.' She led him to the rug in front of the fireplace. 'Lie down.'

He lay helpless while Sue knelt astride him.

'Please ...' he begged, 'please ...'

She lowered her hips. He was entirely in her power, his balance and reason had vanished. There was only her body enclosing him, suffocating him, enveloping him, promising him ecstasy. She was irresistible and this was the crowning hour of Wilmot's life. He was a maestro and this was the performance of his lifetime.

'You don't have to do anything else, James. You've proved yourself to me. Now lie still and show that you trust me,' the little-girl-lost voice, tinged with pornographic visions, drove James Wilmot over the edge. Lost in a churning sea of ecstasy he couldn't hold back. The walls of Jericho came tumbling down as Wilmot experienced the climax of his life.

'That was great, wasn't it?' Sue kissed him gently.

James stared at her in sleepy wonder. 'You ..., oh my God, I've never ...'

'I know ... nor have I'. Sue stroked his cheek, watched as his eyes closed. Then she rolled away from him and reached into the pocket of his jacket. It only took a minute to find the codes and scribble them down. She slipped his phone back and leaned back and watched him. She'd give him another ten minutes or so and then wake him up and fuck him stupid again. James Wilmot would pay dearly for his evening of pleasure, but Sue would make sure that she was worth every cent.

# 21

## 5 July 2006 – morning

My hired car turned slowly into the entrance of the Sisters of Mercy Convent on the northern outskirts of Port Elizabeth.

Dogs barking, children laughing and playing on the grass told me I was in the right place. The new orphanage was a low, modern building, set among vegetable gardens. There were swings on the lawn and I saw a cluster of housemothers, dressed in pink, playing with the children. As I got out of the car a well-padded woman broke away from the group. With children clinging to her skirt and hanging from her arms, she made her way to me, laughing. Mama Elsie was active for a woman in her seventies. She'd hardly changed since we last met.

'Thabisa,' she called. 'Is it really you?'

'Mama Elsie, yes, it's me,' I said. I was enveloped in a bear hug that felt like a big, warm blanket engulfing me.

'Let me see you, child.' Mama Elsie held me at arm's length. She shook her head vigorously. '*Ai*, but you are like your mother. And your eyes! I can't believe the ancestors haven't called you for themselves, to be a *sangoma*.'

'I'm too much trouble for them,' I said dryly.

Mama Elsie's real name was Mashadi Nombuso Tswane. She was seventy-five years old, a younger half-sister of Chief Solenkosi Tswane. She had worked in the convent and orphanage for more than forty years, ever since her husband died in an accident in a gold mine in Johannesburg. Now, at a time when she should be sitting in the sun and dreaming, she cooked, washed and cared for orphaned children.

'What can I do?' she asked me. 'So many children are left without parents because of this terrible sickness. We must all try to help.'

'You are doing good work, Mama,' I said.

'Somebody must look after them. I will work as long as I can.'

After a rough-and-tumble game on the lawn with the children, and the exchange of traditional greetings with some of the other housemothers, I took Mama Elsie's hand. 'Let's talk.'

Mama Elsie led me down a maze of corridors to a small cottage at the back of the orphanage. The full folds of her skirt swung and her movements flowed with dignity and authority.

'This is my place,' she said.

It was small, but cosy. Mama Elsie's red blankets were folded neatly on the end of her bed. Cups and saucers were stacked next to her cooking pots on a shelf. The shabby chair held a pink velvet cushion.

Mama Elsie took a red tray, laid it with a blackened tea kettle and flowered cups and saucers. She added a large slice of cake. 'Let's sit,' she said. In valley tradition, we settled ourselves on a grass floor mat and wrapped a blanket around our legs.

Only after we'd had tea and exchanged small talk, did she fix her eyes on me.

'So, my child, what brings you here? We haven't seen you for many months. Not since the orphanage was built.'

'Forgive me, Mama,' I said. 'Now that I'm in Johannesburg, I can't travel that freely. I have a very busy job.'

Mama Elsie's face creased with amusement. 'Yes, the world has grown very busy. There are new people everywhere and everyone is rushing. I can't think why we are all so busy these days. In the valley it's still quiet. That is why I like being there. There is time to think. When will you go back my child, and see your grandfather?'

'I saw him last week. He is well.'

Mama Elsie looked at me in surprise.

'So you have returned to the valley?'

I nodded. 'It was police business.'

'This world is selfish, full of bad, dangerous people,' said Mama Elsie. 'We need the police more than ever before to keep them in order. It is good to live in the city, where so much happens, but it is a wonderful thing to go back to your roots, Thabisa. There's no need for explanations. Everybody is linked to you.'

I sighed. 'Yes, Mama, that's true. But what about you? It's far for you to travel. It must take you a long time to reach the valley. How do you manage the cliffs? It's a very hard journey.'

'I manage,' said Mama Elsie firmly. 'I like to see the people and hear the valley news every year. So I manage.'

I didn't comment. I knew Mama Elsie enjoyed relaxing into the rhythms of rural life, sitting with old friends in the sun, sipping bush tea and gossiping. I smiled to myself. Mama Elsie had the best of both worlds. She might long for the valley, but she also admitted to enjoying the town way of doing things: running water, the electric hotplate, cotton sheets on her bed, the small fridge in the corner. But most important of all, her work was here.

Mama Elsie interrupted my thoughts. 'Nothing is as fine as one's own home-place, Thabisa. Remember our river? All through the village you can see it shining and hear it sing. It's a beautiful thing to go home, Thabisa.'

I smiled and nodded. Mama Elsie continued: 'I never wanted to leave, you know, but your grandfather arranged a husband for me when I was sixteen.'

'That was very young, Mama. Did you want to get married?' I asked.

'Your grandfather insisted,' Mama Elsie continued. 'He cared about the cattle. He got good *lobola* for me.'

'Yes, you're right,' I said quietly.

'Don't look so sad, my girl. I was very lucky. He chose a good husband for me. Nzeku. A very shy, kind young man. He had already left the valley to work on the mines. He had a good job, so I left my home and went with him. It was very hard at first. We lived in the township. *Ai* – such a noisy, loud place! But listen to me going on like this. You know all my stories, Thabisa.'

'I do, Mama, but I like to hear you tell them.'

Mama smiled. 'Just like the children here, Thabisa. You all love a story.' Her eyes softened as she gazed back into the past. 'Yes, Nzeku was a good man. We never had children, which was very sad for us both. Then he died in the mine accident and I came here to this convent. At first I was a cleaner, but later I became a housemother.'

I took her hand in mine. 'You are happy, Mama?'

'This is good work, Thabisa. As a young woman I dreamed of being a nurse, you know. I did not want to get married so young, but that was our custom. You were lucky, Thabisa. Solenkosi allowed you to go to school. And now, you have the chance to work, to choose to be a wife and mother.'

'My grandfather doesn't see it like that,' I said. 'He is disappointed in me.'

'Don't be too swift to condemn him, Thabisa. He hopes that one day you will give him strong sons. Well, great-grandsons, I suppose they will be.' Mama Elsie chuckled. 'We are all getting older.'

'Why did he let me go to school, Mama?'

'He wanted somebody to learn for the valley. Your teacher, Mrs Talbot's husband, spoke to Solenkosi about this. He was a man who knew how to make your grandfather listen. He spoke perfect isiXhosa and he was a kind man. He showed Solenkosi how bright you were. An asset to the valley.'

She stopped and looked at me directly. 'But this is not why you are here, Thabisa. You did not come to talk about old times in the valley. Something is troubling you ... Tell me, what is it?'

I smiled. Mama Elsie had always been able to see into my heart. I had spoken to her in my troubled times, when my grandfather had forced me to leave the valley, and again when I was at New Brighton police station. She listened carefully and gave good advice.

'Mama, I've come to talk to you about my father and uncles. About what happened to them.'

Mama Elsie sat still for a few moments. Then she drew in her breath and shook her head. 'He was a rebel, that boy. He married our gentle Pomola, and broke our hearts.'

'Are you talking about my father?'

Silence. Mama Elsie shook her head. 'All of them. I remember all of them. So young.'

'What happened? Please tell me, Mama Elsie. I have often tried to ask but nobody answers. Who else will tell me?'

'Pomola wanted to marry Zikhali, but he was not amaQaba and Solenkosi refused. Instead, Pomola had to marry Fezile, Solenkosi's choice from when they were infants. The *lobola* was paid.'

'So Fezile was my father. But then who was Zikhali?'

'Your mother was a beauty, tall and slender. She held herself like a queen. She was a tribal chief's only daughter. Many young men desired her, but Solenkosi insisted she marry the one he had chosen.'

Typical Solenkosi Tswane. Bending everyone to his will. But that didn't answer my question. 'Who was Zikhali, Mama?'

'Your mother met him at a neighbouring village, two days' walk from the valley. It was at a chief's wedding, a very happy occasion. There was singing and dancing.' Mama Elsie's eyes glazed as she looked back into the past. But now wasn't the time for one of her stories of the joys of valley life. There was something darker hiding here and I had to know what it was.

'What happened?'

'Zikhali was a handsome young man. He was worldly; he had been to school in Umtata. He and Pomola were drawn to each other. They spent three days talking, walking together. Your grandfather was not pleased. Pomola was promised to Fezile. A good man, quiet, well-spoken. He loved your mother very much, even when she was dazzled by the charm and good looks of Zikhali. Later, after we returned to the valley, Zikhali came to see us with his father and uncles. They stayed for several days, tried to persuade your grandfather to change his mind, and allow Pomola to marry him. His family promised better *lobola*.'

'What happened?'

'Solenkosi refused to go back on his word. The *lobola* had already been given. Promises must be kept. Zikhali left. He was very, very angry with Solenkosi. Your mother married your father, and when you were born, she was happy enough.'

I sat quietly. There was a long silence.

'You were an early baby, very small, but the *sangoma* passed you through the *umsi* and the smoke made you stronger. Your mother was happy.'

A thin blade of doubt slid through me. What did she mean?

'How early!' I asked.

'I don't remember this ... it's now too long ago.' Mama Elsie closed her eyes wearily.

'Tell me about Zikhali. What did he look like?'

'He was handsome. His body was strong and he was tall. He was a perfect body of man, except for one thing.'

'What?'

'In the deep valley between his back muscles, the bones of his spine looked like a ladder. Up the ladder crawled the *inyoka*.'

'A snake? What do you mean, a snake?' My heart skipped a beat.

'In Umtata they painted the boys with skin paint that never comes off.'

'Do you mean a tattoo?'

'It was a big *inyoka*; it crawled up the ladder of his spine from his buttocks to his neck.'

'Was this unusual?'

'Some young men who went to school in Umtata had pictures painted on their arms or legs. I never saw another *inyoka*.' Mama Elsie's lip curled in disdain. 'Who would choose to do such an arrogant thing? A big-headed man. One who has no respect for his people.'

'What happened when my father and uncles were arrested in the valley?'

Mama Elsie poured another cup of tea and sipped it slowly. 'These are painful matters, Thabisa. Some problems have no solution. There are the problems of the dry land where no rain falls, the problem of the great sickness in Africa, which is turning so many children into orphans. Then there is the other kind of problem – the one people make for themselves.'

'Please go on.'

'If people behave themselves like we used to in the valley, when we obeyed the laws we were taught, there are no problems, but your father and uncles were rash, headstrong. If only they could have resisted in some other way, without bloodshed. I am old now, Thabisa. Old enough to see that violence brings pain and trouble.'

'You are right, Mama.' I thought about my father, wondered what injustice and cruelty had driven him. 'But you have said my father was a good man, a quiet man. He must have had good reasons for acting as he did? Sometimes fighting back, against injustice, brings change.'

'There is no answer to this, Thabisa. All I can see, looking back, was a bad time. Too much sorrow and death.' Mama Elsie sipped her tea. We sat in silence for a few minutes.

'Now, you must stop asking and forget about the old days.'

'I must ask, Mama Elsie,' I said. 'Please tell me what happened at the end.'

There was a long silence before Mama Elsie opened her eyes and scanned my face. She shook her head before she spoke.

'The police came and took them. They were hiding in the cliffs above the village. There were caves, we took them food and water.'

'Who betrayed them? I read the beads, Mama. They showed me a snake. I thought they were implying treachery. But it was more than a symbol, wasn't it?'

Mama Elsie didn't answer. She got up and moved around the room. 'Nobody knows for sure, but it was whispered in the valley that it was the *inyoka*.'

'Zikhali,' I said quietly.

Mama Elsie said nothing.

Discomfort rolled through me and I thrust back flashes of memory. Zikhali had a snake tattoo. He had loved my mother. There was a story here. I intended to find out about it.

# 22

Driving back to Grahamstown I thought about what Mama Elsie had said. My stomach tightened every time I remembered her words. A black hole of questions had opened in my mind. Questions that I couldn't answer. Here was a clear link to the snake man Zikhali. The man who had betrayed my family. The man who had loved my mother. I couldn't escape the powerful feeling that here was a mystery, a lost story, just waiting for me to solve it. But how? Where would I start?

I stopped once, at Nanaga farm stall, and sat in the garden sipping lemonade. Bantam hens scratched around me. I smiled at their soft, silky feet – fluffy slippers. I stared at the flower beds for a long time without moving, thinking about the valley, watching people come and go.

When I got back into the car I checked my voicemail. Eight messages from Tom Winter, two from Bea. Nothing from Zak Khumalo. I called Tom Winter's number. He answered immediately.

'Hi Tom.'

'How are you, Thabisa?'

'I've been out of town. I'm on my way back to Grahamstown right now.'

'Can I see you? What does your diary look like for tonight?'

'Tonight?'

He laughed softly. 'Why not? I'm off-duty. Thought you might like to relax, have a chat.'

I hesitated for a moment. 'Where?'

'A newish place. It's supposed to be good.'

'Okay, pick me up at eight.'

When I reached Grahamstown, I stopped by the station. It was after five.

'Thabisa! Back at last. I was just leaving.' Bea bustled through the door. She was dressed head to foot in fuchsia, even her eyeshadow was pink. A big tote bag on her shoulder, take-away coffee in one hand, groceries in the other.

'Update me,' I said, 'why did you call?'

'Nothing much happening.'

'No calls? No messages? Anything from forensics?'

'The bullet was from the same gun as before. No fingerprints. That's what my call was about.'

'Right.'

'Oh and Zak Khumalo is back, staying at the Royal in town. Why he can't stay at the safe house with you, I don't know.'

'It wouldn't be a safe house, that's why.'

'You're mad, who'd *want* to be safe with that guy around?'

I laughed and shook my head.

'Come and have a drink and tell me about Jo'burg.'

'I'd love to, Bea, but I'm going out for dinner this evening.'

'Out? Who with?'

'The doctor,' I said.

'Omigod, I hate to say it, Thabisa, but life's so unfair. That doctor's so cool and Khumalo is totally hot, and they *both* fancy you. I read your horoscope yesterday. It said you're going to have to make a big decision soon. Looks like this is it. Which one do you like best?'

'Don't go there, Bea,' I said. 'I'm not doing any choosing, believe me.'

'Ja ... right,' Bea said. 'That's not what your horoscope says.'

I drove back to the safe house, showered and dressed in a black pantsuit and white top.

Tom Winter whistled when I opened the door. 'Lovely lady.' He kissed my cheek. 'I still can't believe you're a police officer.' He didn't look too bad himself, in a soft leather jacket and open-necked blue shirt.

'You don't look like a doctor without your stethoscope either, but we both are what we are.'

He placed his hand on the small of my back and guided me to the car. Did I like being treated like a porcelain doll, or resent it? Confusing.

As we entered the restaurant, we both took out our cell phones and set them to vibrate.

'It's like looking in the mirror,' Tom said. 'Same wave length.'

'Public servants,' I retorted, 'behaving properly in public.' And Zak Khumalo could go to hell. I was off duty for the next hour.

The restaurant was a bright, tasteful place, the food elegant. We ordered drinks. A sparkling water with a twist of lime for me, a red wine for Tom. I raised an eyebrow.

'I'm off-duty. What about you?'

'Always on duty.' I smiled.

I ordered salmon, baby potatoes and a salad; Tom went for the pasta. The waiter lit candles on the table and we began to talk.

'What have you been up to?' I asked.

'Oh, the usual, saving a few lives here and there. What about you, DI Tswane?'

To my surprise I found myself telling him about my journey to Johannesburg, the story I'd heard about my father and uncles. The words tumbled out. It was such a relief to have a kind, gentle listener, one who I knew would never betray my trust. As I spoke I realised how deeply affected I'd been by what I had learned. So much about my life had been thrown into question and it didn't seem as if I'd be getting answers any time soon. Tom listened intently, narrowing his eyes when I described the bomb attack, their betrayal and execution.

After I'd told him the whole story, I paused.

He stretched out a hand and laid it briefly on my wrist. 'How do you feel about all this?' he asked.

'It shouldn't make a difference to me. I mean, I was raised in the valley, but I left. Still ...'

'What?'

'It's eating away at me.' I took my hand away. 'I want to find out what happened.'

'I don't blame you. I would too.' He reached across the table and touched my hand again.

'Thabisa, don't shut me out. I've been working in Africa long enough to know what happens. There's a lot of anger and disappointment here.'

'Yes, there is, but it's directed the wrong way. When I give police talks at school career days, I see kids dressing badly, skipping lessons, not studying properly, then blaming the system for their problems. It's hard to motivate kids like that.'

'What do you say?'

'I tell them everybody's got absolute power over themselves. The question is what do you do with it? I tell them to get out there, grab what life has to offer and take responsibility for themselves.' I smiled wryly. 'I don't know if I get through to them though.'

'Maybe not to all of them,' Tom said, 'but if you make an impression on one kid, or two, your words can change the way they see themselves. And that's the first step to changing their lives. You worked hard, took what opportunities you could. Look at you now. Those kids, the ones you get through to, look at you and they can see what's possible.'

I turned away and shook my head. 'I worry about the other kids though. The ones who don't make it, who don't have anyone to look up to.'

He stared at me seriously. 'I enjoy looking at you. I could look at you for hours. You're a lovely woman.'

My cheeks flamed. 'Thank you.' I tried to cover my embarrassment by studying the baby potatoes as if they were the most fascinating thing I'd ever seen.

'Good food,' Tom said.

'It's greatthat we both we seem to enjoy food,' I laughed.

'What will you do about your family mystery?' Tom asked.

'I've decided to go to the valley, talk to my grandfather, and see if there's any more he can tell me.'

'Good. That's a start. Do you want any help from me?'

At the thought of Tom appearing in the valley, I burst out laughing. 'I don't think the valley is ready for you,' I said. 'White men aren't thick on the ground there, let alone Australian ones.'

'What did Martin Luther King say? We should be judged by the content of our character, not the colour of our skins?'

'I doubt many people in the valley have heard of Martin Luther King, but my grandfather belongs to Nelson Mandela's tribe, and they all know about him.'

'Really?' Tom looked suitably impressed.

'Don't get excited, Tom. My grandfather isn't anything like Mandela. Take it from me.'

'Why?'

'He doesn't want anything to change. He thinks the old ways are best.' I snapped a bread stick in half with a satisfying crack.

'Don't you think they are in some ways? Easier to understand. Structure, a hierarchy, knowing where you stand?

'South Africa's moved on, Tom, it's all changed.'

'Some changes happen more quickly, others take longer. It's all very well being progressive, but what's the use of destroying everything in a rush?'

I fiddled with my braids and sighed. 'My grandfather will never change.'

'Well, you could try to help him.'

'Me?' I retorted. 'He won't listen to any woman, let alone his granddaughter.'

'But you're the key. Don't you see that, Thabisa?'

'No.'

'You're the link. You're his blood family. Why else did he educate you?'

'He wanted somebody to come back, to help the valley.'

'So, why don't you?'

I looked away. 'He wants more, much more. He wants me to marry somebody he chooses. He wants me to stay in the valley, do beadwork, have kids.'

'You can help him compromise. He's created an educated granddaughter. Work with him, on your terms.'

'He won't compromise.'

'Try him. Use psychology. Talk to him about this tragedy in your family then try and debate. Ask him how you can help him. You can follow your own rules.'

He watched me closely. I remained silent, restlessly rearranging the salt and pepper containers, straightening out the silverware.

'You'll never lose your identity. It's part of you, Thabisa. It's a proud thing, to come from the valley and educate yourself the way you have, but there's room for all aspects of your identity.'

'Hmm,' I said thoughtfully. 'Perhaps.'

Tom listened intently, asked intelligent questions and weighed up my words. Talking to him helped sort my thoughts into some kind of order.

Later, while we sat over coffee, Tom asked: 'Have you ever been in love? Really in love?'

'Have you?'

'You first, Thabisa.'

I paused for a long time before I answered. 'Yes, when I was just out of school, before I went to Police College. He was a student at Rhodes.'

'What happened?'

'He was ... killed.'

'How?'

'He was shot during a rally in Pretoria. Even though the State of Emergency had been lifted. I was there.'

*Shall I tell you what it was like to see the crowd descending on us as we tried to hold them back with a cordon, Tom? Shall I tell you that I saw Victor trying to stop them? He was part of the protest, right at the front of the crowd. He was yelling at them to stop stoning us. All round me, men and women opened fire. My finger froze on the trigger and I watched as the bullets flew. One of them hit Victor in the chest. I broke ranks. Rushed to him. I held him while he died. Shall I tell you, Australian Doctor Tom? Will you understand?*

'I'm so very sorry,' Tom said. 'How old were you?'

'I was eighteen.'

'What a dreadful thing,' he said.

We were silent for a moment before Tom said: 'It's something else we have in common, Thabisa. My fiancée died in a car accident just before we were due to be married.'

'That's terrible. When did it happen?'

'Two years ago. It's the reason I left Australia and came here.' Tom swigged the last of his wine, and then placed the glass firmly on the table. 'Right, that's enough doom and gloom. Let's order something decadent to cheer us up and then I'll take you home.'

Tom summoned the waiter and ordered warm chocolate pudding smothered in raspberry coulis. He even persuaded me to try some and the rest of the evening passed easily.

As soon as we arrived at the Hill Street house, Tom reached for me and drew me to him, wrapping his arms around me. He held me close for a moment.

'We've done nothing but talk since we met,' he said.

'That's okay,' I said.

'It's not enough for me.'

'I think it's great that we've got so much to talk about.'

'Shh.' He stopped my words with his mouth. 'You're beautiful.'

I tried to relax. I wanted to like this kind, attractive man, but I felt nervous, on edge. As we stood embracing in the narrow hallway, I glanced across to a mirror on the wall opposite. Tom's skin looked so light against mine. Light against dark. Beautiful in a way, but unfamiliar. A man with skin the colour of vanilla ice cream. All that paleness.

His body against mine was warm and solid. His kisses were gentle at first, but they soon became hotter, more insistent. The kiss was arousing in a way many unknown things are arousing. I moved away a little.

'Let yourself go, Thabisa,' he murmured against my mouth. 'Relax and enjoy this.'

'I don't really know you well enough,' I said quietly.

He laughed. 'You and I have talked about so many important things.' He spoke softly into my ear. 'You know what? Thabisa Tswane is brilliant, and she knows it. Thabisa Tswane is highly competent and she knows it. Thabisa Tswane is beautiful and loveable, but she doesn't realise it at all. She's the woman I think about when I wake up in the morning and when I go to sleep at night. Believe in yourself, Thabisa, you're very special.'

He lifted my wrist and kissed it. Then he placed his fingers over my veins, checking my pulse. 'Fast,' he said. 'Racing.'

'What does that mean, doctor?' I laughed up at him, relaxing into his arms.

'I hope it means you quite like me,' he said.

'I do,' I smiled. 'I really do.' I melted against him. I felt charmed, almost helpless in the face of his admiration. I was carried along by him; his enthusiasm, his determination, it was all very endearing in a fairy-story kind of way.

Most men I'd known couldn't keep their idea of me as a friend and human being separate once sex entered the equation, but Tom was controlled, gentle and – yes – sexy. I kissed him, his tongue soft in my mouth.

The cell phone vibrated in my pocket. For a moment I was disorientated, wondering where the buzzing came from. I broke away from Tom, opened the phone and tried to concentrate.

'Yes?' I said. My voice sounded wobbly.

'It's Khumalo. I'm just letting you know I'm in Grahamstown. I need to meet with you tomorrow.'

I glanced at my watch. It was one in the morning.

'Zak, do you know what time it is? This call is completely unnecessary. Please don't phone me again unless it's an emergency.'

I heard his laugh. 'Not alone?'

I slammed the phone shut. The moment was lost. I turned away from Tom.

'Thabisa ... why don't we –'

'Sorry, Tom, I can't. It's hopeless when I'm on duty.'

'I know the feeling. Doctors' phones always ring at the wrong times.'

'Tom, I –'

'Don't worry, Thabisa, there's always a next time.'

Tom kissed me and stepped out into the night.

# 23

I tossed and turned. I couldn't get comfortable. The bedclothes were like bandages winding around my body, pinning me into weird, contorted positions. I remembered things I had banished from my mind for years, refusing to allow them to surface. The nightmares were still there. Talking about Victor had unlocked the part of my brain I had carefully padlocked many years before.

I lay in the dark, listened to the wind rattling the window, and remembered.

A concert at Rhodes University, just before I sat my final examinations. Saint Andrews and DSG were both there, all in our green school uniforms. Just kids, mixing with the older university students. Everyone was chatting, laughing together.

Then, there he was, muscular and tall, shining among all the others. Victor Zondwa. My first love. Second-year law student at Rhodes and angry about everything.

'What are you going to study?' he asked me, when he had worked the room and finally introduced himself.

'I'm not going to study further,' I said.

'What?' His tone was low and compelling. 'A girl like you, brainy as hell? What a waste.'

I smiled wryly. 'Try telling that to my grandfather. He wants me to go back to the village, get married and have a dozen children. Even if I was offered a bursary it wouldn't be enough to see me through university. I just can't afford to go any further. So that's why I'm thinking of joining the police."

'The police?' I stepped back as his voice jabbed at me.

'What's wrong with that?' I asked defensively. This guy might be handsome, with his dark perfect skin, strong jaw, but he was pretty arrogant.

'Sorry,' he said. 'Reflex action. I hear the word "police" and my hackles rise. But change is coming and this government can't last much longer. South Africa's going to need a new police force. Joining now, it's actually a good idea. You'll be able to do something really practical for your country. Go for it.'

'So I have your blessing?' I said tartly. 'Thank you *so* much.'

'Sorry,' he said. 'I get a bit carried away.' He smiled at me then and I was glad of the wall behind me, holding me up as my knees turned to jelly.

His head was shaved, the bones of his skull sculpted like a statue in the art books at the school library.

He was so alive and enthusiastic, so full of ideas.

He introduced me to his crowd of friends. He was more of a man than any of the others. I had never been interested in boys, but that evening I felt as if I'd been hit by a two-ton truck.

The talk was all about the importance of the National Peace Accord and the hope surrounding Nelson Mandela's release from jail. I'd been living in a bubble. My whole world had been school, passing exams and athletics. Singing in the choir and going home to the valley for the long holidays. Talk like this wasn't part of my life.

All the while he watched me with his dark, angry eyes. He was attracted to me; I could see it in his body language. I was surprised and flattered. There were several other girls, older than me, hanging around him, but he didn't seem interested. I wondered why. He looked like a man who only dated clever college girls with their own cars.

When the school bus came to take us back to the hostel, Victor asked me if he could visit me on Sunday. 'You're allowed visitors then, aren't you?'

I felt as if I'd been struck by lightning. 'Yes ... yes of course,' I stammered.

The other girls teased me on the way home. 'That gorgeous boy likes you, Thabisa, better watch out; everyone says he's an activist. He may activate you!'

I hardly knew what an activist was, but I felt breathless when I thought about him, my whole body jangling with new thoughts and feelings that fluttered around my body like bees around a hive. Some of them stung. Others were sweet as honey.

He arrived on an old black bicycle, wearing a worn leather jacket and a red beanie. We walked on the sports field while I told him more about the valley, my grandfather and my schooling. He told me about his Umtata upbringing, the university and why he was studying law. He was alert, aware, critical of everything and he shook me awake.

'I'm going to do something for our country, something big,' he told me.

I couldn't believe how white his teeth were, how rich his skin. And then there was the confidence, bursting out of him. Nothing was insurmountable, not even my dreams of continuing my education.

'If I had any financial support I'd come to Rhodes like you and do something like social work. That's what I'd like to do. But the way things stand with my grandfather, that's out. Not that he could afford to help me anyway. I've been advised to apply for bursaries, but there aren't many going.

What do you think?' I asked.

'I reckon you should make the most of whatever opportunities you have now,' Victor said. Go where you can do some good straight away,' he said. 'And joining the police won't limit you, quite the opposite. You'll be able to learn and earn. The police will be desperate for a bright, intelligent woman like you. There's a new world coming, Thabisa, and you can be part of it. Don't let your grandfather sabotage your plans by forcing you into marriage. Because that's what will be coming next in his eyes, isn't it?'

I stiffened. 'I'm not going that route,' I said. 'My grandfather has already got a husband lined up. I've never even met the man. I won't agree.'

'Absolutely not,' Victor said. 'Arranged marriages, *sangomas* and grandfathers making all the decisions. Then the woman becomes the property of the husband's family, to become a workhorse and a baby machine. Surely your grandfather doesn't expect to educate you and then marry you off to some local chief who can't read or write?'

'My grandfather does what he wants. His word is law in our valley, but I'm going against him over this.'

Victor snaked his arm round my shoulders and pulled me against him. I felt as if I was melting into his hard, strong body. I pulled myself away when I remembered where we were.

'Don't sell yourself short, Thabisa,' he said softly. 'You are a beautiful girl. Can we meet outside all this?' He gestured at the school buildings and groups of girls.

'I don't know, Victor, I'm about to sit for my matric, I've got a lot of studying to do.'

'Surely you have some free study days?'

'Well, next week, I've got two days, but I'm preparing for my English paper.'

'Maybe we could meet up in the afternoon?' Victor suggested.

I thought for a moment then nodded.

Later that week, when he smuggled me into his room at Rhodes and we talked for hours, I knew we were two people on the cusp of something special. I looked around the room: notepads, books, tapes, pens, pencils, and files all over the place. The books all seemed to be about South Africa's struggle for freedom and the notepads were filled with his angry, black scribble.

I tried to see through to the core of him, and he wouldn't allow me, but I felt the space between us, ready to ignite. He didn't try to touch me, but I knew he wanted to.

Through my matric examinations we snatched time to be together. Victor was a different person when he was alone with me. In public he was always talking about issues, noisy and angry. He tore other people's ideas to pieces. He put forward outrageous schemes, then debated them with ferocious energy until everyone agreed with him. He was popular and impressive, everyone wanted to know him.

But alone and in private, with me, he was tender, enquiring, funny. I told him all my fears, dreams and thoughts. My heart was racing for new experiences, all involving him.

My body clamoured with new sensations I didn't really understand. There was nobody to talk to about it. Most of the other girls in my year didn't have boyfriends and if they did, they didn't discuss them. Not openly, at least.

After the examinations were over and just before Catherine Talbot drove me back to Encobo for the holidays, Victor and I spent a day together in Grahamstown. We picnicked by the river, talked and laughed. He teased me about my grey eyes. I teased him about his red beanie. Every part of my body was chiming like a bell.

'Let's go,' he said pulling me to my feet. 'A friend has loaned me his place for a few hours.'

'Oh,' I said, and then we said nothing more.

Victor didn't look at me while he unlocked the door to his friend's cottage.

I felt as if I was hurtling toward a cliff face. My school education was finished; I knew I'd done well. I was approaching a new life. I knew I would never be the same again. The only way was to move forward. I wanted Victor but I didn't know what it entailed.

Victor led me into a small dark room, drew me toward him and kissed me. His mouth was hot. It was my first real kiss, and his tongue was in my mouth, insistent, exploring. His hands were under my clothes, his fingers on my breasts. I helped him loosen my bra and he bent and sucked my nipples while I gasped at the pleasure of his mouth.

Then he undressed and stood before me. I stared at him in amazement. I had never seen a man naked before. I tried to understand what I should do next.

He helped me out of my clothes carefully and then he ran his hands over my body.

'You're beautiful,' he whispered. He felt in his jacket and produced a condom.

'We don't want any babies at this point, do we?' he said softly. 'Not now, right?'

We lay on a bed in the corner of the room and he covered me with his body.

'Are you sure?' he asked looking into my eyes. 'Do you want me?'

'Yes,' I said, although I was scared, really scared.

'Don't be afraid,' he murmured against my neck. 'Just relax, try and trust me.'

I wondered for a moment how many other women he'd had, but the thoughts got lost as I clutched at his shoulders and opened myself to him. He was gentle, but it was painful, very painful. Then suddenly, all the pain subsided and tendrils of pleasure curled around my body. I couldn't believe what I was feeling. He was my other half. We were one person.

Victor promised to send his uncle to visit my grandfather as soon as he was able, maybe in a few months. His father would offer *lobola*. His parents were both lawyers, who had met when they were studying at Fort Hare University. They respected their Xhosa culture and would certainly observe the formalities.

'Deep down *singamaqaba* – we are Qaba; we don't want to lose our cultural identity,' Victor said.

We would be married when my training was finished and I graduated from Police College. Meanwhile, Victor would be in Pretoria for a few weeks at the beginning of my training, organising a protest march and we would see one another.

First love had grabbed me round the throat. I could hardly breathe when I thought of him. I was dumb with admiration and pride when I heard him talk at rallies and political meetings, oblivious to the men and woman who gazed at him, coveting him. He was mine. I was the one who got to touch him, rest my face on his shoulder, and run my hands over his chest and his smooth, shaved head. I could un-button him, shed his clothes, and become naked with him. Then we could kiss. And oh God, the kisses ... what they led to.

I entered Police College on winged feet. The other girls complained about the conditions, the food and the discipline, but I hardly noticed them. I enjoyed everything and lived for the times I saw Victor.

In early 1992, when I was still a rookie, he came to Pretoria to help the police organise the protest march on Church Square. Responsible, he called it. Working together for peaceful protest. No more violence, no more bloodshed. The people's voices could be heard if both sides showed respect for each other.

I was seconded to a patrol that evening, with twelve other trainees from the college. We were on duty as cadets to help control the crowd and keep things peaceful.

There were crowds of demonstrators in Church Square and many police officers trying to cordon them off, hold them back. We cadets couldn't understand why the crowd was so aggressive to the police. All we were doing was trying to maintain law and order. Wasn't that what Victor had said, that we new trainees had a part to play in the new South Africa that was emerging? Why did they hate us so much? I watched as fresh waves of students arrived, pushing through the streets surrounding the square, blocking it off on all sides.

Suddenly, horns blaring, blunt-nosed vans swept into the square. The sea of demonstrators parted. The vehicles stopped in the centre and disgorged a force of heavily armed police officers who took up positions, surrounding the square and forming an extra cordon. A thick-set man in police uniform, holding a snarling dog on a leash, grabbed me, yelling: 'Form a cordon ... lift the shields ... don't fall back!'

I obeyed, holding up the plastic shield I had been given earlier.

Then we began to move. The police line advanced relentlessly and I was carried forward with it, my shield locked into place by shields on either side of me. We pushed forward, into the first line of students, forcing them back, crushing them into the wave of bodies behind them.

And then the first student fell. A girl with long blonde hair, down on her hands and knees.

I heard bewildered cries: 'What have we done? How can you attack us like this? This is a peaceful demonstration.'

And then the first stone, followed by another and then another flew past my head. One hit my cheek and blood trickled down my neck. I learned later that Victor and his supporters had promised that there would be no stone-throwing. But other more militant students had told everyone to come prepared. I also learned that the powers that be had promised there would be no aggressive action from the police. Another command that wasn't followed by men shouting the orders, urging the dogs onward, raising their batons.

Police officers moved through the crowd. Resistance was met with truncheons and sticks. Panic filled the square. People pushed, pleaded, struggled with the police and tried to break through the cordon to escape. Benches overturned, people fell and others trampled them, unable to stop the heaving masses pushing behind them.

Then I saw Victor. He was at the front of the crowd, shouting. 'Back off! Don't attack the police! Retreat!'

But they couldn't retreat; the square was clogged and there was no way out. They were jammed in, tight against each other. People were screaming. The police were snatching people at random; dragging them towards the police trucks.

Some young men pushed forward against the cordon. I saw the police officers pull out their weapons.

'No ... no ...' I heard myself scream.

Gun fire, like fireworks, popping and crackling. People falling over. Screaming going on ... and on. Never-ending.

In slow motion I saw Victor fall back and crumple to the ground. Blood gushing down his shirt, staining his jacket red, dripping from his hand. Somehow, I tore free of the cordon. I scrambled through the crowd, punching, pushing them apart, until I reached him. A police officer lashed out at me with his stick.

'Get back in line,' he shouted. I ignored him.

Victor was barely conscious, blood pouring out of a gaping wound in his chest. I tried to stem the flow of blood with my jacket but it wouldn't stop. He looked up and recognised me. He tried to speak, but couldn't. I watched the light fade from his eyes. He fell back in my arms. Eyes wide, staring.

The screaming went on and on and I wondered vaguely who it was. Then I realised, it was me, howling and keening. I knelt in the dust, holding Victor's body, rocking him in my arms. Somebody pulled me away and wrapped a blanket round my shoulders. I was shivering uncontrollably. I watched two policemen throw Victor's body into the back of a van as if it were a carcass, my last glimpse of him before the door slammed shut and the van drove off. I never saw him again.

I sat up in bed, tears pouring down my face as I remembered.

*I still miss him. There is still anguish in my bones and my blood. There always will be. Such a waste. Such a pointless death.*

*However much we love someone, we lose them in the end. If life doesn't steal them, then death will do it.*

The phone rang. I sat up in bed. It was just before seven and early morning light pressed through the curtains. Birds tweeted noisily. I glanced at the screen: 'Zak Khumalo'.

I pressed the button.

'Zak, what is it?'

His voice was tight, professional. 'Thabisa, please get down to the station as soon as you can. We've got Julia McEwen here. She tells us someone has been shot.'

# 24

Driving through the streets of Grahamstown at two in the morning, Julia and Sue saw no other cars, nobody was about but a few late night revellers weaving their way home from the Festival. As they cruised slowly down a tunnel of overhanging trees, peering into the backyards of houses and restaurants, there was no discernible sign of life. The heavy buildings stood out in stark relief against the night sky. It was bitterly cold.

They hadn't spoken much since Sue had unlocked the door to Julia's room and let her out into the kitchen. While Sue locked up and put the outside lights off, Julia leaned against the kitchen door frame, running her eyes over Sue's dishevelled clothes and hair. 'Did you get the security numbers?' she finally asked.

'Of course, I've got his cell phone security combinations, didn't you hear?'

'I tried not to listen. Are you okay?'

'It's no use standing there looking like a disapproving maiden aunt in your bloody diamond earrings and my old dressing gown,' Sue said defensively. 'I've told you before, Julia, sex means nothing to me. I fucked him for information. I know you're too pathetic to take risks, but I'm not, okay?'

'Sue, it's dangerous ...' Julia bit her lip but didn't continue. She looked at Sue's swollen mouth and flushed face. She had heard the animal noises Wilmot had made behind the locked door when he was with Sue. She was deeply worried about Sue and the desperate game she was playing.

'It's not dangerous,' Sue said. 'I was in control. Fucking is theatre, it's dressing-up. A performance, a means to an end.'

'What about love?' Julia said quietly.

'I don't fuck anyone for love.'

'Never?'

'No,' she shook her head. 'If you love someone it's different. That's not fucking.'

'Was it love with Sando?'

'Who knows? This whole "being in love" thing doesn't last. I haven't got a clue what love means. Have you?'

Julia turned away. She felt a surge of despair at Sue's attitude. She was so tough and emotionless. Yet, sometimes, when they were together she could be so warm and funny. It seemed ridiculous to admit that, despite the whole surreal situation, she really cared about Sue. More than cared. Julia wasn't stupid, or naive. She understood the Stockholm Syndrome, and how sometimes victims fell in love with their captors and would do anything for them. She recognised all too well that in his own way Magnus had been her captor. But she certainly had never wanted to become like him, and nor had she loved him for what he did to her. She knew how starved she had been of love, how vulnerable that had made her, but none of that was what attracted her to Sue. Sue was something different. Sure she was fucked up, but who wasn't? Julia could look at Sue objectively and love her courage, her ability to march to her own drum, say fuck you to the world, and really mean it. She was so unlike anyone Julia had met before. Perhaps she didn't actually love Sue, perhaps it was just her exotic, daring personality, but Julia was, against all her expectations, in the grip of something unique. A fascination, a sense of being alive. She had never felt this before.

Images flashed through her mind of Sue; her poker straight posture, the unexpected elegance of her slim fingers, their expressiveness – their touch. Tears threatened and Julia closed her eyes for a moment, remembering Sue's long, beautiful hands on her shoulders and the back of her neck. The new feelings she had of discovery, of life, of appetite. This was more than a captive's admiration for her captor. Maybe it *was* love? The breath caught in Julia's throat. Against all odds and in the most bizarre of all possible circumstances, Julia McEwen was falling in love. And as she fell, she was shedding her inhibitions, her reserve, the icy exterior that had helped disguise the barren pain of her life with Magnus.

Julia shook her head, cautioned herself. This was madness. Sue was dangerous. Everything about her spelled trouble. And this thing with James Wilmot; it went beyond all the risks they had ever taken. How long could they continue like this, wildly careening towards disaster? She wiped her eyes with the back of her hand. This wasn't going to end well, but she knew she'd go along with the ride. With Sue.

'May I ask you a question?' she said.

'Depends what it is.'

'Why do you have sex with so many men?'

'Why not?'

'Hasn't it got to mean something? It's not like just having a coffee with someone, is it? Do you enjoy it?'

'Enjoy?' Sue paused and considered. 'Sometimes.'

'Is it because you like men or despise them?'

'Why not both?'

'Shouldn't you be more cautious?' Julia asked. 'It's dangerous to take risks like this. One of these days you might meet someone brutal who doesn't take kindly to being messed around. You could end up in hospital with a broken nose, or worse. I don't want to have to identify your body on a mortuary slab one day.' As she spoke, Julia remembered Magnus. His brutal behaviour. The scientific precision with which he aimed his blows, inflicted wounds that only showed when she stripped off her clothes and stood in front of a mirror examining deep purple bruises on her belly, the lacerations on her lower back, her buttocks, the top of her thighs. The pain of rape, dry, searing, over and over.

'Cautious?' Sue threw the word back at her with a laugh. 'You've got to be joking! It's more likely to be the other way round. At least I know how to look after myself.'

Julia stared at Sue for a moment, and then said quietly: 'Anything could happen. It's more dangerous to play with people's feelings than to rob a bank.'

'I don't care. What would you know anyway? I'm not a frightened little princess like you, Julia, scared to take risks.' Sue laughed again. But her laughter was hollow and unconvincing.

Julia ignored this. She put her hand on Sue's arm.

'I care about you,' she said softly. 'I really do.'

Sue stared at Julia. For a moment she looked bewildered. Then she turned away.

'Right, let's do it,' she said briskly.

'Whatever we do tonight, it won't be as dangerous as what you did with that man,' Julia said as they dressed in black trousers and zipped up their hoodies.

Sue ignored her. She tucked her hair under her beanie, checking carefully that no tell-tale blonde strands had escaped.

The process was becoming familiar. Julia could transform herself into a man quickly and efficiently. When they stepped out of the door neither of them looked like a woman. It was amazing what beanies, black trousers and hoodies could achieve. The hoodies bulked out their torsos, the narrow black pants disguised their slim legs.

Sue watched Julia approvingly. 'You're getting good at this,' she said.

The two women stood side by side and looked in the mirror. 'Here comes trouble,' Sue laughed and Julia joined her, feeling the adrenaline kick into her bloodstream. They stacked their backpacks with tools and their weapons, then hoisted them onto their shoulders.

'Ready?' asked Sue.

Julia nodded. They walked out into the cold night air.

'I love nights like this,' Sue said. 'When it's dark you can do anything, be anyone. You're invisible. Invincible.' She paused for a moment, then continued: 'I'm sorry about earlier. I didn't mean that, about you being pathetic; too scared to take risks. Considering everything you're quite amazing.'

'I know you didn't,' Julia said.

The Bank of the Eastern Cape stood in a quiet, tree-lined street. Sue turned off the engine a little way down the street; they sat in darkness, lowered the car windows and listened. Somewhere, back along the road in one of the houses they had passed, a dog was barking. Then it fell silent. All Julia could hear was the urgent pulsing of her own blood.

They left the car, shrugged on their backpacks, crossed the street, walking through patches of shadow and moonlight, and approached the heavy, dark wood doors of the bank. No locks visible. Sue motioned Julia to follow as she moved to the right of the building. They crouched against the wall for a few moments while their eyes got used to the darkness, their breath misting in the cool air. Julia looked up. If there were any security lights they hadn't come on. The clouds were thickening, a few stars glinting in the gaps.

They moved around the building cautiously, then recoiled immediately, pressing themselves back against the cold wall. A guardhouse stood in front of them, a figure sitting inside. They waited for a few minutes. There was no sign of life. Then Sue moved quickly to the right, keeping low, her knees bent, her head and shoulders hunched forward. Julia waited, pressing herself against the wall, listening. Sue crept back. She touched Julia's shoulder, breathing: 'He's sleeping ... just follow me, we'll get past without waking him. Keep close.'

They crept forward, tiptoeing past the guardhouse, past the slumped figure of a uniformed guard, his head resting on his arms. They could hear his snores as they slid past.

They moved carefully along the back wall of the building, feeling their way with their fingertips. About halfway along, they located a discreet door, its security panel set in a grid.

Sue inserted James Wilmot's access card and the door clicked open. They stepped forward cautiously, flashing their torch lights in short bursts to light the way. They were inside the bank. Sue moved swiftly to a flashing monitor pad and punched in the numbers she had extracted from Wilmot's cell. The bleeping stopped. She turned, grinned at Julia and gave her the thumbs-up.

They were in a spacious, dark-toned foyer. A marble staircase to the side led down steeply and they followed it down three flights, emerging into a large area with a heavily barred security gate at the end. It was completely dark. The flashlight illuminated a computer pad to the side of the grid. Sue tapped in the code and the steel gate opened. They were in the vault. It was a huge, echoing place. Banks of safety deposit boxes ran down both sides, and an untidy stack of crates, cartons and old computer screens were pushed against the back wall.

Sue swung off her backpack and lowered it between her feet. They stood for a moment, silent, their backs flattened against the cold brick wall, listening. Then Sue stepped forward, opened her backpack and fished out a chain with a key dangling on the end. 'It's box 2805,' she said. They shone their torches over the walls, scanning the numbers.

'Oh shit,' Sue said. 'They're not in sequence.'

'When did Sando give you the number?'

'Months ago.'

Sue scoured the numbers down each side of the walls. Nothing matched.

'Maybe it's an old box,' Julia said, 'not opened for ages?'

'If that's the case ...' Sue darted forward and began tearing at the crates and boxes at the back of the vault. Julia joined her and together they pulled away crates and computer screens.

'Gotcha!' Box 2805, rusty, covered with cobwebs, on the bottom row. Sue struggled to unlock it. She finally stood up, holding a dusty envelope. As she walked towards the backpack near the security gate, she froze.

'Oh God,' she breathed, 'someone's coming.'

Instinctively, Julia dived behind the debris at the back of the vault, lying flat, frozen still as the footsteps got closer. Sue stood motionless, staring at the shadow moving down the steps towards her. Julia saw her reach for her gun, then hesitate, realising that it was still in her backpack.

A flashlight shone, lighting up the muzzle of a pistol. James Wilmot. Pointing his pistol right at Sue's chest. He was red, panting and out of control.

'Don't move. Don't you *dare* fucking move,' he yelled.

She saw him looking at Sue's black tracksuit, webbed belt and empty holster. Roaring with frustration, he stuck the pistol in his belt, dropped the torch on the floor and came for Sue. He grabbed her arms, pulling her round towards him. He yanked the beanie off her head and her hair tumbled out to frame her face.

'I knew it!' he shouted, stabbing his finger into her face. 'Bitch! Fucking bitch! You took me for a fool.'

Sue jerked away from him and dived for her backpack. Her gun. She wasn't going to make it – it was too far away. Julia lay motionless, watching as Wilmot lurched forward and punched Sue between the shoulder blades, knocking the breath out of her. Sue gasped, fell, scrambling for the backpack. He was right behind her. He seized her ankles, sliding her back towards him, grabbing her face, squeezing it, forcing her head to the side. Then he pulled her up by her hair. She cried out. He hit her hard across the face with the palm, then the back of his hand. Then he grabbed her by the throat and started squeezing.

'It was all a game, wasn't it? A fucking game,' he yelled. 'You little cunt. And you thought I was stupid enough to fall for it? Bloody, cock-teasing whore!' He was panting, triumphant, and totally unaware of anyone else being in the vault.

Julia lay silently, patiently – waiting. She needed perfect timing for maximum surprise.

Sue tried to wriggle away from Wilmot. She swung her foot upwards into his crotch. It didn't stop him. He kept up the pressure, muttering obscenities, pushing harder and harder onto Sue's neck. Julia heard hoarse gasps as Sue fought for breath. Then Wilmot shifted, and for a moment, he had his back to Julia. As he moved the torch rolled on the floor, lighting the vault walls with jumping yellow shadows.

She had to strike. Now.

Julia stood up, raced forward, and leapt onto Wilmot's back. She pulled his head towards her, tearing at his hair, clawing at his eyes, pummelling him with her fists. He shouted in shock, and let go of Sue. She tumbled across the floor into the darkness near the security door. Wilmot twisted and turned his body, desperately trying to dislodge Julia. But she hung on, kicking him, screaming at him, digging her fingers into his eye sockets. Finally he managed to heave her off his back. He grabbed for the gun stuck in his belt. Julia landed lightly on her toes, twisting to face him, pulling at the gun, wrestling with him, trying to force it out of his hands. Wilmot swore, kicked out at her. She jumped to one side, kicked back, smashing her foot into his knee.

'Fuck you!' He bellowed with pain, moved forward, pushing the gun against her, grappling with her, his foul breath and spittle spraying her face.

His gun went off.

Julia felt as if she'd been kicked in the chest by an elephant. The blast shredded her eardrums. For a moment everything was quiet. Wide-eyed, she watched Wilmot stumble backwards. He clutched his chest; fell on both knees, blood gushing past his fingers, pouring down the front of his shirt. He groaned as he fell against the safety deposit boxes, staring down at himself in disbelief. He looked up at Julia for a long moment. He opened his mouth as if he wanted to tell her something. Then his body jerked, crumpled back and lay still.

'Oh God ... oh my God ...' she whispered. She couldn't take her eyes off him.

'Is he dead?' Sue's hoarse voice broke through the fog settling in Julia's mind and she looked around wildly, seeking a way out of the horror. She was frozen with shock. Shadows spiked the walls as the torch rolled, lighting up the bloody scene. She felt less than human. She could smell her own fear and wretchedness. She had to get out of the place, breathe some clean fresh air. Somewhere in the back of her skull a voice was shouting, 'You've killed a man ... You've killed a man ...'

'Let's get out of here.' She almost choked on the words.

'The envelope ... don't forget the envelope ...' Sue said. She could hardly stand. Julia supported her. She looked over at Wilmot.

'We can't just leave him.'

'We have to.'

Trying not to look at Wilmot's body and the pool of blood spreading over the floor, Julia half-dragged Sue up the stairs, through the foyer and through the security door. Sue stumbled; Julia had to stop and haul her along as they crossed the cobbles and made their way to the car. The guardhouse was empty, but Julia couldn't see the guard anywhere. She opened the passenger door, pushed Sue inside and got into the driver's seat. They had left the keys in the ignition to make escape quicker.

As Julia started the engine, there was a shout. Somebody was running towards them. Glancing in the rear-view mirror, Julia saw the guard, powering along the street, almost at the boot of the car.

'Stop! Stop!' he yelled.

He reached them, banged his hand on the boot. Julia rammed the car into gear and moved forward. He wrenched open the back door of the Toyota. He half made it into the car, but she picked up speed, jerked the wheel hard to the right, and as they swerved across the road, the car skidding, screeching and tilting on two wheels, the guard lost his grip and went tumbling out of the car and across the road like a rag doll thrown down by an angry child.

Julia drove at manic speed through the quiet streets, then forced herself to slow down, heart thumping in her chest. She pulled into a parking space and killed the engine. A security company van raced past them. Julia slid down; her head level with Sue's where she lay silent on the passenger seat. She checked the mirror, and then quickly gunned the engine into life. She swerved into a side street and took two more turns. When she was finally sure they were not being followed, she drove sedately back to Graham Street, straight into the garage and activated the door. It slid down, sealing them from the night.

It was only then that she started shaking. She looked down at her hands and saw the blood on them. She tried to wipe it off but it was deep under her nails and in the creases of her knuckles. If she thought about her bloodied hands and James Wilmot's face, she would collapse. She tried to concentrate on taking one breath at a time. One minute at a time. Like a soldier going into battle.

Battle. The thought helped Julia to move. She muscled Sue out of the car, into the bathroom. She was seriously hurt. The mirror and basin were soon splattered with blood, violently red against the white porcelain, demented crimson splashes from a mad artist's brush. In Julia's hyped-up state, the mess blurred into hallucination. An unfamiliar landscape and she was walking in it. But as her horrified frenzy died away she felt stronger, more in control.

She soaked towels and bathed Sue's face, which was already bruising. One of her teeth was missing. Her nose was swollen and shapeless. Her right eye was almost closed. A raw graze ran around her neck, and her left wrist was swollen. Julia brought ice packs, arnica oil and disinfectant from the kitchen.

'Paracetamol?' Julia reached into the cupboard and produced a packet. Sue nodded.

'Thanks,' she whispered.

'Let me look at your mouth,' Julia said.

Sue turned so Julia could inspect the damage.

'It's a mess; you're going to need stitches. You'll have to see a dentist.'

Sue pressed a hand against her ribs. 'Fuck, that's sore,' she slurred. Her mouth had swollen grotesquely; her lips were thick and rubbery. She looked just like Donald Duck.

'You'll live,' Julia said. 'You're going to be very sore for a few days, but you'll live.'

Sue was too shaken to speak. She shook her head in disbelief. Finally she said: 'You saved my life, I can't tell you, I'm –'

'Don't say anything,' Julia said. Then she picked up the envelope from the safety deposit box and threw it down on Sue's lap.

'I hope you think this was worth it. Now we've got absolutely no chance of getting out of this mess. I've killed a man and the security guard saw our faces. It's over.' She slumped to the bathroom floor and buried her face in her hands.

Finally Sue found her voice. 'Don't be crazy, you didn't kill him. The gun went off. He killed himself.'

'I'll never know that for sure.'

'He was just a stupid, dick-driven male. Men who beat up women don't deserve to live.'

'Shit, Sue! Give the guy a break. You were robbing his fucking *bank*! I reckon he was entitled to be a bit pissed off with you. It's over. It's really over, we're finished. We'll have to go to the police.'

'Don't be an idiot. It's not over. Nobody knows us, there's nothing to identify us. The guard didn't get a good look at us. He's probably got concussion after that fall, anyway.'

'Or *he* died as well.'

'Rubbish! These guards are tough, he'll survive.'

'What about the people in the bank who saw you with James Wilmot? The police aren't idiots. You were seen at game reserves and restaurants with him. You can't believe they won't trace you quickly?'

'All the more reason to get out of here first thing in the morning,' said Sue. 'They'd never recognise me now, anyway,' she added, trying to smile.

'Where do you go from here?' asked Julia.

'I'm holding the ace card. Sando's papers. If he wants them, he's going to have to deposit a hell of a lot of money into my offshore bank account. Enough for us to go away. To Australia or New Zealand maybe. We can start a new life. I can just see us lying on a beach somewhere in the Indian Ocean, cocktails in our hands – a classic movie ending.' Her sore mouth twisted in a smile. 'We'll prove that crime does pay. Somewhere there's a place for us, we've just got to find it.'

'What do you mean, "us"?'

Sue shrugged.

'We're damaged people, you and I. We should be together. I'm making you an offer, Julia. Nobody's ever done as much for me as you. Maybe that's what love is.'

# 25

Dawn was breaking when Julia finally sat down on the sofa with a cup of coffee. Sue was asleep. Now that all the hype was over she finally had time to take stock. Her head was still filled with images of James Wilmot's body sliding down the wall of safety deposit boxes. The way he'd stared up at her. But now she felt no guilt. He'd asked for it.

Leaning her head back against the cushions, Julia analysed her feelings. She was in control now. The dynamics had shifted. Now Sue was the vulnerable one. She, Julia, had become more ruthless and determined than she had thought possible. She pressed her head hard against the back of the sofa, feeling her brain working, her thoughts becoming colder, more logical.

First of all, so overwhelmingly, that it would be top of her list until she'd found a way, she wanted revenge on Magnus. She would seek him out and corner him like a trapped animal. She would punish him, however long it took. The longer the better. The slower, the more painful and more shameful the better. The new Julia would have no compunction about what she did. She knew how to plan and execute a crime. She had already killed. Magnus would pay for the years of abuse and humiliation.

She visualised Magnus tied up and at her mercy. She would burn him, twist cigarettes out on his face, stub them into his eyes. She would cut him, in all the places that hurt the most. She would push him down into a bath of boiling water and hold his head under until he almost died. She shuddered with pleasure just thinking about it.

Next Julia's thoughts turned to the woman who had turned her life upside down. Sue had snatched her at her most vulnerable moment, perhaps even saved her life. The intense attraction that had sprung up between them had forced her to become a new woman. A dangerous woman. The old Julia had gone. The darkness in Sue matched something similar in her, there was no escaping that. But she couldn't save Sue. She had to save herself. She would have to cut out all sentiment and forget Sue if she was to survive. The new Julia knew there was only one person in this game. The murder of James Wilmot had changed everything. She would be the survivor. Much as she cared for Sue, she cared for herself more. There was no room for sloppy emotions in this game.

Sue had told her things she would rather not have heard. Some things she couldn't begin to imagine even thinking about, let alone doing. But whatever she had done, however evil she'd been, no other person had ever touched Julia so intensely. But the time for sentiment was over. The new Julia wasn't going to allow anything to stand in her way, not even Sue. Not even the thought of the two of them alone, in love, and far away from this poky blood-stained little town. It couldn't happen. It was fairy-story stuff. Julia didn't do fairy stories anymore.

After Sue's suggestion that they go away together, Julia had taken her hand. 'This isn't a good plan, Sue,' she'd said quietly. 'I'm not the right person. Get away from here and start a new life, away from all this mess. You'll do much better without me.'

'I don't want to do better without you.'

'You don't mean it. Look at the two of us. We're from different worlds. I don't even know what I want to do next. I'm still waiting to find out.'

'For fuck's sake,' Sue cried. 'You're not thinking of going back to Johannesburg, are you? To that plastic life? All those charities and orchid shows. Do yourself a favour, Julia, get off it!'

'Of course I'm not going back, don't be crazy.'

Sue's wounded face crumbled; she began to cry. She leaned her head against Julia's shoulder and her body shook with sobs. Julia helped her to the nearest bed and propped her up on a pillow. She talked calmly to her until she quietened. It was the first time Julia had seen her vulnerable, and with it she felt the shift in the balance of power. After she'd recovered a little, Sue started talking about her past.

'I've always been self-destructive – any shrink could tell you it must have something to do with my childhood,' she said, lying on Julia's bed, her bruised and swollen face resting on the white pillows.

'I had a crappy childhood, crappy everything you can imagine. My mother ran away with hippy dropouts, all free love and fuck the consequences. She didn't have a clue who my father was. My grandmother brought me up. We lived in an inner city council estate in south-east London, where everyone drank, took drugs, had sex. I'm talking about kids here, heroin addicts as young as nine years old. Girls of twelve having abortions. It wasn't that I didn't enjoy playing chicken on the motorway, stealing rich kids' bikes, setting things on fire. But it wasn't a great start to life. No jobs waiting when you finished school – if you finished. No bright shiny university degree followed by a bright shiny future. No hope.'

'But you're so much more than your past,' Julia said.

It was as if she hadn't spoken. Despite her sore, twisted mouth, Sue wasn't going to stop telling Julia these sad, horrifying things.

'I used to fantasise that I had another family somewhere,' Sue continued. 'Perfectly ordinary people, the kind I saw at the supermarket, cousins who worked in shops and offices, uncles who mowed lawns at weekends, aunts who baked cakes. They all existed somewhere in my imagination. They were out there, looking for me. But they never turned up.'

Sue's voice rose in pitch as she talked. She was near to tears again.

'Everyone felt sorry for me with my third-hand school uniform and my weird pink hair, but they stopped feeling sorry when they caught me sucking the English master's dick after class. They didn't throw *me* out; I was only thirteen, so *he* got the bullet. Then I started a girl gang and we terrorised the neighbourhood. We performed cutting rituals before girls could join; really painful things. We even drank each other's blood. We beat up old ladies, kidnapped kids and beat them up too. We stole things, set houses on fire by sticking petrol bombs through letter boxes.'

Julia's stomach turned. She might be getting harder, but this was horrific to listen to.

'Didn't you ever have a decent boyfriend?'

'Plenty of sex, but nothing you'd exactly call "decent". I liked bad boys best. First abortion at fourteen, the second at sixteen, botched job, so it meant I'd never have kids. Not that I ever wanted them. I avoid love and all that crap.'

She lay silent for a moment.

'You know what, Julia? I've always been the woman that bad, sick guys pick on. They're like heat-seeking missiles, targeting me, screwing me up. But I'm over it. Men suck. I want a new life.'

Julia watched her intently. 'How did Ollis Sando get such a hold over you?'

'I guess I built up this fantasy world, where we were the stars, but it got out of hand and I couldn't control it. I was the ideal plaything for Sando. Promiscuous, defenceless, no friends or family, ripe and ready for adventure. A true victim. Then everything started to go wrong.'

'How?'

'Sando wanted me to have sex with a Russian investor.' Sue's voice wavered. 'It was bad. He was a monster. My wrists and ankles had rope burns for months afterwards. Sando hadn't meant it to go as far as it did.'

'What happened?'

'I pushed him off a balcony.'

'A balcony?'

'The twelfth floor of the Michelangelo Hotel.

'Oh, my God, Sue, I read about that in the newspaper. It was reported to be suicide. Wasn't it headline news about a year ago?'

'Yes,' Sue turned away. 'Sando fixed it, gave out the story that the guy was depressed.'

'And now Sando's blackmailing you?'

'Yes.'

'Couldn't you call his bluff?'

'He videoed it. The Russian broke two teeth and smashed my cheekbone. I had plastic surgery afterwards. You can see everything on the video, and it's definitely me pushing the disgusting bastard off the balcony.' After he'd untied me and was ready for some other perverted activity, I laced his drink with some sleeping pills, and then got him outside to look at the lights of Sandton. He was small, drugged and mean, so it wasn't hard to tip him over.'

'Oh, my God ...'

'Sando and I did such crazy things. I keep wondering if he meant it to go on for as long as it did. Did he want me to tell him to stop? I don't know why I didn't. Except that *I* loved all the darkness and violence too. I can't deny that – try to make him out to be the only one who was twisted and sick. Maybe I need it in my life.'

'You've got to see that Sando was the villain here, Sue, what a twisted creep. You were just another victim.' Julia took Sue's hand and kissed it. 'Are you feeling better?' She smoothed Sue's hair back from her forehead.

'The room keeps swimming in and out of focus. I need to sleep.' Sue stroked Julia's hand and looked up at her with such naked trust and affection that Julia felt a moment's remorse for what was going to happen next.

'Julia,' Sue said, 'I mean it, about us going away together. I hate sloppy stuff and all that crap, but you're very important to me. I've never trusted anyone more.'

'Thank you,' Julia said. She lay on the bed with Sue, smoothing her hair, and holding her. But she already knew what she was going to do.

Thin, wintry morning light was streaming into the house. Julia washed her coffee cup, wiped down the sink and tidied up the kitchen before she returned to the bedroom. Sue was asleep in the narrow white bed, the bruises on her face a vivid contrast to the white sheets. Dark marks circled her throat in a purple band where Wilmot had choked her. But she was sleeping peacefully, her thumb in her mouth, like a child.

'Goodbye, Sue, forgive me,' Julia whispered as she bent down and kissed Sue lightly on the forehead. The Judas kiss.

Then she took the car and drove to the police station.

# 26

6 July 2006 – 8.00 a.m.

When I arrived at the police station, Julia McEwen was already in the interview room with Zak Khumalo and Director Mandile. I knew at a glance that this was the woman I'd seen at the arts festival. Sometimes being right was no pleasure at all. This was definitely one of those times. Under any other circumstances, this tall, elegant woman, dressed in a black tracksuit, would be on her way to gym for a workout with her personal trainer, but here she was, in the interview room of the Grahamstown police station. Not the best of settings. She looked cool, composed and unruffled as she faced us.

I introduced myself. Julia McEwen responded with a nod.

'Please tell us your name,' I said.

'Julia Anne McEwen.'

'Are you the wife of Magnus McEwen and is your address Bright Water, 91 The Fountains, Houghton, Johannesburg?'

'Yes,' Julia said calmly.

I watched her across the interview table. Her hands lay quietly in her lap. She wore diamond studs and her dark hair was short and spiky, following the graceful line of her neck. It didn't seem possible that she could be involved in violent crime.

'Why have you come here today?'

'I've already told these officers. I've come to report that a man has been shot.'

Zak shifted in his chair. 'Please, tell us what happened.'

I could see that Zak was unnerved by Julia McEwen's calm, cool demeanour. I had to admit that I was too. But I believed that she was in deep shock. I had seen so many people after traumatic shootings or accidents, who had that weird aura of calm about them – as if they had been muffled in cotton wool.

'Since I was taken hostage a few months ago, I've been living in this area with my – well, the person who abducted me. Last night we broke into the Bank of the Eastern Cape in the High Street. There was an ... incident. The manager was killed in the vault. Accidentally.'

Zak pushed back his chair, its legs scraping the floor noisily. He looked at me, eyebrows raised. 'Zak Khumalo, leaving the room at 08.45 hours,' he said as he left.

'May I have some water?' Julia McEwen asked.

While I poured a glass from the water filter in the corner, I watched her staring blankly at the ceiling lights. I wanted dozens of questions answered. I passed Julia McEwen the glass and she lowered her eyes from the ceiling and gave me a cool, assessing look.

'Thank you,' she said.

'We want to hear about your abduction and what's happened to you since. But before we get to that, please tell me what happened last night. My colleague Detective Inspector Khumalo has gone to visit the scene. He will be back shortly to corroborate your statement so please be as accurate as possible.'

'We broke into the vault. The bank manager followed us. There was a struggle and the gun went off.'

'Who pulled the trigger?'

The words curled in the air between them like dark smoke.

'My abductor killed him.'

'Please describe what happened.'

'We were all struggling together. It was pitch dark. He attacked us. He could have called the police, or the security guards, but he attacked us. He fought us. My abductor had a gun and shot him.'

'What about your abductor? Where was he standing?'

'She. My abductor is a she.'

'She? A woman?'

'Yes. She was standing next to him with the gun. She pulled the trigger. Her name is Sue Kellon.'

Director Mandile drew in his breath sharply.

I almost smiled, Director Mandile had been made a fool of. After all the leads, all his important detective work, he'd been foiled by two white women. If Julia McEwen hadn't handed herself in, he would still be out there looking for two black men.

Two hours later I emerged from the interview room. Some of my questions had been answered, but certainly not all of them.

Julia McEwen told us she had escaped from a house in a pan-handle off Graham Street in which she had been held captive, after the murder of James Wilmot. She explained that Kellon had been injured during the fight with Wilmot and wasn't physically able to restrain her anymore. So she had taken her chance and escaped. She had remained calm and composed throughout the interview. Only once did she demand a lawyer, after she accused me of treating her like a suspect and not a victim. When I'd suggested contacting her husband she stared at me coldly. 'That won't be necessary,' she said.

All the way through the interview, I felt things were not quite real. There were so many gaps. So many of the questions that McEwen answered in her cold, steady voice seemed wrong. I couldn't believe her story. My instinct was that she was lying through her teeth.

Julia McEwen finally reached the end of her capacity for answers. We'd have to talk to her again, but for now it was enough. We would have to act fast.

I sat at Bea's desk for a moment, straightening my back, feeling vertebrae crackle. My neck was stiff and my watch told me that I hadn't eaten for a long time. I needed a big, starchy sugar lift, a double espresso and a slice of chocolate cake. By some miracle, Bea arrived with a tray at that very moment. Lemon meringue, not chocolate, but it would do.

'Here you are, Thabisa,' Bea said. 'A sugar-caffeine rush is what makes the world go round. You okay?'

'I've been better.'

'I came to work past the BEC building. There are police crawling all over it, pavements taped off, the lot. Serious, hey?'

'Yes, it's serious.'

I had only taken one sip of coffee when Zak arrived, wearing a black nylon-web gun belt and a bulletproof vest. He looked cool and confident.

'I need to speak to you, somewhere private. Come with me,' he said. He took my wrist, moved me through the corridor to Mandile's office without breaking stride. His long legs forced me to run to keep up with him. I started to argue but he ignored me. He kicked the door shut, sat on Mandile's desk and faced me. His eyes narrowed so I couldn't see what was in them.

'It's all true,' he said. 'The manager is in the vault. He's been dead about four hours by the look of things.'

'Has the body been properly identified?'

'Yes. His wife's in Australia holidaying with their kids. We got one of his staff to ID him. Not the greatest thing for somebody to do just after breakfast. It's James Wilmot, manager of the bank for over twenty years. He was sixty-two, just about to retire, poor sod.'

I thought of the man planning his retirement, maybe a holiday to see his kids in Australia; now that future remained frozen. Everything can change in an instant.

'What did McEwen have to say?' Zak asked.

'She's answered all the questions, but I don't believe it's as straightforward as she says. I don't trust her. It's not just that she's in shock. It's all too pat, too simple. I don't understand why she was still hanging around with her abductor.'

She had every opportunity to get away and yet she didn't even try. She went along, doing the heists, bank robberies, being an accomplice, even to murder.'

'Probably Stockholm Syndrome,' Zak said. 'Like Patty Hearst. They fall in love with their captors and won't leave them.'

'Only in this case, the captor is another woman.'

Zak looked surprised.

'Another *woman*? That's got to be a first. Well, I guess the same rules apply.'

'The other woman's name is Sue Kellon. She's at a house off Graham Street. It runs off Worcester Road. We've surrounded it with six armed police officers who we seconded from Port Alfred and Kenton. She's armed and dangerous. We need proper back-up, a Crime Prevention Unit to go in and get her.'

'We'll have to get one from Port Elizabeth. There's not enough support here.'

'Mandile's already called for it. They should be here in about an hour. But it's too long to wait; I'm worried she'll get away, especially when she discovers that McEwen has gapped it. I think we should go in now.'

Zak watched my face closely. 'We could take a support team from here and an ambulance. We're all highly trained professionals. It should be enough but I'm not sure,' he said.

'McEwen wants to come with us; she's convinced that she can talk Kellon into giving herself up quietly. If McEwen has been a captive of this woman it sounds unlikely, but perhaps she could come along as a last resort?'

'Why isn't she under arrest?'

'She hasn't been charged with anything yet.'

'I don't like it.'

'I think it might work; they were obviously very close.'

'At least one of them is a murderer, Thabisa. They're dangerous.'

'I think it's worth a try to let McEwen negotiate before anyone gets hurt.'

'I still don't like it.'

'It's the way I want to play it, Khumalo. We don't want a blood bath if we can avoid it.'

'Okay, it's your call, but I'm not in agreement. I would rather just go in there and get her.'

'I think it'll work better my way.'

Zak Khumalo's mouth twitched. I was pretty sure it wasn't a smile.

'Let's look on the bright side,' I said. 'Maybe I'm right.'

My gut instinct was that this wasn't as simple as it looked. Something wasn't right. I wanted to see the two women together. That might answer my questions, put things into perspective.

I was wrong. I was so wrong.

# 27

For the first time since she had abducted Julia, Sue slept deeply. As she woke, peace flooded through her. With surprise she realised her rage was gone. She had lived with it for so long it took her a moment to identify the sensation of its absence. It was like the silence when one discovers the rain has stopped or the wind has died down.

She climbed out of bed, stumbled into the bathroom and splashed water on her face, wincing at her gruesome reflection. She looked terrible.

'Julia, where are you?' She walked into the kitchen.

Nobody there.

Late morning light poured through the window. She opened the fridge, took out a tub of yoghurt and ate it, wincing with pain from her damaged mouth.

'Julia?' she called again.

She opened the door of Julia's room. Empty.

A noise outside attracted her attention. She peered through a crack in the curtains and looked out of the window. An armed police officer was standing in the garden. A walkie-talkie crackled instructions.

Julia had gone to the police.

Sue ran to her bedroom, scrambled through the cupboard for Sando's envelope. Then back to the kitchen, to find a matchbox. She held the envelope in the sink and burned it, watching flames eating the sheets of paper that she had risked her life to steal. Sando was safe. Then she prepared; her dues for all the lost lives, horror and confusion were about to be paid.

She was nervous, but that didn't keep her from weighing the pros and cons, trying to guess what might happen and how she might possibly survive. She put on a designer dress, wincing as she pulled it down over her lacerated face. Next, leather boots as soft as butter. She'd always believed in dressing for the occasion.

She felt a great flare of anger about Julia, and then bleak sadness. The only person who had ever really cared about her had betrayed her. She was alone again, she had always been. But she wouldn't cry over spilt milk, she would get into battle mode and fight this out. Fight it until her last breath.

As she waited for them in the cottage's sitting room, she held the Glock steady. She smiled wryly. Just like in the movies. She wouldn't go quietly. Courtrooms, explanations and jail didn't enter the equation. Not for Sue Kellon. She'd go down fighting.

When the cars came up the pan-handle and turned toward the cottage, she took a deep, calming breath. She looked over the top of the weapon, finger on the trigger, holding her breath, ready to shoot anyone who came through the door.

Car doors banged. Four dark silhouettes stood against the sunlight alongside two police cars, behind them an ambulance, with medics tumbling out of it.

Next, a loudspeaker. A disembodied voice shouting: 'Miss Kellon, we know you're in there. Come out with your hands up ... put down your weapon, come outside ...'

*Choose. You don't want to be taken alive. You can kill one, maybe even two.* She could see Julia standing next to a woman with braided hair, and two men, one much taller than the other.

Julia's voice came over the loud speaker: 'Give yourself up, Sue, please ... just come out with your hands up ... nobody's going to hurt you ... please Sue ...'

She'd always thought she'd be safe from this sort of ending. Somebody else would sort it out for her. Ollis would step in and save her. There had been no fear at the beginning, only happy times. The trap had been so easy to fall into; his laughter when he held her, his lips travelling over her skin; his mouth whispering dirty, sexy words against her neck.

*'A little fear is good, isn't it?'* his words flickered in the silence. *'It's good to push yourself further.'* She was doing that now. As far as she had ever gone. *'I'll be there to help you. You'll be safe with me.'* But he wasn't there. Nor was Julia. Sue pushed her feelings down deep to where they couldn't sabotage her. She was alone – just as she always had been. Nobody and nothing was safe. No one could be trusted. No one should be loved. Life was full of traps.

*When you wake to life, real life, you understand it's just a road and travelling it entails countless choices.*

*Whether you want to or not, you've got to walk that road alone. What it comes down to in the end is the choosing.*

She had never chosen well. Even when she chose Julia. Or had Julia chosen her?

The door was kicked in, the silhouettes entered the room, black against the sunlight. They were all aiming their guns at her.

'Put down your weapon. Put down the gun or we fire,' a man shouted.

Sue's finger hovered on the trigger, aiming at the woman with the braided hair, but she heard Julia screaming at her, from somewhere outside, begging her not to fire. 'Come out Sue. Please. Sue, I love you. I love you.'

The familiar voice stirred something inside her and she hesitated, turned fragile, at the wrong moment. And with that, she lost her chance.

*Stupid bitch,* she told herself. *You've blown it this time.* The sunlight outside blurred and wavered before her eyes and everything was a confusion of liquid sunlight and shadows.

Sue blinked. Shook her head. *You had your chance, you stupid cow. And now, it's all too late.* Without warning she fired at the tall policeman. He crumpled to the floor.

A sudden, splintering shock of pain in her chest, the world white and slow. She was sliding, slipping, falling. The last sound, a rush of frantic feet, a voice yelling, 'Let me through. Let go of me.' Her last sensation, Julia's thin arms around her, her voice again screaming: 'No – No! Sue, don't die ... don't die ...'

A long weightless drop, then clouds skimming around her, closing over her and she was flying.

# 28

'No!' Julia shrieked.

She flew at me, her eyes wild.

'You bitch,' she yelled. 'You've killed her ... oh my God, you've killed her.'

She threw herself at Sue. 'Don't die, don't die,' she sobbed, cradling her body.

My bullet had sent Sue Kellon slumping to the floor, crystal-blue eyes glazed, staring up at the white ceiling. Globules of red all over her chest, running down her arm and dripping from her limp hand.

Through a daze, I saw Zak stand. The ceramic plates in the bulletproof vest had saved him. I heard myself whispering ... *Thank God, thank God, he's not dead.* He looked shaken, but he was alive.

I'd had to fire that shot. I'd aimed and fired. Just as I'd been trained to do.

Zak came to me; put his arm around my shoulders. My knees gave out and I slumped against him. The room was full of people, police, paramedics, hectic movement. From the corner of my eye I could see them working on Sue Kellon, hooking her to an IV line, shouting orders and running with equipment.

I couldn't breathe. The paramedics brought oxygen, but I couldn't breathe. There just wasn't enough air in the room.

Zak scooped me up, and carried me out into the garden, away from the insanity of the house. He was talking to me, but I couldn't hear what he was saying. He moved me to a garden chair and knelt beside me. His lips were moving but I couldn't hear his voice. A roaring storm filled my ears. His words reached me from a great distance. 'It's okay, Thabisa, it's okay, just breathe deeply, lean on me, just relax, I've got you. You're safe.'

They came through with Sue Kellon on a trolley, rolling her past us, her eyes wide open and staring. They'd put an oxygen mask over her nose and mouth. Blood everywhere.

Julia ran beside the stretcher. Zak reached out to stop her.

'It's too late,' he said quietly. 'She's gone.'

She slapped his hand away.

'Don't touch me, you fucking murderer. I'm going with her,' she hissed.

Zak gestured to a nearby police officer, 'Cuff her,' he said. 'Take her to the hospital.' The young officer did as he was asked. Julia McEwen fought him, kicking and screaming, but she finally stumbled against him and he led her away.

Zak bit his lip and turned back to me. 'Are you up to following them to the hospital?' he asked

I nodded. My teeth were chattering. I was shivering with nervous energy. 'Breathe,' Zak said. 'Try and take deep breaths.'

We followed the paramedics through the streets of Grahamstown.

'It's too late, she hasn't survived,' Zak said. 'You had to fire. There was no other choice.'

I nodded and tried to inhale slowly. My feelings of guilt were overwhelming. I knew all about shock and grief. I'd seen countless examples. I'd been to the site of a hundred fatal accidents, but the bodies in the bags weren't people I'd shot. Not an attractive young woman, somebody my own age, dressed to kill in a beautiful black dress, who had stared into my eyes as I fired. Tears ran down my face and dripped onto my shirt.

Zak pulled over to the side and put his arm around me. He didn't speak, he just held me.

'I feel terrible,' I said. 'I hesitated for a moment, but when she shot you –' I broke off, unwilling to finish the sentence, even inside my own head. And then the meaning of what I had just said penetrated. 'Oh my God, Zak! She shot you. Are you okay? Are you okay?'

'I'm touched that you care so much about my health,' he said with a wry grin. But then his expression changed and grew harder. He tightened his grip around my shoulders, turning me, forcing me to look at him, to watch his dark eyes scan my face.

'Thabisa, we're trained to do this, it's our job.'

'I know ... but ...'

'We had no choice. If you hadn't stopped her, she'd have killed us all. Shots to the head would have been next. Bulletproof vests and plates aren't a hundred percent insurance, you know.'

'I know, Zak, but it was bad, really bad ...'

'I know it was.'

'You could have died.'

'We could all have died,' he said, 'but we didn't. I'm going to have an enormous bruise, want to have a look?'

'No thanks,' I said.

We sat for a few minutes until I got control of myself. Zak pulled out into the traffic again. 'How are you doing?' he asked, breaking the silence between us.

'I'm okay. It's just ... I've never deliberately shot anyone before.'

Zak parked in a private lot reserved for emergencies. We entered casualty together. It was a small unit, crowded with people. I saw Tom with a huddle of other doctors and nurses. He excused himself and hurried over to me. He took my hands in his.

'We know what happened,' he said. 'She's dead, Thabisa. There's nothing more we can do.'

I nodded. The moment after those words were spoken, they splintered into a thousand shapes. I had seen them all. People collapsing, howling, freezing in shock, sobbing with the pain of it all.

My work should have conditioned me to this. Police officers, firefighters and ambulance crews have to learn detachment techniques early. Normally I was able to cope, I didn't get sucked in to personal feelings, but this was different. I had shot and killed this woman. As my shock subsided, and I felt calmer, I could feel my public, police-officer mask slipping back on again. But I knew I would see Sue Kellon's face in my dreams for a long time to come.

Tom, Zak, and the medics looked calm and in control. All of them were good at hiding emotion. Everyone in the emergency room had been trained to compartmentalise, it was part of the job, but perhaps they all felt like wrecks inside. Just like me.

I moved to where Julia McEwen sat, her head slumped in her hands. I reached out.

'Come, Mrs McEwen,' I said. 'Lean on me, let me help you up.'

Tom moved forward. Julia sagged between us, unable to stand. We led her into a small, emergency room and helped her to a narrow bed. She lay there, covered in Sue's blood, her arm flung over her face. A police officer stood outside the door.

'Leave her here, Thabisa,' Tom said. 'We'll try to stabilise her. She's in shock.'

'We need to interview her, Tom,' I said. 'When will she be able to answer questions? She's been involved in some pretty brutal robberies and at least one murder.'

Tom stared at me, plainly shocked by this information.

'She should be okay in a few hours. Maybe later this afternoon? I'll let you know.'

Director Mandile arrived, sidling up to stand next to me, bustling with self-importance, claiming glory for the capture of the criminals, promising a lurking reporter from the local newspaper press information when it was available.

'Yes, yes,' I heard him say, 'we just went in there and dealt with it, we didn't need any help from Port Elizabeth. We are perfectly capable of solving difficult national crimes in Grahamstown. I personally directed operations; you can quote me on that.'

I just gave him a withering look and walked away. Officious little man.

I stood in the bright winter afternoon. The hospital looked down over the town and rolling green hills beyond. It was the kind of crisp, clear day when university students rode bikes in parks and office workers chose to eat their lunch outside. A day when no one deserved to die.

It all seemed so normal, but the horror of what had happened pressed against the backs of my eyes and clogged my throat.

All I wanted was to get back to Hill Street, normalise my life and erase the horror of the past few hours from my thoughts. The thought of Sue Kellon's dead body was a dull ache in my chest.

I walked back into the hospital emergency unit, searching for Zak. I found him talking to the obnoxious Mandile. He turned as I approached, rolling his eyes in the direction of Mandile.

'Zak, I'll stay here and wait for McEwen to recover. Why don't you go back to the station and wait for me to bring her in for questioning?'

'Absolutely not DI Tswane, I think you should go back to the safe house and change.'

He gestured at the blood stains all down my shirt.

I tried to argue, but the sight of the blood was enough to make me agree with him.

'I think we can leave this in the capable hands of Director Mandile until McEwen can be questioned. I'll drive you back,' Zak said smoothly.

Mandile agreed. 'Yes, yes, just leave it all to me; I'll let you know when she is ready to be transported back to the station.'

'Nothing's going to happen here for a few hours,' Zak said quietly. 'Let's get out of these clothes and freshen up.'

Zak drove me back to the house. His eyes were shadowed with fatigue. It was one of the few times I'd seen him anything but cool and in command. It was strange. Seeing Khumalo vulnerable didn't make sense, but then, nothing about this day made sense.

'You okay?' His voice was devoid of emotion.

'I'm managing,' I said. 'What about you?'

'It's never easy.'

I fumbled the key into the lock with hands that wouldn't stop shaking, dropping it twice before I pushed open the door. Zak followed me in. He was wearing his police face again. Wary. Emotionally inaccessible.

'The trick is to focus on what we're trained to do,' he said. 'It's our job. We had to choose who was going to die. It would have been you if Julia McEwen hadn't yelled at her to stop.'

I closed my eyes. 'I know.'

I focused on Zak for a long moment. 'We should have waited for the back-up team. You were right.'

'We all have to make difficult decisions at times in this job. Sometimes we make mistakes. We're police officers, aren't we? And days like today are when the job takes it right out of you. Only problem is, when it takes it out of you like this, there's nothing to fill the hole that's left.'

For a second we looked at one another, a clear moment of shock and loss. I bit my cheek hard. If anyone thinks police officers can shoot people then go off and eat a Wimpy breakfast, they're terribly wrong. Trauma and guilt aren't easy companions.

'Why don't you make some coffee while I have a shower, Khumalo. I'll be down in a minute.'

'I'll hang around 'til you're done. Just to make sure you don't fall over.'

'I'll be fine,' I said.

'Shall I scrub your back?' Zak gave a small smile. I knew he was trying to make me feel better. I was grateful for that.

'Beyond the call of duty,' I said.

I went upstairs, and stepped into the shower. I had just killed a woman and it felt as if her blood was all over me; my hands, my breasts, embedded in my finger nails, streaked down my legs. Standing under the gushing hot water, letting it pour all over me, I felt I was washing away some of the trauma and guilt. I wanted to stay there all day long, stand there letting the water wash me clean.

When I heard Zak's footsteps coming up the stairs two at a time, I grabbed for a towel.

'Are you alright?' he asked and pushed open the bathroom door. It was steamy and I could hardly see him, but his broad shoulders took up almost all the room. I wanted to move forward and bury my face against those broad shoulders, feel his power and strength. I stepped forward and the towel fell. I stood there naked in front of him, unmoving. His eyes ran over my body, but when he looked into my eyes, they were full of something soft, something gentle and kind.

He pulled me to him, wrapping his arms around me. Every move he made was instinctive and sure. He wove himself around me, caressing the air between us. He rested his cheek on the top of my head. 'I can manage most things. I just couldn't manage seeing you killed in front of me. You may have saved my life, Thabisa. When a person saves your life, they become very special to you, very special.'

His eyes focused on me. I trembled as he pulled me closer. His hands moved over me, and I didn't stop him. He lifted my braids and bit softly into the back of my neck. I could feel his teeth as he breathed in my hair, my body. He guided my face to meet his, ran his tongue over my lips caressing me softly at first, then more firmly. I was drunk with his mouth, the hair on the back of his neck, his powerful shoulders, his hands and the danger of it all. It took a few seconds for the full realisation to hit me. I was naked, wrapped in Zak Khumalo's arms and kissing him back.

'This is a mistake,' I said, struggling to pull away. A last ditch stand against the tide of desire that was flooding through me. Lust is like vertigo; you get dizzy and fall into danger. Falling for a friend or colleague is disastrous, it's like stepping into a shower that you know will scald you. But nothing mattered. It was too late.

'Are you afraid?' he answered.

'Yes,' I said.

'Do you want this, Thabisa? Say it ... or I'll stop now.'

I knew that if I stopped to think, my logical, practical self would win and I would send Zak away. So I shut out the voice of reason.

'I want you,' I said and moved closer.

'I've wanted you for so long, Thabisa. But only if you're sure.'

'I'm sure,' I whispered, aware my quick intake of breath gave me away. The need for comfort in this man's arms was escalating into white hot desire.

I gasped as his fingers made contact with my flesh. He moved his hands over my scars, testing the raised flesh left by the ritual punishment. Then kissed the raised scars, staring down at me with such compassion I almost wept. I wrapped my arms around his neck with a strength that alarmed me. Complications, problems, implications ... all reservations melted as I locked my body against his and surrendered. Zak picked me up, carried me into the bedroom and slammed the door shut with his foot.

# 29

6 July 2006 – 5.00 p.m.

Zak dropped me at the station before he went to his hotel to shower. When he returned he was dressed in his usual black. I watched him cross the street. Look at him, I said to myself. A dark swagger of a man. As he walked through the traffic women watched him. Inside the station a young policewoman hung off her desk, flicking her hair as he passed her.

He was all lean planes and angles and hard muscle. And now I knew those cool brown eyes were liquid chocolate when he was aroused.

He smiled when he saw me.

I smiled back.

I would have to think very carefully about Zak Khumalo. But not today. Today I could only remember his mouth, his powerful body moving with mine, his eyes watching my face as I cried out in pleasure. I could only remember the dark bedroom, the single bed, far too small for two, the sheets tangled round us as he explored my body. The way he gazed down at me, then traced my mouth with his fingers.

My cheeks flushed and I buried my face inside a document on Bea's desk in case people could read my mind and see the pictures inside it. My whole body was chiming like a bell. Surely everyone could hear?

Bea kept glancing at me suspiciously. Today she was way beyond voluptuous in a sparkly silver spandex dress and four-inch spike heels.

'What's up, Thabisa?' she asked eventually. 'There's something going on here.'

'I hate to say this, Bea,' I said, 'but you're trespassing.'

'So there is something going on, I knew it!' Bea did an exaggerated eye roll. 'Okay, I won't ask another question. But whatever it is, I wish I'd got some of it too!'

Mandile had brought Julia McEwen back from the hospital. By six that evening we were in the interview room with the tape recorder, the plastic-moulded chairs, the dead plant and the tiled floor.

Mandile wanted to conduct the interview, of course. He was bursting with self-importance, already had his notebook out. When Zak told him that wasn't going to happen, he hissed, 'What do you mean? You can't do this; it's my case.'

'Sorry,' said Zak, 'DI Tswane is the best interviewer in our unit, and this is a Serious and Violent Crimes Unit investigation. She conducts the interview. Just leave this to us, that's why we're here.'

With bad grace, Mandile sat back in the corner of the room, casting spiteful glances at us both.

Julia McEwen looked waif-like in Bea's borrowed jeans and an oversize blue jumper. Her face was gaunt, her pale eyes enormous. A pulse hammered in her throat. She sat silent, blank. I watched her raise one hand to brush her hair off her forehead, saw a blue vein beating at her temple. She had long, slender fingers, bare of any rings.

She looked fragile, broken, but what was going on in her head? She was a mystery woman right down to the bone.

For a sliver of a moment our eyes met, and I saw the vacant expression I'd seen many times at car crashes and murder scenes, a look saturated with shock and pain. This wasn't the detached calm she'd shown when she first came into the police station. This was something else. Real shock. Julia McEwen had been exposed to what a life of crime really was.

'Would you like to tell us everything from the start, Mrs McEwen?' I asked gently.

Julia McEwen stared blankly at the wall in front of her.

I waited. I was good at waiting. One of the reasons Matatu had chosen me for the Eagles. I had an instinctive feel for interviews like this: when to wait, let a silence grow, when to push for an answer. If you leave a space empty long enough, eventually somebody will speak to fill the silence. There was no need for rough tactics, just a need for patience. I had learned the art of silence from my grandfather; nothing would make him speak unless he wanted to. So I waited until Julia McEwen's eyes focused on my face. Finally, she nodded slowly, her face haggard.

I switched the recorder on. Julia struggled to speak.

The process of taking a statement was often long and boring, but this was riveting, almost unbelievable information. Her abduction from the restaurant, the first heist, the killing at Kenton-on-Sea, robberies, hold-ups, attacks. Sue Kellon and Julia McEwen had rampaged across the Eastern Cape causing mayhem and grief wherever they went. Several times, Zak, and I, and even the petulant Mandile glanced at one another in disbelief at Julia's descriptions.

'Why did you and Sue Kellon break into the bank vault last night?'

'To get documents.'

'What sort of documents?'

'They were for Ollis Sando. He was her lover.'

Julia didn't seem to realise the significance of what she had said. I glanced at Zak, who raised his eyebrows and shook his head.

'Ollis Sando? The politician?' he asked.

'Nonsense', Mandile said. 'She's talking fiction.'

'Sue knew Ollis. Intimately. They were involved for many months. She knew the name of his wife, she even described a long scar on his back. Ollis and Sue were in this together. All of it.'

'Together? What do you mean?'

'She was being blackmailed by him.'

'Can you tell us how this happened?'

Julia described Sue's affair with Sando, her voice high and unsteady. Zak, Mandile and I listened intently, occasionally asking questions.

'What was the hold he had over her?' I asked. 'It was evidently so strong she risked her life for him.'

'It was like some sort of weird power-play between them. That was her driving force. He kept pushing her to see how far she'd go – until it all went too far. With the death of the Russian businessman, Ivor Petronov.'

'That's the man who committed suicide in Johannesburg last year?' Zak asked.

'It wasn't suicide.'

Zak narrowed his eyes.

'Are you saying that Sue Kellon was involved in Petronov's death?'

'Yes. She was ... involved.'

'Did she say ... how?'

McEwen nodded. 'Sue killed him and Sando fixed it to look like suicide. You police officers really do need to look deeper than the surface evidence.'

It was an odd remark. And one that made me think Julia McEwen wasn't as fragile as she looked. She was more in control than we thought. It was time to push a little, see what came up.

'Right, Mrs McEwen,' I stood, folded my arms and faced her. 'Knowing Sue Kellon was a murderer who was involving you as an accessory, why didn't you attempt to escape? People were wounded and killed. You had plenty of opportunities. We know she allowed you out on your own. Walks, shopping. Right down to the toy shop where you bought the helium canisters. She didn't have a gun on you then. You had plenty of chances to escape. So why didn't you?'

Silence.

'Please answer my question, Mrs McEwen.'

I watched McEwen's face closely, taking a clinical interest in her reaction as she thought what to say.

'You liked her, didn't you? You liked it all. The planning, the excitement – even the killing? Your reaction to her death was ... excessive, if you were just a "captive" as you claim to be.'

Julia McEwen's eyes were flat, coldly speculative. Her hands slithered across her lap and she raised her shoulders in a shrug. 'No comment,' she said.

Complete silence.

Zak cleared his throat, and then spoke, 'We're going to charge you, Mrs McEwen. Director Mandile will read out the charges. After that you will be taken to Port Elizabeth and held in custody pending a trial. Do you understand?'

'Yes,' she said.

'Do you wish us to contact your husband?'

She looked up quickly. 'No.' She spat the word. 'Definitely not.' Yet another side of Julia McEwen.

Director Mandile's stale smile was stapled across his face as he read the charges out. 'I am a police officer. I am arresting you on the following charges: Armed robbery. Assault with a deadly weapon. Accessory to murder. You have the right to consult with a legal practitioner of your choice, or should you prefer to, to apply to be provided by the State with the services of a legal practitioner. You have the right to remain silent. Anything you say may be used as evidence in a court of law. You have the right to apply to be released on bail.'

He closed her file with a satisfied snap. 'I look forward to meeting you again, Mrs McEwen. I hope you find the accommodation in Port Elizabeth to your liking.'

He turned to us, with narrowed eyes.

'I hope DI Khumalo and DI Tswane that you will let me have your reports as soon as possible. I want to check that you have recorded everything correctly.'

Julia McEwen remained seated, staring blankly into space as Mandile left. As I walked across to her and asked her to stand, she rounded on me.

'Why did you kill her, you bitch?' The charm and grace had vanished. She strained forward in her seat, her face contorted into a snarl. For a moment I thought she would attack me, but Zak moved forward and held her back. She tried to push him away. She stretched out her hands towards my throat, yelling, 'Fucking police! Brute force and violence, that's all you morons know. You didn't have to kill her. I know who you are, *DI Tswane*. I'll come for you one day.' Then she spat into my face.

Zak pulled Julia McEwen roughly by the arm. 'I don't think DI Tswane has to worry about your vendetta,' he said. 'You're going to be behind bars for a hell of a long time, Mrs McEwen.'

He handed me his handkerchief. I wiped the glob of spittle off.

In the main reception area, Julia McEwen stood facing me, a police officer on either side. As they led her away, she turned back to face me.

Then she smiled. A slow, dangerous smile.

But it wasn't Julia McEwen's smile that kept me awake that night, tossing and turning that night. It was the thought of a scar crawling up a broad back.

'What sort of scar?' I had asked in the interview.

'It went right up his back from his buttocks to his neck. It could have been laser tattoo removal, Sue thought. Of a snake.'

# 30

Men swung in a circle, singing and stamping, striking their fighting sticks on the ground. Women clapped and ululated. I'd arrived in the valley just as a ritual killing was about to take place.

It was a Saturday afternoon, and I'd travelled all day. I'd left Grahamstown before dawn; four hours later I left the car, put on my backpack and started to hike the great folds of the mountains, praying I wouldn't meet a leopard.

As I descended into the gorge, I was struck by the beauty of it all. A green world swirled below me. Far down in the valley, I glimpsed round mud huts, spirals of smoke. The sun was burning, and I longed for a cool swim in the river, but more than that, a long talk with my grandfather. I felt strong, hoping that I could make a breakthrough. He needed to know what I'd come to tell him.

Tom's words echoed in my head as I made my way down: 'You're the key ... ask yourself how *you* can help *him*.'

When I arrived at my grandfather's homestead, it was deserted. His youngest wife, Nomvula, was sweeping the huts. She looked up in surprise as I appeared, and blushingly explained that the whole village was attending a ceremony for the Malumi family, at their homestead.

'Why aren't you with the others?' I asked.

'Ngosi told me to stay behind and sweep,' Nomvula said quietly, averting her eyes.

'Did she indeed? Well, now you've swept, so let's both go and join in. Ngosi used to say that sort of thing to me all the time when I was living in the valley.'

Nomvula suppressed a smile.

I linked arms with her and we walked along together with Nomvula gazing in undisguised admiration at my hair and clothes.

'Your name is so pretty,' I said. 'Miss Rain.'

Nomvula spoke shyly. 'I was born when the spring rains came.'

'You're lucky to have a nice name. I never tell anybody my first name, it's *so* awful.'

Nomvula giggled. 'What is it?'

'*Nontozakuyithini*! – Oh that will never do!'

Nomvula burst out laughing, covering her mouth with her hand. 'Why did they call you that bad name?'

I grinned. 'Probably because I wasn't a boy, but at least I got a nice second name. Can you tell me why this ceremony is taking place?'

'It's a sacrifice for the Malumi grandchild who is sick,' Nomvula said. 'They are brewing the beer and a black-and-white ox is being prepared.'

My heart sank.

It was late afternoon and already the sun was low. Voices and drums sounded ahead. As we rounded the brow of the hill, red cliffs reared in front of us. Below lay dark green forests, four grey huts and a cattle fold. Spilling between us was a vivid flood of people dressed in red, pouring down the hill.

My timing was unfortunate. It had been many years since I'd attended a sacrifice and I certainly wasn't looking forward to this one. I felt my stomach turn at the thought.

Malumi's homestead had been swept and branches of mountain trees laid for the sacrificial fire. His family made a colourful group, some with faces painted white and others bright yellow. They were seated on the floor, and a small girl lay on the lap of her grandmother. She was crying softly, her small head barely moving. I watched through narrowed eyes. The child was probably suffering from malnutrition. She should be in hospital, not lying here far from the help she needed.

Malumi appeared in the doorway. He held himself proudly, wearing an intricately beaded headband and carrying a sawn-off spear. His family shuffled to their feet, heads bowed.

A figure seated at the far end of the homestead raised his hand. My grandfather, seated in the position of honour.

Very slowly, in single file, Malumi, preceded by my grandfather, led his family out. They followed him, chanting and dancing, to the cattle fold. The rest of the villagers joined the procession, most of them stained bright red with ochre, their foreheads smeared with white paint. White lines under their eyes gave them an alien appearance.

A general thumping of feet began as the villagers stamped in rhythm, moving forward, following Malumi and his family. Above the rhythmic pounding, women ululated, their cries lending an eerie effect to the occasion. The noise swelled until it felt as though the hills were pulsing with sound. It was as though the ancestors were watching, floating amongst us, reaching out to us, sending us strength and wisdom.

I squeezed between the crowds. Their comments followed behind me as I made my way to the front. They were laughing, commenting on my appearance. '*Tyho! Tyho! Lomfazi!* – Goodness me, look at this woman!'

They eyed my jeans and white T-shirt with scorn. The old crones, led by Ngosi, were crowing with mean laughter, hissing, and taunting. I rounded on them, flashed my pale eyes in their direction and hissed back. That stopped them.

I finally squeezed through the crowd and stood near the front. My grandfather was standing at the entrance to the cattle kraal. He noticed me and I lowered my head in respect. When I flicked my eyes up and looked at him again he was still staring at me, eyebrows raised. At least he didn't look angry. I had too much of importance to discuss with him to become embroiled in one of our usual arguments. But all of that had to wait until the ceremony for Malumi's grandchild was over.

The Malumi family sang a traditional song; the guests repeated their words in another key. The result was vibrant, their voices swelling in splendid harmony. I found myself singing along, swept back to my childhood by the familiar words. My body moved involuntarily to the rhythm of the chant. With every beat my muscles contracted and my bones seemed to vibrate. The ancient ritual of the music was in my blood and it couldn't be denied.

But I knew what was coming next, and I dreaded it. It was taboo for women to enter the cattle fold, and at the gate the dancers paused and the singing stopped. The crowd pushed forward. I found myself near the front, in full view of what was about to happen.

Malumi and all the men moved into the cattle fold and stood in a circle. The pungent smell of dry manure wafted around me, bringing back vivid memories.

I felt like a visitor from another planet witnessing an otherworldly ceremony. Was it only nine days since Sue Kellon had died? Only last night that I'd slept in a soft bed? And only this morning that I'd showered under hot, running water, using my favourite Body Shop soap? It all seemed to have happened long ago, to a different person.

A woman, dressed in white, pushed past me, thrusting herself in front of the crowd. She lunged backward and forward, her legs moving spasmodically, her feet raising red dust. She went on dancing wildly until Ngosi, skinny legs rattling so fast I thought she would trip, pulled her back into the crowd. Ngosi, with her narrow eyes rolling, lips thin and unsmiling, spittle running down her chin. She looked even more creepy than usual.

Now, all eyes were fixed on Malumi as he approached the black-and-white ox. It was held immobile by men with ropes tied to its horns and legs. I watched knowing what would follow. The creature's chest was rising and falling in terror. It thrashed about, taking great gulps of air. Some of the men held onto the animal to subdue it. Others held up flaming torches whose brightness lit up the cattle fold, chasing away the evening shadows. Their bare upper bodies glistened.

Malumi, holding a long spear, held up his arms invoking the ancestors to listen. He called out in a loud voice: 'We call upon the ancestors to help us. I call upon you all to witness that I make this sacrifice to my ancestor.'

The people roared out in one voice: '*Camagu*! – We are with you!'

Malumi stabbed the ox and the beast bellowed with pain. Then others moved forward to slit the throat and a geyser of blood spouted into the air.

The world tipped. It was barbaric, a gory scene from the Old Testament. A howl of approval lifted to the sky as the ox fell to its knees. A good omen: the ancestors would help the child.

Malumi and his sons performed a prayer dance. The drumbeats thudded; their voices rose and fell in an ancient rhythm. The faith of their song touched me. My throat tightened with the need to cry. A small breeze wandered across the valley. There was a throb of thunder and lightning played beyond the mountains.

I watched transfixed, staring at the scene. It felt familiar to me, and yet there was so much I didn't want to understand, had forced myself to forget. At once repelled and fascinated by the ritual of blood and fire, I had a strong sense of the transfer of spiritual power that was happening in front of my eyes. Something unique was taking place, something to be acknowledged with respect but also a shiver of supernatural discomfort. From time to time in everyone's lives something big is glimpsed for a moment or two, and that was what was happening to me. For a fleeting moment I grasped the thread of feeling that was winding around me and saw the bigger picture.

I watched the crowd swirling around me, faces glowing. I thought about the desperate lives they lived, how many died early, aged by hard work and malnutrition. How rituals like these give life meaning, connecting us to something bigger than ourselves. And then, a thought hit me – a thunderbolt sent from the darkening sky. Who was I to say that my life was any less desperate? Perhaps the valley people would see my city life as pretty undesirable. The rush and bustle of the city, never stopping to appreciate the slow passage of the seasons, the joy of sunrise, the comfort of knowing that life is being lived as it has been for centuries, unspoilt by technology and progress.

I thought of the rituals of life that make an urban man happy: anointing a new car weekly with polish, feeding bank accounts, slotting plastic cards into machines and buying more and more stuff. Suddenly the valley way seemed beautiful in its simplicity. I thought how nice it would be to wake up one morning and not have to worry about the mortgage, the electricity account, getting my car serviced, answering my buzzing cell phone every few minutes, organising my Facebook, coping with rising prices, traffic jams, the escalating crime rate in Jozi, getting hijacked at the robots on a dark night.

Not everything in life revolved round a Sandton apartment, a good job, an attractive boyfriend and a favourite perfume. It was far more elemental. Something was present in the valley for all people that night, something from the dark past linking all human beings as they struggled to make sense of their lives. As quickly as the thought came, it left, but I felt different.

I moved towards my grandfather, then knelt on the grass and greeted him in the traditional way. When I looked up he was smiling thinly. At least he didn't look irritated.

'Back so soon? Why is this, Thabisa?' He spoke kindly. I was surprised, but relieved.

'I have some questions, important issues I need to discuss, Grandfather,' I said.

He gestured me to sit next to him. I settled down at his feet. I noticed Ngosi scowling and murmuring under her breath as she watched me.

'There will be time to talk later, Thabisa, this is not Johannesburg, rush, rush, rush. Big city, fast action. This is the valley and things will be told in their own time.'

I sensed a softening in my grandfather's attitude towards me, and wondered why. Perhaps he had watched me during the ceremony and seen how I had been affected.

He bent to speak to me, his words echoing the thoughts racing through my mind.

'I know from watching you at the ceremony that you are still a child of the valley. It's in your blood. The ancestors spoke to you. I could read it on your face'.

I couldn't deny it. 'Yes, it's true, but I can't change my life. I am what I am, Grandfather. But I would like to come back and visit you without feeling like an outcast in the valley.'

My grandfather paused. Several emotions played across his face and then, for the first time in my life, I saw that he was considering my point of view.

'I can't make you change, Thabisa,' he said slowly. 'I can't force you to do what I want you to do. Sometimes, I even tell my fellow elders about my granddaughter who chases criminals in the big city. They laugh, but we all know that change has to come.'

We stared at one another, both stubborn, both determined. He, an autocratic, overbearing traditional man, me a career-orientated, focused young woman. Both bearing the same blood lines. It was in our veins, part of our DNA. I knew that we would always take opposing views, but we had each moved part of the way to understanding and respecting one another.

Solenkosi looked towards Ngosi and some of the other old crones, skinnering behind their hands as they watched us.

'Stop!' he commanded. 'Stop that and return to the village, now. You are no longer welcome at this feast.'

All but one scuttled away. Ngosi sidled forward.

'What is this young woman who was cast out in shame doing here?' she demanded. 'Don't the scars on her body remind her she is no longer part of the valley?'

Much as I hated the old battle-axe, I had to admire her fighting spirit. It was going to take more than a few harsh words to silence her.

My grandfather rose from his seat. 'You have gone too far in this matter,' his voice silenced the people around us. 'I will send you from the valley if there is any more of this conversation. This is my granddaughter. She is my blood. You will show respect from now on, or you will leave the valley and make your way in the world outside. You have disgraced my house with this behaviour.'

Ngosi gave me one last ugly look. Then she turned on her heel and scuttled away. I knew I would never win her over, but as long as I got to speak to my grandfather and make him listen to my story, I was happy.

My grandfather turned to me and said quietly, 'I had no idea the punishment you endured as a young girl was so severe. I would have stopped it had I known. It is my shame that I allowed my granddaughter to be so badly hurt.'

I gripped his hand and held it for a moment.

'Thank you,' I said.

When the meat was cooked and all had feasted, everyone settled in the Great Hut. I sat with my grandfather, watching the men, women and children I had grown up with. They sang with their whole being, clapping, bodies swaying and bending. There was too much noise to speak, so I sat quietly, knowing what would happen next.

Tall and terrifying, the *sangoma* sprang into the space, as if by magic. His left eyelid, arm and thigh were painted white, the right side black, the rest of his body smeared with blood-red clay. He strode into the crowd, face covered by a bizarre mask. He wore animal skins dripping with white beads. His skirt, made of monkey tails, swirled around him and he carried a long, thin stick. The crowd gasped in fear, turning away, trying not to meet his eyes. I found him pretty scary too, although my logic told me not to be so foolish.

No greetings were exchanged. He appeared to be in the grip of intense rage, lashing out with his stick. The crowd shrank back. He inspired awe and terror in everyone. He asked no questions, only making statements.

In the valley, people's fears, fantasies and emotions are deeply embedded in witchcraft. The *sangoma* is their priest; he speaks directly to the ancestors, and rules over their rites and rituals.

Without his powers of magic, the valley people couldn't survive. He stops a storm simply by placing certain herbs under a stone; he divines illness by the lines on a man's face. By holding up an earthen pot he protects the valley during a lunar eclipse. He is all-powerful.

Although I dismissed traditional healers as primitive, far removed from the life I was now living, I was apprehensive. They were always unpredictable. Sometimes it was almost laughable, but dark comedy was their speciality.

As he leapt and pranced, the *sangoma's* monkey tails flew faster and faster, his bead necklaces gyrated, and he shone with sweat. Tossing his head, leaping and kicking, he moved with a magic rhythm.

Raising his stick high above his head, he cried out in terrible voice: 'You have come about a bad happening!'

'*Siyavuma*! We agree,' the crowd shouted, clapping their hands.

'You have come about a woman whose mother is killing her!'

The crowd disagreed. '*Asiva* – We do not hear.'

He made another attempt. He whirled round, lifting his stick high. 'You have come about a sick child!'

'Yes!' shouted the crowd.

The *sangoma* moved to the family of the sick child in a series of frightening darts; leaping, prancing, shaking his stick in the faces of the family; moves that held the crowd spellbound. Was he going to help her? Wasn't he? Eventually he presented the family of the sick child with a heavy necklace made of bark and herbs telling them that she should wear it until she was cured.

Was it my imagination or did the child's grey pallor lift as soon as he put the necklace round her neck? Or was I just caught up in his drama and my fevered imagination?

Jet-propelled, he leapt forward again. Terror rippled through the crowd. He held his stick high. Then he pointed it straight at me.

'You have come here on a secret mission!' he shouted at me. The crowd was silent. 'Do not tell me that this is not so. I have been told why you are here!'

All my logical training and schooling didn't stop a trickle of fear running down my spine. I bowed my head. My grandfather chuckled.

'Oh, so that's why you are here, eh? Well, we'd better return to the homestead and talk about this secret mission. Come.'

Solenkosi Tswane rose to his feet and stood majestically, head up, shoulders back, every inch a leader. He raised his hand to the *sangoma*, signalling him to leave the gathering.

The people made a path, bowing deeply as we passed, careful not to let their eyes rest on the face of their chief. I noticed my grandfather's dignified and assured manner. I saw how he delighted in the children of the valley, patting a small head there, stroking a small cheek there.

When we reached his homestead, I sat at his feet. He looked down and said, 'Whatever you are about to say to me is not important, child. Your heart speaks for you. You have travelled far to come home.'

I felt tears welling as I looked at him. 'Thank you, Grandfather.'

I felt that at last there was a chance that things could change. Although our paths were different we were still blood of blood, bone of bone. I reached out, took his hand and held it between mine.

'I have come to tell you of a great wrong that has been done. Do you remember the man who betrayed my father and uncles in 1977?'

He nodded slowly.

'That same man is bidding to become the next President of South Africa.'

My grandfather pulled his blanket around his shoulders and lit his pipe. After a few puffs, he said: 'Tell me about this man.'

I told him about Sue Kellon, Julia McEwen and Ollis Sando. I described Richard Bowles and the Truth and Reconciliation Commission, Lucas Makanda and his family. I told him of the records in the Grahamstown bank, now destroyed, and the death of the bank manager. Then I told him about what Julia McEwen had said about the mark of the snake, the symbol of treachery, tattooed on this man's back. This Ollis Sando was the same man. The man who had betrayed our people.

Solenkosi Tswane was leaning close, to hear me better. After I'd finished, he sat back and looked at me. For the first time in a long time, I didn't see censure in his eyes. He took both of my hands and held them together, placing his own above and beneath. The gesture carried comfort and courage. 'You have behaved bravely in telling me this,' he said finally. 'It must be taken higher. I will speak with our leaders.'

'We can't stop him, can we? Even with proof from the beads?' I said.

'There must be more proof than beads in modern law. Who would believe the beads against such a man?' I bit my lip. He was right. My grandfather and I were the only witnesses who could tell what the beads said, and even that would be based on symbols and what they meant according to the way we had been taught to interpret the beads. An art passed down from generation to generation. Never recorded in the way a court of law would recognise. A clever lawyer would be able to tie it all up in knots in no time. I could just hear it: 'Are you sure Ms Tswane? This long mark here symbolises a ... *snake*? Isn't it meant to be something more, ahh ... *phallic*?' And then the laughter which my grandfather and the other elders would have to sit through. There was no way our testimony would be enough. Even if we authenticated each other's statements, we didn't have powerful enough proof.

'I must consult my ancestors over this matter,' my grandfather said. 'Before I speak to the leaders, I must talk with the spirits.'

I tried not to look doubtful. My grandfather smiled, reached out and touched my braided hair. The simplicity of the gesture touched me deeply. I remembered Tom's words: 'Ask how *you* can help *him*.'

'How can I help in these matters?' I asked. The least I could do was ask, even though I knew he wouldn't allow me to help, of course. I was a woman. Women don't help in matters like this.

Right on cue, he answered, 'No woman can help in matters such as these. To help me, you must marry and have children, Thabisa, to continue the bloodline of our family, but I see my granddaughter is stubborn, like me. I hope one day we can reach agreement over this matter.'

He drew a deep breath. 'I will talk to you now about this man Zikhali, who is Ollis Sando, before we go to the bead room again.'

I nodded.

'He wished to marry your mother, but it was forbidden. She was already promised. He was a proud and angry young man, well-educated and clever. It was rumoured that he told the authorities of the three young men, who were seen running from the scene, your father and uncles. He identified them. A month later, they were taken into custody. They all confessed and were executed six weeks later. Then he claimed the three million rand reward, and it was said that he travelled to a far land. Until you revealed the actions of this Sando to me, we had no knowledge that this man, seeking to be president, was the same Zikhali. But it is him, Thabisa. He carries the mark of the snake. He must be stopped.'

We walked together to the Great Place and my grandfather held the lantern while I stepped inside. The beads were waiting. They leapt off the wall into my mind, hypnotising me as I read the story of the snake man who had betrayed the valley, his passion for my mother, his fury when they couldn't marry and his revenge on the family of the man who stood in his way.

I reached forward and touched the beads with my fingertips. The symbols I had learned at my mother's knee swam effortlessly into my subconscious, forming patterns I could read as clearly as a book. The jagged point for a dagger, the long straight line for a snake; a broader deep green line meant the valley, the jagged blue one the mountains. Alone, they were nothing. It was only when they joined with others that they made sense. Colour changed their meaning. A long red line symbolised treachery, a thinner black line, a tall man.

I thought back to my history lessons at school. The Egyptologists and archaeologists tried to make sense of the hieroglyphics they discovered inside the pyramids. The codes that had helped them break the ancient scripts and the ones used to read the valley beads were much alike.

My eyes scanned the beaded landscape of village life, the stories worked in, generation after generation. I stopped. There was something here. The symbol for man, the symbol for snake, the symbol for young woman. A young woman standing alone. She was pregnant, beaded in pale red. Something slid into place, something I shouldn't have missed. Wouldn't have missed the first time if I had been allowed to see more. There was no man beaded close to her, no shapes or colours to suggest a wedding celebration.

I had a reputation in the Unit for being a good code-cracker and puzzle solver. Frame by frame the beads led me on, drawing me into the story. The story of my mother. Who beaded this in? It could only have been one person. Ngosi. The evil old woman must have guessed my mother's secret and beaded the story to record my mother's shame, so that it could never be forgotten. A message to the world that not only do I, Thabisa, carry the blood of a white-skinned woman, I also carry the bad blood of a man who is not my mother's legal husband. I stood staring at the beads and the colours shifted into a sickening kaleidoscope of colour, all shouting the same message.

Finally, I turned to my grandfather: 'He's my father, isn't he? This is the secret you have all kept from me. Sando is my father? Tell me the truth.'

'Whoever he is, he must be stopped.'

'That's not answering my question. Is he my father?'

'And if he was?'

My mouth tasted metallic, like faintly sour milk.

'We have to stop him,' I whispered.

*I had stirred my ancestors into action. Now they were whirling, a dust storm, looking for justice, looking for vengeance.*

# 31

18 August 2006

News-flash

Doctors at Greenacres Hospital, Port Elizabeth, have confirmed that Ollis Sando, slated by political forecasters worldwide as the next President of South Africa, died in Port Elizabeth this morning. The cause of death appears to be heart failure.

Tributes from around the world have been pouring in to the Sando family. Leaders of African states have sent heartfelt condolences to the family, and the White House and Downing Street have expressed shock and concern about Sando's sudden death.

Yesterday, Sando attended an Imbizo with Traditional Leaders in the Eastern Cape. A spokesman stated that after dining with the Leaders, Sando retired to bed, but became ill during the night. He was rushed by helicopter to Greenacres Hospital.

His condition deteriorated rapidly during the night and early morning and he died at 10 a.m. today.

Although rumours that a snake was found in Sando's bed have been discounted as 'typical sensationalist misinformation' by a spokesperson close to Sando and his family, police have not yet ruled out the possibility of foul play.

Ollis Sando (54) leaves his wife, Sitina, formerly an Ethiopian beauty queen, now a minister in the Department of Health. The couple had no children.

# 32

A perfect day. The sky was a deep and thirsty blue as we headed for the sea, rocketing down the road to the beach in Tom's open-top Golf, with a picnic basket in the back. We stopped at Salem, watched cricketers on the green, and paused to visit the little church where the graves of the 1820 settlers pushed up the earth.

'These guys had a hard time,' Tom said. 'They thought it was all going to be milk and honey when they came here, but it turned out to be hell on wheels, really hard for them.'

'They had to fight my ancestors,' I said. 'My people fought them stark-naked, covered in red clay, when they stormed Grahamstown.'

'I'll think of that every time I stand on Signal Hill,' Tom said. 'Any chance of a re-enactment, Thabisa?'

I laughed. He was easy to be with. *He's a good guy.*

We passed game farms where blesbok, impala and wildebeest grazed calmly, unaware of passing traffic. We saw elephants in the distance and watched the Kariega River winding through gorges on its way to the sea.

It was my last day before returning to Johannesburg, a day for the beach, for the sand dunes, for the river.

We had met up earlier at Tom's place, the top floor of a grand old house in Worcester Road; a cleverly converted studio apartment with high ceilings, white walls and lots of light. The whole apartment was filled with the warm smells of good food cooking and music. A procession of clay Nguni cattle stretched across a white bookcase, their vigour and character vividly evident.

'Interesting work,' I said, picking up a tiny figurine. 'Where did you buy these? They're beautiful.'

'I made them,' Tom said.

'They're wonderful. So you're a sculptor as well as a doctor?'

'I try,' Tom said. 'I just wish I could be better at it.'

'You're really talented. I love these.'

I touched the tiny works of art gently. Tom had caught the splotched patterns and colours of the cattle perfectly. Some were ceramic, others just plain clay.

'I go up to the university and take the ceramics classes when I can,' Tom said.

'You must be top of the class. You're really good.'

'You should see the others in my class. There's some real talent there.'

'None better than you,' I'd said, replacing the perfectly sculpted figure. 'I'm a valley girl, remember. I know all about cattle.'

We packed a picnic, and piled food, wine and swimming things into Tom's car. The weather was glorious. A champagne Eastern Cape day.

I leaned back against the headrest, enjoying the chance to forget all about work and do nothing but enjoy a day out in the country.

'How are you feeling now it's all over?' Tom asked.

I smiled wryly. It had been a hectic few weeks, but now I'd finished the reports, and tied up all the loose ends, I was keen to leave Grahamstown.

'Better,' I said.

'You've got a tough job.'

'So have you.'

Tom leaned across and dropped a kiss on my cheek, 'Let's forget about our tough jobs and have a good day, okay?'

I grinned. 'Okay, tell me where you've been this week?'

'Monday Grahamstown, Tuesday Umtata, Wednesday Port Elizabeth, Thursday East London, Friday Grahamstown, Saturday Kenton-on-Sea with Thabisa Tswane.'

'You travel a lot.'

'Which is why I can't get to my ceramics class as often as I'd like. I'm in Umtata all next week.'

'My grandfather goes to Umtata next week to collect his grant.'

'It's good that you've reconciled. What happened?'

'I'm indebted to you, Tom. I wouldn't have done it without your advice. I tried your approach and it worked.'

'What are you going to do about the valley?' I decided to tell Tom about the beads, and the bead room, and my ideas. He listened intently to what I had to say.

'This is amazing, Thabisa,' he said. 'Shapes, patterns and colours can be proved to have a meaning in early history. Look at the Egyptians and their hieroglyphics – and now your valley. I visited Easter Island a few years ago, and they have these amazing petroglyphs carved into the stone. Nobody has been able to decipher them, because the local population who could have passed the information on, was wiped out by invading forces. A wealth of information, gone in a flash.'

'I've asked my grandfather to allow me to teach three young women how to read the beads,' I said. 'I figure that if I fall under a Jozi taxi, the valley loses one of the few people who know how to attach meaning to the symbols and the colours.'

'Has he agreed?'

'Believe it or not ... yes! And he's agreed to allow his youngest wife, Nomvula, to get some training, and maybe set up a school in the valley. We'll start small, with the younger kids. She'll make a brilliant primary school teacher.'

'What an amazing woman you are, Thabisa!' Tom shook his head, laughing, as he pulled into a parking lot. 'Now, let's go, we've got a boat to catch.'

'Boat? What boat?'

'Not only am I a doctor and a sculptor, I can also handle a boat up the Bushman's River. We might even see elephant at some of the game parks along the way.'

Bright boats on the river, the cream and aqua of water and sand dunes – it was a perfect day. I relaxed after the drama of the past few weeks. Tom was easy company. He was patient, didn't press me for explanations of what had happened. I didn't give any. It was enough to lie back on the boat trailing my hand in the water, watching the river as we floated past. Tom caught a fish, and we saw elephants playing in the water. An idyllic day.

When we returned to Grahamstown, Tom said, 'Right, where shall we eat? Any ideas?'

'Why don't we stay in?'

He looked at me in surprise. 'Really?'

'Yes, got any food?'

'I make great pasta. Can you do salad?'

Tom lit candles all over the apartment and we chopped, stirred and cooked together, Tom's iPod playing French café music in the background. I felt chilled out for the first time in months. Words came easily when we were together. We chatted about our childhoods, our dreams and ambitions, history, politics, movies and music. Several times Tom made me laugh out loud.

After we'd eaten and cleared up, he came up behind me and lifted my hair. His mouth was warm and soft on the back of my neck. He pressed up against me; I pulled him to me and we kissed. Then he took my hand, drew me into the bedroom.

I pulled back.

'What is it, Thabisa?'

I looked at him. I didn't know what it was, and I didn't know what to say. 'I'm sorry, Tom. I really like you so much. I enjoy being with you. But I just can't ...'

'Is it too soon for this?' he asked.

'It's too soon for me. I just want us to be friends.' The worst thing to say to any guy, but I couldn't lead him on.

Tom slumped onto the bed and ran his hands through his hair.

'Thabisa, we talk about life and art and politics and our families and everything else in the world. That's the best thing about us, the way we talk. I don't think it's too soon. We know each other very well. But you have to want me. *I've* wanted *you* ever since that first day when we met in the hospital.'

Sure, we could talk about everything under the sun – except intimacy. In that area there were things unsaid and undone that loomed large between us. I didn't know how to resolve it – or if I even wanted to. A relationship with Tom would be a serious commitment.

Everything in my life had been coloured by the passionate afternoon with Zak after I had shot Sue Kellon. But Zak wasn't a friend and confidant like Tom. And lust wasn't the same thing as compatibility at all. Surely a proper relationship should have all the elements – the person who shared your life should be everything: friend, confidant *and* lover. Why couldn't Zak be more like Tom and Tom be more like Zak?

'I don't want to get it wrong. Too much has happened to me recently.'

'I'll wait. For as long as it takes, Thabisa.'

He ran his finger softly across my cheek. Nothing he said had indicated that he might be upset, but it was there in his eyes. Disappointment.

What was the matter with me? Tom was such a good guy, smart, handsome. Everything a woman could possibly want. And yet, none of this was enough. It didn't feel right, and I didn't know why. I wished I could try to explain it to him, but how could I, when I couldn't figure out for myself how I was feeling? I could feel tears coming and I walked into the kitchen and stared through the window. I looked at the soft green garden below, a sharp contrast to my tumultuous feelings.

He followed me. 'What exactly is this about, Thabisa?'

I couldn't answer.

'Is it because we're from different cultures? Is that it?'

'No, Tom. Never. You know that.'

Tom took me by the shoulders and turned me to face him. 'I'm not asking you to do anything drastic, Thabisa, just give me a chance. Let me show you what a good guy I am.'

I smiled through my tears. 'I know what a good guy you are, Tom.'

I suddenly realised why I was feeling so confused. I wasn't in the right frame of mind to make any major decisions. It was all too much to digest: Sue Kellon, Julia McEwen, Zak, my grandfather, the beads, Ollis Sando. What I needed, more than anything, was space to breathe, and time to decide where my life was going.

'Can I come and see you in Johannesburg?'

'Of course.'

'Let's take it from there.'

I felt lighter, like I could finally breathe.

# 33

Three months later

November 2006

The meeting of the village elders took several days. It was hosted by Chief Solenkosi Tswane in the valley. It was an important occasion. Big decisions had to be made. Chief Tswane had requested dancing before the ceremonial meeting took place. I had not been invited to join the initial ceremonies.

I smiled to myself. Change might be happening in the valley, but it was coming slowly, and at the pace dictated by my grandfather. One of these days I might settle down next to my grandfather and watch everything as it happened. But not today. For now I had to imagine the dancers dressed in their best, brightest clothes and bedecked with beads, the great showing of magnificent turbans and ceremonial skirts of all kinds: white ones, ones made of brown ox-hide or sheepskin, and some that had been freshly ochred for the special day. I'd seen the women donning the beaded leather belts and cummerbunds that drew attention to supple waists and swelling curves, watched as they fastened traditional bead headbands, throat bands, anklets and very long necklaces. During the dance the necklaces would be flicked over their shoulders and they'd sway with a life of their own. I might not be able to see the dancers, but I could hear their voices, the shrill call to the ancestors, for it was through their spirits that all decisions were made about the valley.

As the women sang they stamped to the rhythm, and I listened as the tempo picked up, pictured their bodies spinning and twisting, the beadwork patterns and colours interlinking with the dancing, painting bead pictures as they moved.

And then the sound changed, became deeper, hoarser as the men came surging into the circle, blowing shrill whistles, shouting and stamping, dancing and leaping in fierce mock battle. They too would be adorned, in beaded body harnesses and girdles that flashed in the sun. Hard feet pounding, strong voices singing, a feast of music and drama. After the dancing, the elders and Chief Tswane rose and entered the Great Hut for their meeting. I remained outside for this too, along with all the other women and younger men. I wondered when this would change, if ever. Would we, the younger people of the valley, ever be allowed to hear the deliberations of our elders?

The meeting seemed to go on forever. It dragged past lunchtime and into the late hours of the afternoon. Finally they emerged and Chief Tswane spoke with the news of their decisions. The valley children were to be educated. I leaned back on my haunches and smiled. This was a huge breakthrough, more than I had dared hope for.

Nomvula sat next to me, her hand on my arm. When she heard her name her grip tightened, and then a huge grin split her face. She was going to Grahamstown, to do a special literacy course at a Grahamstown girls' school. After that, to Johannesburg for a course in rural teaching skills, on condition that she stayed with me.

Nomvula was mad with excitement; one moment shy and frightened, the next overwhelmed by all the new possibilities. I promised her that it was all going to be fine – I'd even arrange for a trip to the beauty salon for hair braiding, *when* – not *if* – she got through the first course.

After the long discussions, my grandfather called me in to the Great Hut to speak in private. The village elders withdrew.

There was a long silence. Chief Solenkosi had welcomed me warmly when I'd arrived in the valley, but even then I had sensed there was something on his mind.

Finally, he spoke. 'Do you see how it is now?' he asked me. 'We will help the children to read and write.'

'I'm glad of that,' I said. 'You have shown much wisdom in these decisions. Thank you for this great step.'

My grandfather remained silent for several minutes. I waited patiently.

'I have received an offer of *lobola* for you,' he said slowly.

My heart thudded in my chest.

'From whom?'

'From the Zulu, Khumalo. He offers me much money, too much for an older woman in my opinion.' He smiled, softening his words into a dry joke and I smiled back. 'This Zulu has promised that you will give me strong great-grandsons. He says you will be happy.'

'What did you say?'

'I told him that I would speak to you.'

'Thank you. I need to think about this offer.'

I turned to go. What did this tell me about Zak? Traditional Zak, versus Modern Zak? Surely a smart, urban man asks the woman before he makes an offer? This was so entirely like Zak. Unpredictable as ever. But even as I thought this, it made me smile.

'Wait.' My grandfather called me back. 'There is another offer.'

'Another?'

'This offer is for more money, twenty splendid cows and a special fund for children's education here in the valley.'

'But who –? Who made this offer?'

'A white man. A doctor, so he tells me.'

My heart lurched. Tom had warned me that he wasn't the kind of man to give up easily ... now he was proving it.

'When? How did this offer come about?' I asked.

'Doctor Winter from the hospital visited me when I was last in Umtata. He brought me twenty clay cattle as a promise. Look ...'

He gestured to a box behind his seat. I opened it. Nestling in white tissue paper, twenty tiny ceramic Nguni cattle stared up at me.

'Thabisa, I want you to be a happy woman. These troubles have shown me the strength in you. I am an old man now but you have taught me something very important. I do not have to decide everything for you. I want you to choose for yourself, for your own happiness. Which of these men will make you the best husband? They are of different cultures. I have long wished for a Xhosa man for my granddaughter, but change has come to the valley and we must accept that new bloodlines will result. If you accept the offer of the white doctor, you will have to face big changes. You will have to go far away from the valley. But he is a kind, good man who will provide well. The Zulu is a proud, strong man. Your life will be an adventure with this man. He will match your strength and passion. Which man do you wish to accept?'

I bowed to my grandfather and took his hands in mine. For the first time in many years, he embraced me warmly.

*What should I tell you, Solenkosi Tswane? I will never stop being part of this community where everyone knows everyone else and where life is cut down to human size. I can live in the city, work as a police officer, drive my car and have my urban life, but in my heart I will always be a part of this life, where the sun wakes me and the darkness sends me to sleep, where flocks and herds, ploughing and reaping, dancing and singing fill the days. I will never forget where I come from.*

I stepped out into the warm night feeling light and weightless, sad and tender, old and sweet. I was filled with the strong sense that everything would be right.

I looked up at the stars that I'd loved all my life, shining down on the thatched roofs and cattle byres of the valley. My feet sank into red dust.

I passed a group of old men sucking on their clay pipes. Two women strode by, beads clicking, as they carried water buckets from the river.

I stood there in the dusty red night. The sweetness of home skipped and shifted around me. I shrunk into the valley again, expanded inside it.

I could see clearly now.

I turned back and entered my grandfather's homestead. He stood waiting for me with a solemn expression. I took his hands in mine and said, 'I've made my decision.'

# 34

February 2007

Everyone came to the wedding. It was a day of pure enchantment.

For many years it was spoken about in the valley. It was whispered that the couple had already held a modern wedding party in Johannesburg, but, of course, that wasn't a *proper* wedding. That could only take place in the valley. The modern idea of city weddings couldn't take the place of the real thing. Traditional celebrations were essential, however modern the couple.

The visitors packed their city suits and high-heeled shoes into rucksacks, laced on their trainers and picked their way down into the valley. They came from far and wide, the bridegroom's family having brought many colourful guests from far away. There were people there from every culture, but most had observed the valley traditions and wore red ochred shawls over their finery.

The bride was beautiful in her red ochred dress, with a deeply-fringed collar of turquoise beads that fell to her waist, where a wide waistband echoed the turquoise beading. She wore three headbands of white pearl-like beads, and matching ankle bracelets. She seemed to float, as she walked towards her bridegroom, so light were her steps and so joyful were the looks they exchanged. Although he was from a different culture, the bridegroom looked like a prince, so proud and distinguished. He wore a beaded turban that made the guests gasp when they saw it. He was a very tall man; this headdress made him look like a giant.

Two oxen were slaughtered. The villagers wore their finest beads, their red shawls and blankets, *gogos* walked in front of the pair, sweeping the ground with their brooms, singing the bridal songs. With the setting of the sun, the bridal pair walked together to the place where Chief Solenkosi Tswane waited for them.

There were wild cries of exultation; everyone sang and rattled tin cans filled with stones as they passed. Love and warmth, friendship, spontaneity and joy filled the valley as the bride and her groom approached the bridal hut.

When they arrived there, the master of ceremonies lifted his beaded knob stick, and called out in a loud voice: 'Those within, answer us.'

The reply came clearly: 'We await you,' and they entered the hut.

The bridal procession entered slowly, and Chief Solenkosi Tswane stepped forward to take their hands in his.

There was a great cry as the entire assembly swept forward, singing the traditional song in adulation:

*Today we had a wedding*
*Everyone attended*
*Who was there who did not know?*
*Everybody knew!*
*A great and happy wedding.*
*Hurrah! Hurrah!*
*Rejoice! Rejoice!*

The villagers talked about the other guests for months afterwards, especially a friendly white lady called Bea, who wore a sparkling purple gown and danced with them till dawn.

Old and young, everyone danced and sang and feasted until the sun rose. It was a night to remember.

Apart from the food, the drink and the music, the best thing for the villagers was to see their chief so happy. At last his face was wreathed with smiles; he danced with them, sang the valley songs, and looked with pride on his granddaughter and her husband.

'This union will bring strong sons,' he said time and again.

The bridegroom agreed.

The bride blushed and said: 'Not yet ... we'll see. We'll see ...'

# 35

Six years later

## 23 April 2012

I turned to the mountains and looked at the clouds invading the sky from the south. The valley was lit by a strong, late-summer sun, the mountains bright red in the light. I was standing in the soul of my country; in a land of red earth, green acacia, cattle bells and rushing water.

I climbed to my favourite spot, the ridge where, over the centuries, a mountain stream had carved out a chain of small pools and little beaches. I sat down, propped myself against a smooth rock and closed my eyes. It had been a long three weeks away from the rush and hurry of my Johannesburg life.

Today the new school had finally opened its doors and tears had prickled behind my eyes as the children sang their school song, filling the deep valley with their childish voices, the sound of hope: for a better South Africa, a better world.

I glanced up the cliff path. My family would be arriving soon. I'd hear them before I saw them tramping down the path. The new road from Encobo made it easier to get into the valley these days, but at the end where it joined up with the winding path through the mountains, the descent was steep.

A dart of movement. I looked over my shoulder towards the mountains. It wasn't the children, or my husband. Somewhere, far inside my skull and deep in my body, something hummed; a sound too low to hear, like a warning chime. I had felt it several times recently and each time when I had looked harder, stopped to listen, there had been nothing. My senses were on high alert, even though it had been quite some time since I'd done any active police work.

Matatu had been contacting me regularly lately, urging me to come back to the unit. 'Part-time,' he'd said. 'You name the hours.'

'Soon,' I kept promising him, 'soon.' I missed the thrill, the chills, the adrenaline rush, but I had plenty to keep my hands full on the home front. Would I be able to juggle it all? I wasn't sure, but some days I was tempted to give it a go.

Just because I was no longer actively engaged with the Eagles, didn't mean that my special training had gone out the window. I sat still. Nothing. Only the wind and the trickle of water. Probably a bird, I told myself, or a snake moving to catch the last of the afternoon sun. The bush is full of wildlife that knows how to remain unseen.

I opened the three-week-old newspaper. Only yesterday's news arrived in the valley, but I enjoyed reading the papers anyway. There was always a lot of catching up to do. Sadly, the news was predictably dispiriting. Eighteen years after the first democratic elections and there was trouble and dissension all over the country. Blaming and complaining, moaning and bitterness. Why couldn't everyone just get on with it? Work like a team to make a nation we could all be proud of?

And then I thought of the valley – and smiled. So much had been achieved in six years. Not only in the valley, but in my own life too. There had been some difficult choices to make, compromises to negotiate.

That first year felt like a dream now, a pretty topsy-turvy one. Tom hadn't given up on me that easily – had offered me a new life in Australia. So tempting. Turning my back on it hadn't been easy. But if anything, it had helped me to see how much I loved my own country. How much I wanted to give back. I realised then that I could never leave; that it was time to live life a different way.

It took a while, but once it was up and running everything gathered momentum: starting the charity to build a school in the valley, fundraising, learning the ins and outs of construction, deciding what to buy and what wasn't necessary. And all the while, as the foundations were dug and the walls grew higher, I found myself working shoulder to shoulder with a man who shared my dream, someone who had changed out of all recognition. A man who loved and respected me, helped me, cherished and encouraged me. They say it only happens in fairy tales, but it can also happen in the bustling rush of a Johannesburg life and the quiet moments of a deep green valley. Believe me, I was there to see it happen. Day by day, the friend, companion and lover I had always dreamed about materialised before me. And night by night too ... I blushed as I thought of our passionate nights. Time and kids hadn't dimmed our attraction for each other. Far from it, it had just grown stronger.

I blinked, let my eyes slide down the page of the newspaper. I felt the nape of my neck tighten. A black and white photograph, taken in a small private cemetery. She was wearing black and her face was pale, but composed.

Julia McEwen.

I scanned the article:

**Jailed wife attends murdered McEwen's memorial**

Julia McEwen, sentenced to fifteen years for her part in the murder of an Eastern Cape bank manager was seen yesterday at the funeral of her husband, Magnus McEwen, a well-known mining executive.

Magnus McEwen was found murdered at his Houghton home in Sandton eight days ago, shot dead in an execution-style killing. The autopsy revealed evidence of torture prior to his death. According to information leaked to the press, the execution bears all the trademarks of a Solarin execution, the notorious Nigerian gang, many of whom are serving life sentences for several counts of torture and assassination in South Africa.

Speculation is now rife that Magnus McEwen may well have been involved in drug or arms deals with the Nigerian underworld. There has been no official confirmation from the police on any of these allegations.

McEwen's body was released to the family after the autopsy was completed and the coroner's report was finalised.

Julia McEwen was released on the grounds of good behaviour two days after her husband's death. She had served six years of her sentence.

According to sources close to the widow she is devastated by her husband's death. 'All Julia wanted was to go home, to be with Magnus again," a close friend said, "and now that's never going to happen. Once the estate is settled, she will have to pick up the pieces of her life. We would appreciate it if the press allows her the privacy she needs in this difficult time.'

No arrests have been made at this point, although police have indicated that they have several leads to follow.

'Oh my God,' I whispered, 'she's out.' I remembered Julia McEwen's dangerous smile, the way she had snarled at me as she was led away. How, at her trial, she had shouted: *'When I get out of jail I'm coming to find you. You'll never be safe.'*

'Stop it,' I said aloud. 'You're jumping to conclusions here.' Julia might be out, but her husband had been killed while she was safely behind bars. By all accounts Magnus McEwen had been a hard businessman who lived an extravagant lifestyle. Nothing concrete linked him to the Solarins, but it wasn't beyond the bounds of possibility that he'd got on the wrong side of the Nigerians. I shuddered at the thought of what they must have done to him. The Solarins weren't known for their gentle good nature. Lucky for Julia McEwen that she hadn't been home when they came calling. That is, if they had, of course ... It was all conjecture at this point. I wondered where the case would lead, whether any of my colleagues from the Eagles had been called in on it.

'Mama! Mama!'

There they were. I saw them coming down the path and scrambled to my feet, all thoughts of Julia McEwen forgotten. I ran towards them, holding out my arms. I had missed them so much for the weeks I had been in the valley, helping prepare for the school's opening. They climbed into my embrace, kissing and hugging me like two wriggling puppy dogs.

Solenkosi and Thabo were identical twins with dark honey skin and my grey eyes. They were four years old. The boys ran ahead of me down the path and into the homestead of their great-grandfather. His wisdom and dignity subdued their high spirits for a few moments. He shook their hands and embraced them, addressing them in isiXhosa. They returned his greeting solemnly. Then away they raced, chasing one another, joined by an exuberant dog and two confused chickens, swirling about in the dust.

'Hey guys,' I shouted, 'just cool it, okay? Your grandfather wants good grandsons, not naughty ones.'

'We *are* good,' said Thabo, pulling Solenkosi's sun hat off and throwing it in the air.

I turned round. 'Come along, Dad, bring some discipline to your sons, a couple of weeks away from me and they're out of control.'

Zak stepped forward, smiling, and swept me into his arms. I felt light and buoyant, as if I'd float away if Zak let go of me.

'Hey, we've all missed you, me most of all,' he said quietly, his lips on my hair. 'Don't leave us again, my heart can't take it.'

He shouted to the boys: 'Listen guys, Mama's back, now you've got to behave, right?'

He turned back to me and took my hand. 'I never thought you had such a sobering influence on our kids. They only behave when you're around. So, next time we *all* come to the valley.'

Pure joy and exhilaration – the same feeling I had every time I looked at Zak and the boys. Of course, it was an illusion that everything could always be alright in this complicated, dangerous world, but whatever dangers lurked out there, if Zak was beside me everything would be fine. I thought of Julia McEwen and flicked the thought away. I had Zak, my family, the valley and the great red mountains towering against the blue sky. That was enough, for today.

I smiled up at my tall husband. He put his arm round me and we walked down to my grandfather's kraal.

### 23 April 2012

High in the mountains, in a cave above the valley, a woman put down her binoculars. A slow, satisfied smile lit her narrow face.

## Acknowledgments

Thank you to Colleen Higgs for her decision to publish my book, and the wonderful editor she teamed me up with, Máire Fisher, who has been an absolute star, strengthening my writing, making great suggestions and giving me insights into my characters that I hadn't even considered. Thank you Máire, you are a wonderful editor.

Thank you to Brigadier Mene, of the South African Police Services who gave generously of her time and experience and helped me understand the difficulties of becoming a police officer during the apartheid years in South Africa.

Thank you to Associate Professor Andrew 'Mugsy' Spiegel from UCT for his help and advice on Xhosa culture.

I acknowledge Joan Broster, distinguished author of *Red Blanket Valley* (published 1967). I met Joan in 2006 in Port Alfred and her descriptions of the life and rituals of the people of the Red Blanket Valley and her recollection of a young girl selected to receive an education provided inspiration for *Now I See You*. The rituals and words of the wedding song (page 201) were taken from *Red Blanket Valley*.

To my friends and family who have been so encouraging. A special thank you to the wonderful members of The Write Girls creative writing groups for their support and enthusiasm.

Last, but not least, an enormous thank you to my husband, Jack Holmes, for his constant support and practical advice, not to mention his patience. It's not easy living with a writer!

## Other fiction titles published by Modjaji Books